OTHER HIGH CRIMES

a novel by

David Arthur Gordon

Macaulay & Wittenstein
Publishers
Oklahoma City

Library of Congress Cataloging-in-Publication Data

Gordon, David Arthur.
Other high crimes : a novel / by David Arthur Gordon.
p. cm.
ISBN 1-885823-00-2
I. Title.
PS3557.06546084 1994
813'.54---dc20 94-36622
CIP

Published in the United States of America
by Macaulay & Wittenstein Publishers Inc

Printed in the United States of America

The President....of the United States shall be removed from Office on Impeachment for, and Conviction of, Treason, Bribery or

OTHER HIGH CRIMES...

Article II, Constitution of the United States

ONE

Roger Anthony Morrison was born in Veritas, a small New York town of about five thousand people on the east bank of the Hudson River, half-way between New York City and the state capital of Albany. It was the site of Veritas College, a small private liberal arts college, the only thing of any importance in the town, and Veritas was without question a college town.

After the Second World War, especially during the 1960s when federal money from Washington poured down in a torrent on the small colleges of America, the money pouring because every young man and woman had the right to go to college even though he or she might not be college material, Veritas set up an academic program in computer science. This was the vocation of the future, and every institution of higher learning was trying to carve its place in the new academic discipline. A liberal arts college like Veritas, although reasonably good on balance, could not possibly have as good a program in computer science as a university with an engineering school, but Veritas did its best, and Roger did his best in that program at Veritas.

Roger was a rather unassuming young man, quiet and studious, and although he dated young women from time to time, he decided he would find no permanent interest in any of them until he finished all his education, and that meant another three or four years in law school after he was graduated from Veritas College with a degree in computer science.

The young ladies found him to be pleasant, a gentleman, somewhat old-fashioned, someone they considered a misfit at the time the country was caught up in the sexual revolution of the 1960s, Roger not particularly handsome in the manner of male fashion models, but adequately good-looking. He was six feet tall, weighed about one hundred and eighty pounds when he left Veritas, and had dark brown hair and eyes. He played a good game of singles tennis, and swam in the college pool whenever he could, all in all keeping himself in very good physical condition.

Upon graduation from Veritas with honors, Roger applied for a position as a computer programmer in the office of the District Attorney of New York County, the county having exactly the same boundaries as the island of Manhattan, the very same boundaries as the Borough of Manhattan, one of the five boroughs of the

City of New York. He did get the job, and that gave him the opportunity he longed for to attend the four-year evening program of the Manhattan College of Law, an independent law school on the approved list of the American Bar Association. Neither Roger nor his family had the financial means to send him to law school, and this arrangement was exactly what he needed, a job in Manhattan and a law school in Manhattan.

The emphasis at this particular law school was not to study the subtleties of jurisprudence but to prepare its students to pass the New York State bar examination, and pass it he did four years after he entered the academic program. Now a Member of the Bar of the State of New York, Roger requested a transfer from his position of computer programmer to an apprentice assistant district attorney, a transfer readily granted to a highly satisfactory employee.

The District Attorney of New York County was an elected officer of the county, and there being five counties in New York City, there were five district attorneys, but because Manhattan was the most important borough of the city, the District Attorney of New York County was the most important, his rather large organization having many divisions, each specializing in one area of crime, divisions for homicide, arson, rape, robbery, fraud, forgery, drugs, and other crimes. With his background in computers, Roger was assigned to the Fraud Division, specializing in the more sophisticated cases involving fraud by computer.

At first, Roger did not prosecute cases himself, but

instead assisted others with more experience, until he himself developed enough practical skill to handle cases in the courtroom. But before he was actually appointed a full-fledged assistant district attorney, he was interviewed by the famous Mark Bernard Rosenblueth, the "Manhattan DA," considered by many people to be the most important prosecutor in the United States.

That interview was an experience Roger would not wish to repeat, for when Mark Rosenblueth was finished with him, Roger was literally in urgent need of a shower, but when it was all over, Roger understood the purpose of the very heavy interrogation, and his unlimited admiration for the legendary Mark Rosenblueth was undiminished.

Mark Rosenblueth was born in Brooklyn of an orthodox Jewish family, and earned his law degree at the New York University law school. After becoming a member of the New York State Bar, he lived for several years in the Borough of Brooklyn serving as an assistant district attorney in Kings County, Kings County being to the Borough of Brooklyn what New York County was to the Borough of Manhattan, and Mark then moved to Manhattan to become chief assistant district attorney of New York County about twenty years ago. When the New York County district attorney left to enter private practice twelve years later, Mark ran in the county-wide election to replace him, and was elected. He was now fifty-one years old, very tall, about six four, with prematurely greying hair but all still there, and a physique that reminded his friends of his prowess on the football field, both in high school and in college. Very bright, he was impeccably scrupulous and fair.

The common-law crimes of murder, manslaughter, rape, arson, assault and battery, kidnapping and robbery were without question under the jurisdiction of the Manhattan DA, for they came under the sovereignty of the State of New York, unless the crime was committed on federal property such as a post office or a federal office building or the Brooklyn Navy Yard. But in the areas of fraud, narcotics, and certain other crimes, there was often a question as to whether the Manhattan DA had jurisdiction or whether the crime fell under the United States Attorney for the Southern District of New York, the U S Attorney not elected by the people but instead appointed by the President of the United States with the advice and consent of the Senate. All too often, Roger found his Fraud Division in conflict with a similar division of prosecutors in the office of the U S Attorney, and the two chief prosecutors were not entirely cooperative with each other.

Roger lived in a large cooperative apartment building west of Central Park, between the park and the Hudson River, in the mid-Seventies, in a large building but in a small apartment in that building, for it was all he could afford in a good location within easy walking distance of the park and the American Museum of Natural History. A cooperative apartment building was not a condominium arrangement. Instead of the occupant owning his apartment, he owned a share of the corporation that owned the building, and the apartment he occupied was "assigned" to him according to the investment he made. For all practical purposes, it was like a condominium, but legally something else.

All of the occupants of the building were either single or if married were without children of school age, for the changing population of the city made it no place for young children, and as if to emphasize that this was so, the apartment building had a very sophisticated security system including the latest closed-circuit television. Indeed it was so sophisticated that it was impossible to deceive the security guards watching the monitors, and a continuous record was made of what was seen by each of the many cameras.

Central Park was still a safe place during daylight hours, where Roger replaced his interest in tennis with an interest in jogging. Each weekday evening, and on the weekend after his morning run and shower, he spent much of his time reviving his interest in photography, an interest that soon became a rather expensive one. While in school, he had inexpensive equipment, but now his cameras and processing equipment were the finest available. He had a top-grade Leica 35 mm camera with all the accessory lenses, a Rolex, a Graphlex plate camera, and only recently Roger added one of the best of the new Japanese 35 mm SLRs to his working collection. He had professional-quality enlargers, and he used his only bedroom as a "darkroom," which meant that he had to treat the rest of his flat as a studio apartment. This considerable financial burden was easily borne because photography was his only dependent, although he obviously could not claim it on his income tax returns. Roger was now thirty years old, four years out of law school, a very competent photographer as well as a rather good lawyer.

It was a Tuesday, and Roger arrived home much later than usual to find a large number of police squad cars, their roof lights still blinking and whirring, parked helter-skelter on the street in front of his apartment building. He managed to get through the police officers at the front entrance, not by proving he lived there, but by showing his photo ID card identifying him as an assistant district attorney. He took a few minutes to help other occupants to also enter by vouching for them, and then noticed a plainclothesman in the entry lobby giving instructions to one of the uniformed police officers as though he were in some position of police authority. Roger walked over to him, and introduced himself.

"I'm Roger Morrison...an assistant district attorney in Mr Rosenblueth's office.... What's going on...?"

"I'm Lieutenant William Salinger...of homicide.... Are you from the homicide division of the DA's office...?"

"No...the Fraud Division...."

"Then what brings you here...?"

"I live in this building...."

"Then perhaps you know the victim...."

"What victim...? What happened...?"

"One of your fellow occupants...a Dr Dinah Steinberg...was found dead in her apartment.... According to the medical examiner...she's been dead for about twenty-four hours.... She was with Columbia-Presbyterian...and after being absent without prior notice for more than a day...they sent someone here to see her.... The person knocked...but no response...and finally the hospital got the security people here to open the apartment entry door.... There she was...strangled by hand...lying on her bed...fully clothed...no sign of rape...or burglary...or break-in...."

"My God...," was all that Roger could say for the moment, and then, "Is the body still in the apartment...?"

"Yes it is...but the medical examiner will probably remove it shortly...after all the usual photos are taken...."

Photos, thought Roger. "Will you excuse me while I go up to my apartment.... What apartment is she in...?"

"721...and yours...?"

"314.... I'm going to get my Leica...it has an excellent close-up lens...to take some photographs of her neck.... We might be able to pick up some fingerprints on her skin.... It's a long shot...but I might be successful...."

"Good idea.... I'll join you in her apartment...and I'll call up right now to make sure her body's not removed...."

"Can I take one of your officers with me...? I want him to witness my using a fresh spool of film...right out of the sealed package...."

Roger and one of the officers went up in the elevator to the third floor to his apartment, where Roger loaded his camera with a new spool, and they then ran up the stairway to the seventh floor, to Dr Steinberg's apartment. Lieutenant Salinger was already there, instructing the medical examiner's people to let the body remain where it was for more photographs.

That the victim was strangled was obvious, and Lieutenant Salinger again remarked that the murderer used his hands rather than an object of some kind.

"That's all the more reason to photograph all the neck skin.... If the killer was not wearing gloves...he might have left a fingerprint or two...."

Using a strong magnifying lens, Roger slowly scanned all around the neck, and found two prints in the front, one on each side of the Adam's apple, and then several smaller prints in the back of the neck, symmetrical about the spinal column in the neck. The killer obviously had not worn gloves. As Roger very carefully took his close-up shots, William Salinger was commenting that the absence of gloves and the absence of a break-in indicated that the victim probably knew her killer and that the death might not have been premeditated but done in anger. What did it matter, Roger thought. It was still a killing in cold blood.

When Roger was through and stepped back, he noticed for the first time what a beautiful woman Dr Steinberg was. There she lay, fully clothed with no blood anywhere, but with those death bruises on her neck. And now that Roger had the fingerprints, the police might be able to identify the murderer, assuming the killer had a set of his fingerprints somewhere on file, even on the civilian side of the FBI.

TWO

Roger assumed an air of authority, as though to take over the investigation at this point, suggesting to Lieutenant Salinger that the body could now be removed.

"Lieutenant...I think you should have one of your men retrieve the security video tapes for the past several days.... I have a strong feeling the killer is one of the occupants of this building.... I might be wrong if our security guards can't identify everyone on the tapes entering and leaving the building...either as a pedestrian or through the garage...over the past few days.... And one of the occupants is Supreme Court Justice Robert Berger.... I think he's in Apartment 805...but I'm not sure.... You can check the registry downstairs.... Please ask him to please come to my apartment...."

"Why do you need him...?"

"The photographs I took may be the only solid evidence against the killer.... I need Justice Berger to authenticate the photo prints as soon as they come out of the developing tanks...those I took of Dr Steinberg's neck.... If he's not in...then I'll need you and your two detectives to act as witnesses.... And if we can't identify the fingerprints from the FBI files...even on the civilian side...then a prosecution might not be possible for years...and in the meantime...those photographs have to be kept safe...."

"Very good point...Mr Morrison.... You should have been a detective...."

"But I am a prosecutor...and I know what kind of evidence will not fly in the courtroom.... I can always put myself in the shoes of defense counsel...and understand how he might argue against evidence for the People.... As I said...these photos will be our only evidence...and we have to handle them right...."

Lieutenant Salinger left to find Justice Berger, but by the time he reached the judge's apartment, the word of the murder had already spread throughout the entire building. William Salinger explained to the judge the need for his presence in Mr Morrison's apartment, and offered to have a police officer remain with his wife until he returned.

"I'm glad to see you...Your Honor...," Roger cordially said to Justice Berger. "This is a ghastly crime...and it could be that the only evidence we might ever have against the killer are the photographs of the fingerprints around her neck.... After I took the shots...I gave my camera to Lieutenant Salinger who's been holding it ever since.... He'll certify in writing to this effect.... What I would like you to do...Your Honor...is come into my darkroom with me and Salinger...watch me remove the film...and then develop and print...."

"I understand...and then you want me to authenticate each print...and that authentication together with Lieutenant Salinger's statement made in my presence...will prove that the fingerprints were those taken from the victim's neck.... But defense counsel could always argue that the prints were already in one of the frames in the film inside your camera...even before you took the shots...."

"I took care of that...Your Honor.... When I went up to my apartment to get my camera...Sergeant Malloy accompanied me...and witnessed my removal of the existing roll of film...of my breaking the packing seal of a new roll...and then inserting the new roll in my camera.... We shall also get his statement...in your presence...Your Honor...."

"I think you've thought of everything...Mr Morrison.... I'm impressed...."

"And so am I...," added Lieutenant Salinger.

"This has to be an air-tight case...once we find who belongs to the prints...."

All three went into the darkroom, while Sergeant Thomas Malloy waited outside and the other detective sergeant, Juan Ramos, went downstairs to the main security desk to retrieve the security tapes. The photographs were excellent, and showed a complete set of fingerprints and palm prints taken from the neck of the strangled woman. Roger made five duplicate sets, and had every print in each set authenticated by Justice Berger.

Roger then sat down at his typewriter, and prepared five duplicates of a statement by William Salinger that he witnessed the taking of the photographs, and that he carried the camera containing the film directly into the darkroom where the film was processed in his presence. All five copies were witnessed by Justice Berger. A similar statement by Sergeant Malloy that he witnessed the loading of the camera with new film was also executed in five copies, and all five copies witnessed by the judge.

With all appropriate formality, one of the sets of photographs was deposited with the Clerk of the Court, Supreme Court of New York for New York County. Another was deposited with the Clerk of the Court, County Court of the County of New York, the court of general jurisdiction for criminal cases, the Supreme Court handling only civil cases. A third set was placed by Lieutenant Salinger in the police file for this case. A fourth set was placed by Roger in the homicide files in the office of the District Attorney, and the fifth set was kept by Roger in his own personal files.

A copy of the set in their files, authenticated by the New York City Police, was sent to the Federal Bureau of Investigation in Washington to be checked against their millions of fingerprint records, both on the criminal and the civilian side. The civilian side contained the fingerprints of all persons, in and out of government, who ever received security clearance to access classified information. It also contained fingerprint records of every member of the armed forces, of law enforcement agencies, and of other special groups. A thorough search of the FBI files found no matching record.

Several days later, Roger was personally commended by Mark Rosenblueth for his initiative in gathering the evidence, and officially placed him in charge of the case.

"I got a phone call from Justice Berger this morning...telling me how competent you were in handling the only available evidence to make sure it would stand up in court...once we find the bastard who killed her...."

"I greatly appreciate your confidence...Mr Rosenblueth.... Could you formally request the police to continue the assignment of Lieutenant Salinger.... He's been most cooperative.... I feel we can work well together...."

"It will be done...and now let's find out who belongs to those prints...."

Back in his new office, larger and completely private, Roger had two telephone messages. One was from Lieutenant Salinger, but when he looked at the other his heart literally skipped a beat, for it was from Dr Steinberg. Needless to say, this was the call he returned first, and his ring was answered by the switchboard operator announcing "Columbia-Presbyterian," and that caused a double skip.

"May I speak to Dr Steinberg...?" Roger asked, and

when Dr Steinberg's extension was answered by "This is Dr Steinberg...," Roger literally stopped breathing for a moment.

"This is Roger Morrison...of the district attorney's office...," he responded with some trepidation, "...returning your call...." but her call from where? Roger thought.

"I'm Naomi Steinberg...Dinah's sister...."

"Sister...," thought he as he composed himself. "I should've realized it...."

"I returned this afternoon from a meeting in Stockholm...to get the dreadful news...and I had to go to the city morgue to formally identify her body.... Just got back to my office.... Do you know who did this terrible thing...?"

"I'm sorry to say we don't...not yet.... I'm the prosecutor for the case...and I'll be working with Lieutenant Salinger of the police...."

"Yes I know.... He took me to the morgue...and told me that you were involved in the case...that you lived in the same building...that my sister and I did.... Did you know my sister...?"

"No...I didn't...but can you join me for dinner...to talk about certain aspects of the case...?"

"I can't tonight.... I just finished my internship...and starting a new residency in gynaecology.... I have to be on duty this evening.... Why don't you join me for dinner in the doctors' dining room...if you don't mind the setting...say at about seven...."

"Not at all...and I can be there at seven.... How will I know you...?"

"I'm a younger version of my sister...."

"I'll be there...."

Roger next called William Salinger, and was told that the fingerprints could not yet be identified by the FBI.

"And we found absolutely no other evidence in her apartment...not even stray hairs.... We went over it again with a fine toothcomb...and found nothing.... Luckily...we have the fingerprints...but how do we find the owner...?"

"Were the security guards able to identify everyone in the video tapes...?"

"Every single one...which means that the killer was probably an occupant of the building...."

"Yes...that would take care of the building security system.... Before I forget to tell you...Mr Rosenblueth assigned me to the case...and I asked that you be continued on it...."

"I know.... His request went directly to the Police Commissioner...and you'll have to put up with me until we catch the killer.... Sergeants Malloy and Ramos will be doing the leg work for us.... They're very competent...and hardworking.... What we now need are the fingerprints of all the occupants of the building...but if anyone refuses...then the only way we could get the prints would be to get arrest warrants and fingerprint them at the police station.... We can always arrest them on suspicion...."

"I agree...and I see no difficulty in getting warrants if we need them.... I've been working on a scheme to obtain fingerprints photographically rather than using the messy black-ink technique.... That should at least convince those...who might otherwise refuse because of the black ink all over their fingers...to willingly cooperate...."

"If they're as good as the ones you took of her neck...that will do it.... Let's set the equipment up in the building manager's office...gather all the occupants together in one place...and then ask them to have their fingers and palms photographed one by one...."

"Good.... We'll do it tomorrow evening.... I'll have the manager issue a written notice to each occupant to meet with us at a stated time...and I should have my equipment set up by then...."

Roger subconsciously decided to say nothing to Lieutenant Salinger about his meeting that evening with Naomi Steinberg until after he had met her, and also after he found out what her social situation was and what Salinger's marital situation was. William Salinger's were rugged good looks, and Roger realized he was acting like a school boy being concerned about the police lieutenants's possible competition for a young woman's attention, especially of a young woman he had not yet met except by telephone.

THREE

Without question, Naomi Steinberg was every inch the replica of her older sister, but Roger felt she was even more beautiful. Strawberry blonde with green eyes. Five feet five inches tall. A full, old-fashioned figure, with just the right geometric proportions, and all the features of a sensual face rather than the chiseled features of a human statute. She looked up at him and smiled as he approached her table and then sat down opposite her. She was wearing her medical white jacket, and he a dark business suit.

"I'm glad to meet you...Mr Morrison...," said she in a pleasant well-modulated voice, "...but I regret it's under these dreadful circumstances...."

"And I'm delighted to meet you...Dr Steinberg...and I too wish it were under much more pleasant circumstances.... Please call me Roger.... We shall be seeing much more of each other...."

"Fine...Roger...and I'm Naomi.... I just realized the

telephone message I left for you must have given you quite a shock...since you had no way of knowing that it came from Dinah's sister.... I should have said Dr Naomi Steinberg...Dinah's sister...."

"I must say it did momentarily stun me...but it was well worth it...."

Naomi explained that she had been in Stockholm for a week-long medical symposium, and had then spent several days at a Swedish lake resort without telling anyone where she was, which explained why the hospital could not contact her and tell her about the tragedy until she returned. "What a dreadful thing.... My mother and grandmother are devastated...and so am I.... Dinah and I were very close...and that's why we lived together in the same apartment...."

"Oh...I didn't know you were roommates...." Strange that he had never asked William Salinger whether someone else's things were also in the two-bedroom apartment, or whether the extra bedroom was a guestroom or study. "Do you know whether she was dating anyone special...?"

"No...she was not...and neither have I.... We've both been too busy with our medical work.... Dinah was thirty...and I'm twenty-seven.... She was working very hard doing some research in addition to her regular duties.... I never had anyone in the apartment...and to my knowledge neither did Dinah...but of course our two schedules didn't particularly overlap.... But she would not have invited a man into the apartment...unless she knew him very well...and felt she could trust him.... I'm afraid...Roger...that both Dinah and I have been socially...considerably behind the times.... We both still felt that bed is for sleeping and marriage...." And Roger's heart skipped another beat, but he could at least now understand why he never ran into either sister in the elevators or lobby.

"What about female friends...?"

"We both had a few...mainly other doctors at the medical center...and some of Dinah's might have been in the apartment...from time to time.... Do you think a woman could have possibly done such a thing...?"

"Yes...it's possible.... We can't rule out that possibility.... And speaking of apartments...do you plan to remain...in this one...?"

"No...I don't.... I couldn't.... I've already moved in with Dr Anderson.... She's widowed...without children...a gynaecologist...and has a nice three-bedroom apartment very close to the hospital...."

"I'll need your new address and phone number...and this is my home phone number...if you need to call me...at any time...day or night...," as he wrote it on the back of his business card, and hoped as he handed it to her that she would use it often. He then wrote hers down. "We're having a meeting of all the occupants of the apartment building tomorrow evening...at eight o'clock.... Can you make it...?"

"I don't know...depends on my schedule...but I'll try.... What about...?"

"Using the security video tapes...all the people who went in and out of that building...on the day your sister was killed...and on the few days before...were recognized by the security guards...and known to them.... This indicates the strong probability that one of the occupants is the killer...."

"How will you know...?"

"We have the fingerprints of the killer...."

Naomi gasped. "Then you know who he or she is...."

"No...because the prints are not on file anywhere...not even on the FBI civil side...which means the killer never had government security clearance...never was an officer in the armed forces...and was never a law-enforcement officer...."

"That still leaves a lot of people...."

"Yes it does...but we're going to begin with the occupants...because of the strong possibility that the killer is one of them.... We're going to fingerprint every occupant...and if he or she doesn't do it voluntarily...then we'll have to use police procedure...."

"Which means...?"

"Arrest...on suspicion of murder...and fingerprinting at the police station...and under the circumstances we have probable cause to get arrest warrants...."

Naomi smiled. "If you explain it that way tomorrow night...you'll get one hundred per cent cooperation...and I'll do my best to be there...but it will take days to get all that black ink off my hands...."

"Not to worry.... I developed a new photographic technique...which involves no ink...."

Dinner was buffet-style, and at this point both of them got up and went over to pick up their empty plates to fill with the offerings of the buffet table. Very little was said about the case as they ate, but much was said about each one's background before coming to

New York City. Naomi and her sister were from an old Jewish family in Richmond, the capital of Virginia, were direct descendants of Judah Benjamin, the Confederate Secretary of War. Her father was dead, but her mother and her mother's mother were still alive, both living together in the same antebellum house that Judah Benjamin had lived in during that awful war, the house now entirely modernized but the original architecture retained.

"As soon as it's released...I'm sending Dinah's body as quickly as possible to Richmond...for burial in the family plot.... My grandmother is a very strict orthodox Jew...and she frets that Dinah was not buried as soon as required by orthodox custom.... I'll be in Richmond for several days at the time of her funeral...."

Roger ate very little, too busy watching Naomi without it being obvious that he was actually staring at her.

The following evening, all the occupants of the building, all except the occupant or occupants of apartment 707, but including Naomi Steinberg, assembled in the meeting room of the apartment building. The building manager Alfred Jackson introduced Roger Morrison while Lieutenant Salinger and Sergeants Malloy and Ramos stood by.

"As you are all well aware...," said Roger Morrison, "...Dr Dinah Steinberg was murdered several days ago...and both the district attorney's office and the police are jointly investigating this terrible crime.... As Mr Jackson told you...I am the assistant district attorney assigned to prosecute the killer...once we find him or her...and the police investigation is in charge of Lieutenant Salinger...assisted by Detective Sergeants Malloy and Ramos.... On the sheet of paper...handed out to each one of you...are listed our telephone numbers...and we urge you to call us whenever you have some information to give us...about this case...." Roger paused as almost everyone looked at the sheet he held in his hands. "We have every reason to believe that the killer might be an occupant of this building...," prompting a loud murmur throughout the room, "...and for this reason it is important that we take the fingerprints of each one of you...."

"And if we refuse...?" asked one of the occupants, a prominent securities lawyer.

"Then we'll have no choice but to obtain arrest warrants...which will not be a difficult thing to do...because we have probable cause...and take you down to the police station...there to be fingerprinted.... We must have the fingerprints to continue our investigation...and please remember that this is a murder investigation.... If any of you is concerned about the black ink...we intend to use a photograph technique...which does not require ink...."

"What probable cause...? Just because some young woman is killed by a man she invited into her apartment...."

"The video tapes of your building security system...they indicate that no one other than occupants went in or out of this building on the day of the murder...and the few days before...which strongly indicates that the murderer is an occupant...."

"I notice that Mr Randolph is not here...," said the same legal voice. "Does anyone know where he is...?"

"I think he left town early in the afternoon...," volunteered another voice, "...on the day Dr Steinberg's body was found...."

"Can anyone describe him...physically...?" asked Lieutenant Salinger.

Mrs Berger held up her hand, and was recognized. "He was a very good-looking man...about forty-five...an inch over six feet...I would guess...a lawyer I think.... I met him...only casually...several times in the elevator.... He introduced himself to me.... He was quite a gentleman...."

"Thank you...ma'am...." Bill Salinger then leaned over to Malloy to privately instruct him to check out this Maxwell Randolph. "Get a search warrant...and go through his apartment with a fine toothcomb...."

"What are we looking for...for the purposes of the warrant...?" quietly asked Tom Malloy.

"You'll be looking for fingerprints.... Take some people from the lab with you.... You'll also look for information on his professional activities in New York...and also where he might have gone.... Oh yes...one more thing.... Have the lab fingerprint Dr Dinah Steinberg...tonight...." Tom Malloy left immediately, but Juan Ramos remained.

Because the photographic fingerprint equipment was of Roger's design, it was he who set it up and took the shots. One by one, each person present had his fingerprints and palm prints taken, each one protesting that it was unnecessary because he or she did not kill that very nice Dr Steinberg, and Roger assuring each one that it was all a necessary routine, that he realized that no one present could have done such a terrible thing.

When Naomi Steinberg presented herself, it was all that Roger could do to steady his hands. She spoke in a low voice out of earshot of even Lieutenant Salinger. "I'm leaving on a chartered flight with my sister's body...tomorrow morning.... I had to retain a lawyer...to get it released...even though the police really had no further use for it.... Can you come along...?"

Nonplused, it was all that Roger could do to reply. "I'd be very glad to.... I'll call you later this evening...as to where and when...."

FOUR

Beginning later that same evening, and continuing all through the night, the three detectives and several police technicians went over every inch of the Randolph apartment for any possible clue as to the identity of the occupant, looking for fingerprints, hair, and what-not. There were no fingerprints at all as though the apartment had not been used or the occupant carefully wiped all surfaces clean before he left. There being some evidence of recent use, Bill Salinger concluded that all fingerprints throughout the apartment had been deliberately wiped away. But they found many segments of hair, which the police laboratory later determined were from the same person. As in the case of the fingerprints, what person?

They left the apartment at about five in the morning, Bill Salinger muttering all the while that his wife was not going to put up much longer with these all-night activities, but before he left for home he instructed Juan Ramos, a bachelor, to place the found hair, well wrapped, in the office file before going home. Sergeant Ramos also delivered to the police experts all the fingerprints that had been obtained the evening before from the occupants of the cooperative apartment house, the prints to be compared against the police copies of the prints taken by Roger Morrison from Dr Dinah Steinberg's neck.

While the three detectives and the technicians would be catching up on their sleep at their homes, and the police fingerprint experts would be comparing fingerprints all day long, Roger felt he could be spared, and called Naomi at six in the morning to confirm his going with her to Richmond.

He picked her up at seven, and drove to Teterboro Airport in New Jersey, crossing the George Washington Memorial Bridge in the direction opposite to that of the heavy inflow of morning motor traffic into Manhattan from the New Jersey residential suburbs. Her sister's body had been picked up at the city morgue by a mortician the day before, the body now embalmed, and was delivered by one of the mortician's hearses about a half-hour after Roger and Naomi arrived.

The plane was a two-engine turboprop, originally for passenger use but then converted to handle special cargo and four passengers, the four pieces of human cargo all in one passenger row of four seats, evenly distributed about a center aisle. The casket was loaded aboard, carefully fastened to the fuselage, and the aircraft took off for its two-hour flight to Richmond.

Roger and Naomi sat side-by-side, she at the

window and he on the aisle, both on the starboard side, which did not give him much of a chance to look at her, and during the first half-hour of the flight she did not seem to want to engage in any conversation at all. He noticed tears in her eyes, and instinctively moved his right hand to touch her left hand, and when she felt his, she instinctively grabbed it and held it very tightly while still looking out the window. There they sat for another half-hour, hand-in-hand, saying not a word, Naomi now looking straight ahead, and Roger very often turning to look at her profile.

About half-way through the flight, Naomi released his hand and composed herself. "I'm sorry I've been so unsociable...Roger.... I was just thinking of all the happy years I spent growing up with my sister.... She was always very good to me...especially after our father died...when I was twelve...and she fifteen.... He left my mother and us well provided for...but my mother never fully recovered from his death...so Dinah was my mother...even though only three years older.... She was a wonderful person.... When you find her murderer...you had better keep me away.... I'll kill him.... I'm not going to let him live...even in a prison...for the rest of his natural life...," and then she turned for the first time to look at him, "Do you have any idea...who he...or she...can be...?"

"If the fingerprint check absolves all the other occupants...then I feel certain...that Maxwell Randolph is the murderer.... But who is he...? That's the question...and so far we don't have the answer...."

"But didn't one of the occupants say he was a lawyer...? Isn't there a record of him...and where he practiced...?"

"We checked the records of the committee on admissions of the New York Court of Appeals...and there's no Maxwell Randolph.... There's also nothing about a law office...or any information about his being employed in any organization as a house attorney...."

"Is that like a house officer in a hospital...?"

"Yes...it means he'd be employed by a company...or government agency...or not-for-profit organization...as an in-house lawyer on salary...but we have no information on him...from any source.... It's as though this is another name he uses...and we don't know the others...if any...or the name he was born with.... There's nothing illegal about using another name...as long as it's not being used for criminal or fraudulent purposes.... He's really an enigma.... All we can do...for the time being...is re-submit his fingerprints to the FBI for identification...in the hope that he will have been fingerprinted for their civil side...or perhaps even for their criminal side...."

"But you have his video photograph.... Isn't that also identification...?"

"It is...but that kind of photograph is good only if you've seen the actual person.... The guards knew all the occupants of the building by sight...and could identify which photo belonged to which...but if you tried to use that kind of photo to find someone...someone you haven't seen before...it would very difficult.... We have a police composite...based on what the guards told us...and we've sent it to all law-enforcement agencies...but we don't want to publish it to the world...."

"Why not...?"

"We don't think it's good enough for someone to be able to spot the killer...after looking at the composite...but the killer himself would recognize his composite...and if he does...we're afraid he might simply leave the country.... I have a feeling he's a man of some standing...probably married...probably not a New Yorker...who bought this apartment and assumed this identity...to play around in Manhattan...and your sister got caught in his games...."

"You've suggested...because of no break-in...that my sister knew this man...and let him into our apartment...."

"It would appear that way...."

"Then she kept her relationship with him...whatever it happened to be...secret from me.... She never did a thing like that before.... Why would she now do it...?"

"I realize you and your sister were very close...but I suspect that Dinah might have been very interested in this man...and was afraid you would be competition...in the early stages.... It's irrational...but we sometimes become that way...when we're in some kind of emotional turmoil...."

"That's nonsense...and you know it.... My sister wouldn't keep anything from me...."

"I'm sorry...Naomi...but I don't know it...." Naomi turned away from him, and looked out the window. "I'm truly sorry.... I know what I'm saying is based on circumstantial evidence...but it all fits.... What other conclusion would you draw...?"

Naomi turned back to look at him, and replied, "The same as yours...and that's what bothers me...."

The flight now continued as it had begun, in silence.

A hearse met the plane when it landed at a small airport outside Richmond, and took Dinah's body to Rosenberg & Rosenberg, Undertakers. Roger had arranged for a rental car to be delivered to the airport, and after making sure that Dinah's body was safely on its way, Roger drove himself and Naomi to her mother's and grandmother's home in downtown Richmond.

The house was in the old historic section of the city near the state capitol, in a small enclave of well-maintained large houses dating back to the days many years before the Civil War, and surrounding that enclave, as though the enclave were beleaguered, was an extensive mass of the typical housing of the urban areas of America after the Second World War.

Mrs Sarah Steinberg and her mother Mrs Ruth Benjamin lived in what was probably the finest of the houses in the enclave. Its interior was as though Roger had walked into the past well over a century before, and it was only the fact, that Naomi's mother and grandmother wore modern dress rather than hoopskirts, that made him aware that he was still in the twentieth century.

Mother and grandmother were but older versions of Naomi, and both women were still crying when Naomi walked into the sitting room to greet them, while Roger remained in the entry hall, not wanting to intrude on a family together for the first time since the dreadful tragedy. After a several minutes, Naomi came out into the entry way, apologized to Roger, and asked him to come in to meet her mother and grandmother.

"May I introduce Roger Morrison.... He's the assistant district attorney in charge of investigating Dinah's death.... He lives in the same apartment building we did...but strangely we never met him before...."

"Have you arrested the murderer yet...Mr Morrison...?" her mother asked anxiously.

"I'm sorry to say that we have not...not yet...but we are working very diligently.... I have the services of three of the best police detectives in New York...."

"I knew that you and Dinah ought not to have gone to that dreadful city...," said a very teary Mrs Benjamin.

"Won't you sit down...Mr Morrison...," said Mrs Steinberg.

Roger had dinner with Naomi's family, and remained overnight as their house guest. In the morning, the three generations of women and their house guest from New York attended the funeral services for Dinah Miriam Steinberg, along with many relatives and family friends, and then her burial in the family section of one of the Jewish cemeteries in Richmond.

As they walked back from the gravesite to the motor cars, Roger told Naomi that he would have to leave that evening to return to New York.

"I have a lot of work to do...."

"I greatly appreciate your coming down...with me...and my sister.... I'm staying for a few more days...to keep my mother and grandmother company...."

"Of course.... Will you phone me when you leave for New York...? I'd like to meet your flight...."

By scheduled airline, the plane from Richmond to New York made a stop in Philadelphia, and although the trip this time was on a jet aircraft, it still took two hours because of the stop. Roger missed Naomi as he occasionally looked to his right but did not find her sitting in the adjoining seat, and he wondered whether she missed him. He wanted to know her better, and perhaps that might begin when he would drive her home from LaGuardia a few days later.

FIVE

Roger had been away from New York for two days, and when he walked into his office on the third day, he found a note from his secretary that Mark Rosenblueth wanted to see him when he returned.

"Do you think it wise...fraternizing with the victim's sister...? She might be a material witness...and it shouldn't appear that you and she have some kind of personal relationship...."

"I don't see why it matters.... Our entire case is going to rest on those fingerprints we took from Dr Steinberg's neck.... I have a message from Lieutenant Salinger to call him.... He might have the results of that mass fingerprinting.... And about the younger Dr Steinberg...I am personally very interested...."

"All right...Roger...I'm sorry I called you down...but this case is going to be very difficult.... The press is playing it up...as usual...and somehow they got copies of the video photos...probably from one of the guards.... I think we ought to charge the guards with obstruction of justice...just to deter anyone else from doing such a thing...and we can then drop the charges on some pretext.... As for Naomi Steinberg...the best of luck to you.... She's a very attractive young lady...."

"I'll bring the charges against the guards.... They had no right doing such a thing...and I'm going to charge the newspaper that published the photos with obstruction of justice...by publishing evidence prematurely...."

"Good luck to you...on that.... I'll support you all the way.... It was the New York Dispatch.... I don't know how many cases they've ruined for us by trying them in their newspaper instead of the law courts...."

Roger called William Salinger as soon as he got back to his own office, and received an oral summary of the police report on the comparison of all the fingerprints, and that report was completely negative. None of the fingerprints of the occupants matched those photographed by Roger Morrison.

"And that also includes Naomi Steinberg...," continued Lieutenant Salinger. "She's clean.... I'm sure you especially wanted to know that...."

"That's bad news...and good news.... Let's get together for lunch...with your sergeants...and see where we go from here...."

The Stage Door Delicatessen in the theatre district was the noisiest place in town but it had the best delicatessen in New York City, and this is where they went. All the other customers were so busy talking to each other, around the table or across the table, that no one paid any attention to them, and that is how they got their privacy and the best chicken soup to go with it.

"How was Richmond...?" asked Bill Salinger, as his two sergeants smiled.

"How did you know I was in Richmond...?"

"What else would prompt Roger Morrison...leading assistant DA...to be away from New York...at a time like this...."

"Richmond's fine...and Dr Steinberg and her family are as well as could be expected.... Now...while I was away...did you catch the killer...?"

"We wish...," answered Tom Malloy.

"And we wish those damn building guards had not sold the video photos...," complained Juan Ramos. "That'll just scare the killer off...."

"I'm going to bring charges against them for obstruction of justice...and also against the Dispatch for publishing them...."

"I wish you make an example of all of them...," said Lieutenant Salinger. "That was investigative information...and should not have been broadcast to the world...."

"Well...the damage has been done.... Where do we go from here...?"

"There are a few occupants in your building who were very prominent lawyers...and judges...but are now retired.... No longer active professionally...they go in and out of the building rather often during the day...and while we were interviewing the occupants over the past two days...they said they met this Maxwell Randolph...or whatever his real name is...several times during the day...in the elevator or the hall...and engaged him in brief conversation.... They feel he must be a lawyer...because he seemed to be very knowledgeable about some of the technical aspects of the law...." Lieutenant Salinger paused. "I think we should canvass every state bar and bar association in this country...to get a roster of all lawyers practicing in that state...together with their ID photographs...the ones they sent in when they first applied to take the bar examination...."

"That's a very good idea...Bill...even though there are almost a million lawyers in this country.... As a matter of fact...if we could get the original application papers...we might find his fingerprints on them...."

"Now...Roger...that's an even better idea...but as you say...there about a million lawyers.... How do we do it...without taking the rest of our lives...?"

"There must be some way we can automate the whole search process...and do it by computer.... The main difficulty is...we would have to go around...to all the state capitals...with our equipment...whatever that equipment is.... The state committees on admissions are not going to send us their originals.... We'll have to go to them...."

"You once told me you have an undergraduate degree in computer science...."

"But that's not going to help.... We need a computer scientist who studied at one of the engineering schools...not in a liberal arts college.... We still have some good engineering schools in New York.... Let me think about it.... Your basic idea to go to all fifty states...and let's not forget the District of Columbia...is very good.... I'll have to see what we can do legally...and what can be done using engineering...."

"We'll continue to send the prints to the FBI...but we can't do that too often..... Tom and Juan and I intend to go over those two apartments...once again...until we have the place under a microscope...."

"Under a microscope.... How long do you think it would take to photograph every surface in both apartments...using photographing microscopes...?"

"Probably forever...unless that can be automated...and done by some kind of robot...."

"I think...," mused Roger, "we need some very special technology...to help solve this case...."

They then finished their corned-beef-on-rye sandwiches, Roger paid the check, and off the three detectives went to the apartment building, and Roger went back to his office.

Before he began to prepare two indictments, one against the building guards and other against the Dispatch, Roger went to see Mark Rosenblueth about the feasibility of using the records of the various state bar organizations.

"I think we'll get a lot of resistance...and except in the case of the New York bar...I'm not at all sure we can find a mechanism to compel cooperation from any other state...and I'm not at all sure about New York either...but we'll try it in our own state...and see what happens.... Why don't you see Justice Berger...and try to get a court order...directed at the Committee on Admissions.... They'll probably refuse...claiming they're an agency of the Court of Appeals...which they are.... Does this mean we have to get a court order directly from the highest court in the state...? Who knows...? Let's start with Justice Berger...and see what happens...."

"We could...at first...examine the bar records at random...using some of the statistical techniques that independent auditors use...to save time and effort...."

"It's not the same thing...Roger... You can't use statistical techniques.... It has to be an exhaustive search...but first we have to get the bar's cooperation.... I have it.... Why don't we simply...and directly...ask the chairman of the committee to cooperate...after explaining the problem...and then use the heavy artillery only if the committee doesn't.... It might actually work in many of the states.... If I recall correctly...the New York State chairman...John Paulsen...practices right here in Manhattan.... I'll call him for lunch.... We'll see what happens...."

The Manhattan DA called John Paulsen, and when told that Paulsen was out of his office, he left a message for him to return the call. Later that afternoon, John Paulsen did, and jokingly asked, "OK...Mark...what have I done this time...?"

"Nothing yet...as long as you can find time to have lunch with me...say tomorrow...?"

"Fine.... We haven't gotten together for a long time.... How about the Lawyers Club...at one...?"

"I'll see you there and then...."

John Paulsen was very sympathetic, and anxious to cooperate, but was not sure whether the committee could release the files, even in a criminal investigation, unless there were probable cause that any particular member of the bar might have committed the crime. Mark agreed that he was asking for a dragnet, but emphasized that this was a murder investigation.

"I just don't know...Mark...whether it would be legal.... We'll have to research it...but if you get a court order...then the responsibility is no longer ours.... I would suggest you get a court order to eliminate any doubt.... The committee will appeal the order...to the Appellate Division...and then...depending on who loses there...it will be appealed to the Court of Appeals...and they will make the final decision.... You realize the entire bar will be up in arms...."

"We're not asking to fingerprint every lawyer...but to look for fingerprints on the application papers they filed for admission to the bar.... I don't think that's an invasion of privacy...as long as we keep the contents of the files confidential.... The only thing we're looking for is the name and the identification photo that go with the fingerprints...if we find the fingerprints...."

"OK...Mark...I'm on your side.... Get a court order...and let's see what happens.... You'll have to do the same thing in every state...and you might find special problems in those states having an integrated bar.... This is quite an effort...."

"We have the fingerprints of the murderer...but they're not in the FBI files...not even in the civil files....

We have good reason to believe the murderer is a lawyer.... We must find who belongs to those prints...." Mark paused. "You know...John...our biggest enemy in a case of this kind is the press.... They have absolutely no sense of responsibility.... The Dispatch already published the video photographs the building guards sold to the newspaper...and now how do we proceed for a court order and the subsequent appeals...without the press knowing...and publishing that the suspect is a lawyer...and that we're using the bar files to find out who he is.... If I were the killer...that would be enough of a tip-off for me to get the hell out of the country.... The damn press is forever making it so damn difficult for us.... They could ruin this investigation...and there's ordinarily little we can do about it...."

"You know their argument...Mark...the people have a right to know...."

"I entirely disagree.... The people have a right to know what they need to know...to make a decision for them to make.... The public does not make decisions in a criminal case.... Only the jury does...and they will get all their information from both sides...right in the courtroom.... The only role the public plays...is to make sure the accused gets a public trial...but it's his right...not the public's right...."

"You tell that to that court of nine lawyers meeting in that Greek temple on Second Street...Northeast... Washington...DC.... They seem to have other ideas...regardless of the historical foundations of the law.... Half the time...I feel frustrated because some of their decisions do not make any legal sense.... They literally offend my intelligence.... Oh for the days of Stone...Brandeis...and Cardozo.... They were true giants...."

SIX

Roger, assisted by two other lawyers in the district attorney's office, spent that afternoon and the following three days preparing indictments for grand jury action against the building guards and the New York Dispatch accusing them of obstruction of justice, and also preparing a petition to Supreme Court Justice Berger for a court order to examine New York State bar application papers for fingerprints.

The petition was filed the very next day, and two days later Roger arranged for the convening of the grand jury, to meet in ten business days. As he said he would, John Paulsen opposed the petition perfunctorily, but it was granted. On behalf of the committee on admissions, Paulsen appealed, and won in the Appellate Division. Roger, on behalf of the District Attorney of New York County, appealed to the Court of Appeals of the State of New York. As Mark predicted, the press thoroughly published the entire matter, perhaps too thoroughly, and many members of the New York Bar were up in arms, filing briefs galore with the Court of Appeals against the appeal, all of this making for an overly publicized atmosphere generated by the press.

Roger conferred with Mark, and at first Roger agreed with Mark's suggestion to withdraw the appeal. If Roger had won, the killer would have left the country, or done something else that would have effectively allowed him to escape punishment. On the other hand, Mark thought that a well-publicized dismissal would give the killer a sense of false security.

"Not so...," Roger suggested. "If we ask for a dismissal...the killer will know we're up to something...and he might panic...and flee.... I'm willing to risk my professional reputation...and deliberately lose...without it appearing that I did it deliberately.... That should lull the killer into a false sense of security.... How in hell do you conduct a difficult murder investigation without the press fouling it up...?"

"With great difficulty.... But your idea is very good...Roger.... I appreciate your making the sacrifice...but it won't matter in the long-run.... I feel confident we'll find that bastard...and I think we should not press for indictments against the guards...and the newspapers...for the same reason.... As for the press...it really has the country over a barrel...on everything.... I wish they were required to behave as they do in England...and there's nothing wrong with the fairness of the English criminal justice system....

So Roger deliberately lost the appeal, without it

being at all obvious, and that was the end at the very beginning. The case was back where it began.

During all the many days of court proceedings, Naomi flew back to New York from Richmond, and Roger took time out from his busy schedule to meet her when she arrived at LaGuardia. As they fought the heavy traffic from the airport to Naomi's apartment, using the Queensborough Bridge, Naomi remarked, almost too casually, "I've taken a residency...at the hospital of the Medical College of Virginia...in Richmond.... I'm resigning at Columbia-Presbyterian here in New York.... There's very little to keep me in New York...and my mother and grandmother need me in Richmond.... I came back to say so-long to you...and to arrange to have all my things shipped to Richmond.... Will you be coming down to visit when you can...to let us know what's going on...?"

"I certainly will.... I'm very sorry you're leaving...but I can understand why.... I'd do the same if I were you.... I'll be commuting between New York and Richmond.... I'd like to see you again...," went Roger on and on. He turned his head to look at her, and then had to slam on his brakes to avoid hitting the truck in front of him when it suddenly slowed down.

Things were apparently not going too well for Roger Morrison. He was stymied in the Dinah Steinberg case, and he was sorely afraid he would lose whatever tenuous tie he had with Naomi Steinberg. He was determined to call her every day, and see her every weekend he could possibly get away, but then he also had to find some time to visit his parents in Veritas.

He called her twice daily, once when she got up in the morning, and again when she went to bed, and after a few weeks Roger jokingly mentioned that he ought to buy stock in AT&T.

"My family already have a large block of shares.... Will you be coming down next weekend...? I'm off duty for both Saturday and Sunday...the first time I've gotten a weekend off since I've been here.... Why don't we go down to Williamsburg...on Sunday...? We can make it there and back in one day...and have plenty of time to see the town...."

"I'll be down Friday...early evening...."

"If you do...make it in time for Sabbath dinner.... My mother and grandmother are strictly orthodox...and I can't disappoint them by not being home...for the most important dinner of the week...."

Roger spent the next few days working on other cases, most of them dealing with criminal fraud, and by Friday at noon, he was too impatient to wait any longer. He told Mark he was leaving for Richmond, that he would as usual be the house guest of Mrs Steinberg, and he reminded Mark to call him only in case of a dire emergency. He asked his secretary to get him the earliest reservation to Richmond as he walked out the office door.

"Sabbath dinner...," Roger thought as he buckled his seat belt for the take-off. "I'm a Methodist...anyway one by baptism...and Naomi's a Jew.... My parents are ardent churchgoers...and Naomi's family are observant Jews.... I'm devoted to my mother and father...and Naomi is obviously devoted to her mother and grandmother.... Where do we go from here...? I think one of us is going to have to convert...for his own sake...not for the sake of the other...to make it entirely sincere.... I'm going to discuss the problem with her...but is it a problem...? What do I know about her religion...? Only what I learned in Sunday school...and that wasn't very favorable...but why would my religion find it so necessary to defame another one...to literally vilify Naomi's religion...? I think I'll look into that question...very carefully...."

Naomi picked him up at the airport, and told him they would be just in time for dinner at sundown, the beginning of the Sabbath. Roger was beginning to learn a few things, and one was that the purpose of the Sabbath was a humanitarian one, to give the servants and even the work animals a day of rest for every six days they labored, but then again, as Naomi explained it to him, the whole purpose of Judaism was to civilize mankind. The ancient pagans scoffed at the concept of an obligatory day of rest for laborers and work animals, and this was one of the many things that separated the ancient Jews from the huge sea of paganism about them.

"That is why God created the world in six days...and rested on the seventh...to sanctify the Sabbath...and the only reason Jews were not permitted to ride on the Sabbath was to avoid using horses...for the horses also needed their day of rest...," Naomi was explaining to Roger as they drove to her home. "The original purpose obviously does not apply today...because we use machines...not horses...but the orthodox Jews still avoid riding...to follow a tradition going back many thousands of years...."

"Naomi...you're going to have to teach me about Judaism...and if you like I'll teach you about Christianity...if you already don't know about it...and if you are interested in learning.... Actually...I know very little...except what I learned in Sunday school...and it wasn't very favorable about the Jews...."

"I know that Roger...and my mother and grandmother know that too...and for that reason they are very concerned about the possibility of my getting serious about a gentile.... The Jews suffered indescribable horrors in the name of your religion...inculcated into every generation by your Sunday schools...and my grandmother keeps reminding me about the Holocaust...the culmination of it all...." Naomi then immediately changed the painful subject, and started to talk about Williamsburg.

They did arrive at her stately home just in time for Roger to unpack his things in one of the guest bedrooms, and to wash up for dinner. Roger had never before been in a Jewish home for the Sabbath dinner, to see everyone present standing in the dining room about the table as the mother, in this home the grandmother, placed a white lace shawl over her head and then lighted the Sabbath candles and recited the Sabbath prayer. He did not learn until later that it was always the mother, not the father, who opened the Sabbath day in the Jewish home, for the home was her kingdom. He had much to learn about Naomi's religion and its ways.

The dinner conversation was very gracious, avoiding religion and Dinah's murder case. For the first time, Roger learned that Mrs Steinberg was actually a judge in the juvenile court, and that Mrs Benjamin was actually Dr Benjamin, a retired physician. "What will Naomi think of my father...a factory worker...and my mother...an uneducated housewife...?" Roger's thoughts ran wild. "But I don't think it would matter to her...not one bit...," he continued this silent conversation with himself, "...and if it did...then it would not speak well of her.... The main problem is going to be religion...and my parents' view of the Jews...and Naomi's and her family's view of Christians.... I'm going to have to talk to Mom and Dad about it all when I see them next time.... Jesus...I hope all goes well.... What a wonderful person she is...!"

During a lull at work the following Wednesday, Roger decided to take the afternoon off after two hours in court that morning, to drive to Veritas to have dinner with his father and mother, and to talk to them about Naomi. He reached the house at about five o'clock, just after his father arrived home from his job. His parents were simple people, but to Roger the best father and mother anyone could have. They loved him, and he loved them. He was devoted to them, and would not hurt them for anything. And that is what was bothering him when he stopped in front of their house, got out of his car and knocked on the front door. He had told them he was coming, but that did not stop the air of surprise when his mother opened the door. He had not seen them for several months, and it could be that they only half-expected he would actually come. They missed him, but understood that it was difficult for their son, now a very important man, to get away from New York City.

After Roger greeted his father and mother, the two men washed up, and then the three Morrisons sat down to dinner. George Morrison said grace in the name of the Trinity, and Roger knew he had his job cut out for himself. There was little conversation during dinner, Roger now remembering that this is exactly how it was when he was growing up, a far cry from the few dinners he had with Naomi's family in Richmond, where the conversation was stimulating and interesting, and actually at times went slightly over his head. He was well trained in two glorified trades, computer science and law, but he began to realize that he knew very little else and was rather under-educated about history, philosophy, religion and world affairs.

Roger helped his mother clear the table, just as he had done when he was a young boy, and after the kitchen was settled, he asked both his parents to forego the television set. He had something important he wanted to talk to them about. Roger came right to the point.

"I met a young woman...truly outstanding...a doctor...."

"That's very nice...Roger..," Mary Morrison interrupted. "Are you very interested in her...and is she interested in you...?"

"When can we meet her...?" his father interrupted his mother.

"She's Jewish...."

Mary's tone suddenly changed. "It's a sin to marry a Jew...."

"Why is it a sin...?"

"Because they killed our god...."

"You know...I learned that in Sunday school...and never gave it much thought...until now...until I met Naomi.... Tell me...Mother...how can a god be killed...if he's a god.... I thought a god is immortal...."

"Jesus was the son of God...and it was Jesus who was killed...by those people...by this Naomi...and her kind...."

"If Jesus was the son of God...then he wasn't god himself...and if Jesus was the son of God...why would God not prevent His son from being killed...?"

"Because he was sacrificed by his own Father...to wash away our sins...."

"Then it was God's plan that His own son die...."

"That's correct...Roger.... That's what you learned in Sunday school...and what we taught you...."

"Then why do you blame anyone for furthering God's plan...?"

George Morrison paused for a moment, and then said, "You speak just like Satan.... That evil woman's bewitched you.... I forbid you to see her again...."

Roger returned to New York City the next morning in a completely despondent mood. When he went to his office later that morning, he asked to see Mark at the DA's convenience, and the DA made every effort to see him, intuitively feeling that Roger, his favorite assistant, was having a severe personal problem.

As Roger walked into his office, and even before he sat down, the Manhattan DA asked, "OK Roger... what's bothering you...?"

"I'm in love with Naomi Steinberg...very deeply in love...but my father and mother feel it's a sin to marry a Jew.... They're uneducated...and ignorant...but they've been very good parents...although I'm not at all sure that teaching a son something like that really makes them good parents.... Why would they think that way...? I'm caught in the middle.... I know she wouldn't marry me...unless I converted...and converted willingly...without any reservation whatever...but how could I convert...even if I wanted to for my own sake...knowing my mother and father feel that way.... It would break their hearts...and I love them too much to do that to them.... If you're going to ask how I know how they feel...I went up to see them yesterday...and I got that hate-the-Jews right between the eyes...."

"Slow down...Roger.... Under the circumstances...you have no choice but to stop seeing Naomi Steinberg.... She comes from an old German Jewish family...originally from Frankfurt...in the immediate aftermath of the 1848 uprisings.... I think they're distantly related to the Rotschilds.... Despite her seemingly secular ways...I feel she's very devoted to her religion as well as to her family.... I know I feel the same way...and so does my wife.... She's a converted Jew...converted when she was a young girl...when her parents converted...both history professors at Harvard.... It's too bad you can't make your parents understand...but you yourself must understand that they've been brought up their way...and they won't change.... It's really too bad...."

"It's killing me...Mark...and this on top of the frustration in the Steinberg murder case...and the lingering uncertainty of whether Naomi would actually marry me even if I did convert...."

"Well...I do have some good news...which should cheer you up a bit.... I've been asked to become my party's next candidate for governor...."

"For governor...?" Roger's mood suddenly changed. "That's great...!"

"And I recommended that you become the party's candidate to replace me...as DA...."

"As district attorney...? Why me...? There are so many more experienced people in your office...."

"But they don't have your dedication...and fairness.... I know you'll not go for a conviction just to get a conviction.... I know you won't suppress evidence favorable to the defense...just to win.... I know you won't abuse the awesome power of the public prosecutor...."

Rather than go through the agony of telling Naomi in person what his personal situation was, Roger decided to write her a letter, a rather long letter, and several days after he mailed it he got a reply, by telephone, wishing him success in the upcoming election campaign and offering to help him in any way she could, but making no mention of his situation with his family. They parted friends, but this kind of friendship does not last too long. How can a normal man, very attracted to a very beautiful woman, maintain a platonic friendship with her?

SEVEN

The year was also a presidential election year, and Mark's and Roger's political party held its national presidential nominating convention that summer in New York City at Madison Square Garden, Mark leading the New York delegates. The two main contenders for the presidential nomination were James Monroe Lancaster of Virginia and Sally Abigail Adams Campbell of New York. They had between them an overwhelming majority of the delegates, but that majority was just about evenly split between them.

James Lancaster exuded the picture of an unblemished family man in his upper-forties, a highly successful lawyer, physically attractive with an attractive well-educated wife as homemaker and research professor of education, with four children, one in college, two in high school, and the fourth in elementary school, United States Senator from Virginia for the past eight years, a member of the Senate Committee on Foreign Relations with an outspoken reputation in foreign affairs, an excellent orator apparently without the typical glibness of the typical politician. He exuded confidence and earnestness seemingly without a know-it-all attitude, and above all, he did not sound like a used-car salesman believing in everything his particular customer did. Well, almost everything, but not quite.

Sally Campbell, born Sally Abigail Adams, was a widow in her early forties, with a very attractive full figure, blonde hair and blue eyes, a rather sensual face, about five feet six and only slightly overweight. She had a teen-age son a freshman in college, a teen-age daughter a junior in high school, was formerly district attorney of one of the upstate New York counties, and presently the elected Attorney General of New York. She was tough but she was fair, although it could not be said that she was not a feminine woman, and she had relatively less of the bedside manner than Lancaster did, but she generated around herself a certain strong atmosphere of intellectual honesty that attracted her as a potential President to many people. Where Lancaster tried to avoid certain difficult issues, Mrs Campbell did not hesitate to address them, carefully and without any glibness at all. She was not all things to all people, and she was a very formidable candidate for the nomination.

The out-of-town convention delegates were spread out over most of the Manhattan hotels, but both the Lancasters, with their children, and Mrs Campbell, with her children, stayed at the New York Hilton. Even before the opening night of the convention, James Lancaster phoned Sally Campbell to ask for a quiet business meeting, to discuss a way of breaking the stalemate between them even before it reached the convention floor.

"I don't think it would be good for the party to have a protracted floor fight...," he said on the phone. "It would be wise for us to get together beforehand...and decide the matter between us...."

"Alright...James...where do you want to meet...and how many of your people are you going to bring...?"

"None.... I thought this ought to be privately settled between you and me...."

"I don't see anything wrong with that...but the meeting ought to be private...."

"Then why not meet in your suite...assuming your children have a separate suite...as mine do...."

"Yes...they do...." She hesitated for a minute, never losing sight of the fact that she was a woman and he a man, and although James Lancaster was not publicly known to be other than an unblemished family man, there were certain stories floating about that he was not as unblemished as the public was being lead to believe. "I don't know...perhaps some other place.... I would rather bring along one of my advisors...."

"I would have no objection to some other place...but I think we can more readily settle this matter without anyone else present...to interfere...and if they are present they will interfere...one way or other.... Where would you like to meet...?"

Sally thought for a brief moment, and then said, "I

suppose my suite would be alright... I'll have one of the state police officers...assigned to my office...standing guard outside the door to make sure we're not disturbed...." That was one way of indicating to James Lancaster that she did not particularly trust him, but it seemed like a plausible reason to have someone about, even though on the other side of the door.

"Fine...I'll see you at say ten o'clock this evening...after Joan and I and my children get back from supper.... Is that alright with you...."

Sally hesitated again. "It's a bit late...but I suppose it will be alright.... I doubt we'll be able to settle anything in one meeting...but at least we can begin.... I'll see you at ten...."

James and Joan Lancaster got back from dinner at about nine, and James then excused himself saying he had to meet with some of his delegates. He took the stairs two flights up to Sally's suite, and knocked on the door after asking the state police officer at the door to get something for him in one of the lobby shops. Sally answered, still dressed in the business suit she had worn for dinner.

"Hello...James...please come in.... Shall I send for room service...?" She held out her hand to shake his, but James took it only to suddenly but very gently pull her a little closer to him, to kiss her gently on the cheek.

"Would you do that to a male contender for the nomination...?" Sally asked, rather surprised, and not too happy about it. "I assumed...when I agreed to meet you here...that you would behave yourself.... I have heard certain rumors about you...."

James smiled, and said, "Not one of them true...."

They sat down in separate chairs, and began to talk about the convention voting, but James all the while got up and down and moved about, all for the purpose of getting closer to her when she was off her guard, and finally he was able to very gently touch her cheek from behind. Sally turned about, very indignant, but before she could say anything, James blurted out, "Sally...for heaven's sake...I'm a man and you're a very attractive woman...whom I've admired for many years...."

"That's not what we got together to talk about...," said Sally, suddenly standing up.

"No...it's not...but after we finish talking about business...I want to tell you how I feel...and if you're concerned about Joan...our marriage has been one in name only for many years...and I suspect she'll want out after the election...regardless of whether I win or lose...so why can't I talk about how I really feel about you...and if you're still not interested in me...that way...then I'll say no more about it...."

Sally was a bit flustered, and literally at a loss for words. "I'm not ready for this sort of thing.... It's been two years since my husband died...and during that time I've thrown all of myself into my children...and my work...."

Before she could continue, James moved very close to her, put his arms around her, and kissed her with a most passionate kiss but not roughly. After several seconds of hesitation, Sally completed responded, and the remainder of the evening was commentary.

While lying together in bed, James proposed marriage to Sally after the election and after getting a divorce of course from his present wife. Sally, a mature woman but not behaving with complete maturity, accepted his proposal, and together they came, once again.

The next evening, after the opening keynote address and other political speeches in Madison Square Garden, Sally presented herself on the convention floor, although it was contrary to tradition for a candidate to do so, and asked the permanent chairman of the convention to be recognized. She went up to the podium, and came right to the point.

"The worst thing that can happen to this party...is to have a protracted fight between James Lancaster and myself...for the party's nomination for President of the United States...." A huge quiet fell on the convention floor, and everyone waited for the second shoe to fall. Sally resumed. "At the appropriate time in these proceedings...I myself shall place the name of James Monroe Lancaster...," and before she could finish, the quiet suddenly turned to a tidal wave of cheering, drowning out what Sally next had to say. She stood there, acknowledging the cheering, and when the sound came down to a reasonable level, she finished her sentence, "...in nomination as our party's candidate for President of the United States...."

The cheering resumed at an even greater decibel level, and there were calls that Sally be nominated for vice president. Needless to say, the following evening,

James Monroe Lancaster received the party's nomination for President and Sally Abigail Adams Campbell received the nomination for Vice President, and when James and Sally stood side-by-side with raised hand-in-hand on the podium to accept the cheers, Mark Rosenblueth thought he could detect certain indications of a personal relationship between the two.

Campaigning together gave James and Sally many an opportunity to be alone on many occasions, and they took advantage of each opportunity to make love. Sally was totally smitten, but James appeared to be a bit more in control of himself. Despite it all, they were very careful to keep their personal relationship a secret, but Joan, having been James's wife for many years, did realize that something was going on. James was right about one thing he told Sally, and that was that Joan was not interested in him any more, and had not been for quite some years, and did intend to seek a divorce or at least a separation after the election.

It was obvious from the very beginning that Roger was not a campaigner, and Mark decided that he would do the campaigning for his protege. Although the chief assistant DA was angry that he was not the candidate for district attorney, he greatly helped in the election battle for Roger while Roger was busy working on his important cases. His performance in court in several difficult fraud cases, primarily those involving the defrauding of consumers, was thoroughly reported by the press, and this time the press did Roger a service, but not intentionally.

About half-way through the campaign, near the end of September, John Paulsen phoned Mark to ask him to lunch, and Mark quickly found time to see him despite his very busy schedule.

"I've been very bothered by this Steinberg case...knowing that I could have done more to help you.... I've decided to provide you with access to all the files...unofficially.... What I'll be doing in probably an offense...but I feel confident I won't be prosecuted for it...."

"Certainly not by me...John...nor by Roger...if he succeeds me.... We would both be very grateful to you.... Roger has had one of the engineering professors at NYU perfect an automated means of scanning all the front pages and making records of all fingerprints on them...using some computerized technique called image-processing.... We should be able to go through all the files in one day.... We won't use the information as evidence...because the question would obviously arise as to how we got it...but if we can identify the person...we'll be able to get his fingerprints some other way.... How shall we proceed...?"

"I've already arranged to move the office of the committee to Manhattan...and that includes the files.... We have space in the court house on Foley Square...and the move should be completed in about a week.... You and Roger can come in on any weekend day...and I'll help with any menial work that would be necessary...like taking files out of cabinets and putting them back again.... My offense...if there is one...which I doubt...would take place in Manhattan...and I'm depending on you and Roger to protect me...."

"With our lives...but seriously...we're very grateful to you...and you know we'll keep this all quiet.... After all...we would have to keep it quiet to protect our own case.... You know how nutty the courts have become on this issue of the fruit of the forbidden tree...everything to protect the criminal...to hell with the victim...."

Once the committee move was completed, Roger, Mark and John spent an entire Sunday processing all the application papers for admission to the bar of New York State. Mark and John became human conveyors as Roger ran the top sheets under the photographic device. It took all of seven hours, and the three "conspirators" left with the processing equipment neatly tucked away in two large briefcases, as though they had been busy doing paperwork.

The same evening, in his office, and in the presence of Mark and John, Roger used his computer setup to run through all the photographic images, to compare each one with the photographic image he had taken from Dinah Steinberg's neck at the time of her murder. There was no match!

"Damn it...!" exclaimed all three, almost in unison.

"You know...," said Roger, as though out of the blue, "...I'll bet his fingerprints are on the bar-examination application papers in Washington.... I suspect our murderer was a Washington lawyer...probably still is...taking either the air shuttle...or the Metroliner...to New York whenever he could...to play around.... Probably a married man...and came up to New York on weekdays.... Dinah Steinberg was murdered on a weekday...."

"I know Bertram Augustine...the chairman of the committee on admissions of the D C Court of Appeals...on Indiana Avenue.... Shall I approach him...?" asked John Paulsen.

"By all means...," Mark quickly responded to John's suggestion, "...if you feel he can be trusted...."

"He's a very old friend.... I'll see what I can do...but you realize that we would have to go through this paper and computer processing in Washington...."

"Well...speaking of old friends...," said Mark, "...Robert Ginsburg...the U S Attorney for the District of Columbia...is a cousin of mine.... Perhaps I ought to talk to him about the problem...and ask him to look the other way if your friend is cooperative...."

This was all taking place during a heavy election campaign, but all three thought it was important enough to take some time off from the campaign, which Mark felt he would like to do anyway. It was decided that John would initiate the entire process, and a few days later he took the Metroliner to Washington to see his friend, Bertram Augustine.

Surprisingly, Bertram was entirely cooperative, but insisted that the U S Attorney be informed and also cooperate. It was now Mark's turn to go to Washington, this trip by air shuttle rather than by train, to see his cousin.

"I don't think we have to do this surreptitiously...," said Robert Ginsburg. "You hand me a formal request...and I'll get a court order to search the files.... We can do it all very quickly...and quietly...without the press even knowing about it.... One of the judges owes me a favor...and he'll sign the order in chambers without any formality.... After all...there will be no invasion of privacy.... This is a murder investigation...and I think a legitimate step.... I don't know why things got so fouled up in New York...."

"I don't know why either...Bob...but I'm grateful for your help...."

"Good luck in the election...Governor...." Both cousins laughed.

The U S Attorney in Washington did get the court order, but the election campaign was coming down to the home stretch, and nothing further was actually done until after that important Tuesday in November.

Mark was elected Governor of the State of New York, Roger became the next District Attorney of New York County, and James Monroe Lancaster was elected President of the United States, a clean party sweep at the polls.

All three men assumed office, and the inaugural address of the new President was most memorable without having to plagiarize material from someone else. Mark was there with his family, and Roger also attended. In the evening of January 20th, Roger escorted Mark's eldest daughter, all of sixteen, to the Inaugural Ball, going with Mark and his family. In the distance, across a very large ballroom in the Washington Hilton, he saw Naomi dancing with her escort, a very distinguished looking young man, but he did not think she saw him, and he avoided opening an old wound, especially a very deep one.

Three weeks after the presidential inauguration, Roger and John Paulsen took the Metroliner to the nation's capital, but this time to search for fingerprints. Even though the search was not being done surreptitiously, they and Robert Ginsburg thought it ought to be done very quietly, without office personnel about, and once again there were some very important men playing file clerks on a weekend as Roger ran sheets of paper, one right after the other, under the special photographic apparatus. And this time, when Roger processed the computerized photographic images in his hotel suite in the presence of John Paulsen and Robert Ginsburg, there was a match, a very clear match!

EIGHT

"For God's sake...," exclaimed Robert Ginsburg, "...what's the matter...? You look as though you've seen a real live ghost.... Did you find my fingerprints...?"

"Please don't joke...Bob.... This is unbelievable...."

"Will you please tell us what you found...," implored John Paulsen impatiently. "We've already been through a lot to get this information...."

"I think Dinah Steinberg's murderer is...James Monroe Lancaster...."

"The President...? Are you serious...?"

"President now...but not then.... If I can confirm this...President Lancaster committed a common-law murder in New York County...which falls right under my jurisdiction...."

"You know...Roger...I'll have to resign as U S Attorney...."

"Good...and how about becoming my special

assistant...? I hope you won't mind moving to New York...."

"Not if my wife doesn't mind.... I hope she won't...and I hope that what you have in mind...is that I work on this prosecution...."

"Exactly...."

"Do you realize this is unprecedented...," exclaimed John Paulsen. "How does a State prosecute an incumbent President of the United States...?"

"No differently than anyone else...accused of murder.... I realize it might become a little difficult to arrest him...but the first thing we do...before we get an arrest warrant in New York County...is get a better exemplar of his fingerprints...just to make sure we have the right man.... John...do you think you could also play a role in this case...?"

"I'm not a criminal lawyer...but I'd be glad to help Robert if you intend to put him in charge of the case.... In my younger days...I was quite an expert on constitutional law...and I think there's going to be a lot of that in this case.... It shouldn't take me too long to brush up...."

"Then it's settled.... Both of you become special assistant district attorneys in New York.... And now I have to call Mark in Albany.... I'll be as cryptic as I can...telling him for now that we found the proverbial needle...."

Roger and John took the first flight out of Washington for New York the next day, connecting there for Albany, and went straight to the Governor's mansion.

"Is this some kind of joke...?" Mark asked,

incredulously. "I'm sure you realize this will have to be confirmed...with fresh fingerprints.... I don't think this is enough to get an arrest warrant...certainly not for the President of the United States...without fresh prints.... In any case...as Governor...I'll support you to the limit...Roger.... The constitutional issues are going to be very sticky...and I'm glad you're coming aboard...John...formally.... I remember reading several of your law review articles some years ago...on federalism.... They were very good.... Now let's have some lunch...and when you get back to Manhattan...Roger...keep me continually informed.... Call me on my personal line out of hours...and if you have to get me at my office...use this private number.... There's no extension...and no chance of eavesdropping.... But remember that I'll fully support you...."

At lunch, and right in the middle of it, Governor Mark Rosenblueth exclaimed, "I have it.... I'll tell you about it when we get back to my office...."

"It's really very simple.... I'll try to get a private appointment to see Lancaster.... That should not be too difficult.... Governor of an important state...both newly elected...from the same party...old acquaintances...and so on.... We'll have something to drink...and then I'll ask him for the glass he's drinking from...as a souvenir for my daughter...who collects these things.... That should give us the best exemplar of his fingerprints...."

"Brilliant...Mark...," exclaimed Roger, smiling. "You can have your old job back...whenever you want it...."

Robert Ginsburg resigned as U S Attorney for the District of Columbia to become a special assistant district attorney of New York County, explaining where and when it needed explaining that he was making the change in order to return with his family to the New York metropolitan area.

"Why not ask the President to appoint you a U S Attorney for one of the several judicial districts...in that part of the country...?" asked a reporter.

"There are no vacancies...and I certainly would not want anyone removed to make a place for me...and besides...I would like to get more experience in state criminal law...in the historic common-law criminal offenses...."

John Paulsen, who was on the brink of retirement anyway, took a leave of absence from his law partnership, and several weeks later Roger formally appointed both John and Robert special assistant district attorneys.

Roger was sorely tempted to contact Naomi, to tell her the news, but he thought better of it. He decided he would call her when the first attempt would be made to serve an out-of-state arrest warrant on the man living at 1600 Pennsylvania Avenue, Northwest, in Washington, the District of Columbia, for that is when the issue of federalism would really be put to the test in a well-publicized case. As far as the new Manhattan DA was concerned, James Monroe Lancaster was a prime suspect in an unsolved murder case in New

York County and only incidentally the President of the United States of America.

A new President ordinarily has an exceptionally busy schedule, especially concerning new appointments, but he did find time to greet Governor Rosenblueth, grateful to him for having carried New York State and its many electoral votes for their party and Lancaster's election, for without New York, Lancaster would not be sitting in the Oval Office. They had a private lunch, and reminisced about the time when they knew each other quite well many years ago, both not too long out of law school.

Mark got what he came for, and when he returned to his office in New York City, he turned the glass object over to Roger, together with a sworn statement as to how he got it, and who had held it before he got it. Roger brought along a portable electronic device to measure the unique crystalline structure of the glass, for he did not want a defense lawyer to raise a doubt, in an attempt to quash any indictment that might come out of all of this, as to whether the glass was indeed the glass referred to in the Governor's sworn statement. The parametric values of the measurement were included in Mark Rosenblueth's statement.

Roger then gave the drinking glass to one of his more trusted technicians, without telling him where and how he got it, to compare its prints with the Dinah Steinberg set in the files. The technician found a total match. Without a doubt, Senator James Monroe Lancaster had murdered Dinah Steinberg, and Roger was becoming more and more anxious to tell Naomi, realizing that he wanted to tell her, to see her, to be with her. He still loved her. He would always love her.

The actual fingerprints to be used at a trial would be obtained from the defendant himself, if they could get this particular defendant into custody to take the fingerprints. And speaking of arrest warrants, Roger had already offered Captain William Salinger, recently promoted to be Inspector Salinger, the position of chief investigator for the DA's office, and the offer was accepted. At the request of the new DA, the new Lieutenants Malloy and Ramos were assigned by the Police Department to work under the new Inspector William Salinger.

Trying to anticipate the defense, and the likelihood that they might try to raise a reasonable doubt of guilt by comparing James Lancaster's face to the video images obtained by the security system in that apartment building, a building in which Roger still lived, Robert Ginsburg had those images checked against press photographs of the President. If the video images were not good-enough as visual representations of the defendant, then despite the conclusive fingerprint evidence, the psychological technique of raising the reasonable doubt could be effective.

The video shots were blown up and projected onto a very large screen alongside an enlarged video image of a press photograph. Robert wanted to compare video image with video image, not a video shot with a glossy photographic print. In everyone's opinion, and that included William Salinger, the two images were close enough. But to be more confident, Robert designed an experiment. He had about a dozen office workers come into the projection room, one at a time, and then had the video image of the President, and of other good-looking men of Lancaster's age, displayed successively on the screen alongside the video image from the security tapes. Without exception, each clerk and typist and secretary identified the President's picture. Robert had no intention of using this as evidence, but only to demolish any attempt by the defense to raise this question of the security tapes as an issue of reasonable doubt.

Mark, Roger, John and Robert held several strategy meetings, all at the Governor's New York City office, and finally decided that the best way to proceed would be to present the case to a grand jury just as they would any garden-variety murder case. A grand jury proceeding is ex parte anyway, not requiring or ordinarily not even permitting the presence of the person to be indicted, and in this case the grand jurors were especially reminded by Judge Lipman of the New York County Court that their deliberations were secret, and that they were under oath to keep them so.

James Monroe Lancaster was indicted for the first-degree murder of Dinah Miriam Steinberg on the evidence of the fingerprints taken from the victim's neck and the fingerprints taken from the accused's drinking glass, and the announcement was made within an hour by Roger in a press conference to a startled world. But before he told the world, Roger called Naomi at her hospital office in Richmond, using the private line in his office, to inform her that an indictment had been returned against her sister's murderer, James Monroe Lancaster. He then suggested she follow the news accounts, and before Naomi could say anything further than to thank him for his call, he said good-bye and hung up.

"We will proceed no differently than we would in the case of any other murder...," Roger announced to a packed hall of reporters representing the electronic and printed press from all over the world. "The defendant in this case presently resides in the District of Columbia...and my chief investigator...William Salinger...will go to Washington with an arrest warrant...to execute against the defendant...with the expected cooperation of the Washington police...and bring him back to New York County...to be arraigned.... If there are any procedural roadblocks placed in our way...we shall do our best to overcome them.... The fact that the defendant is the President of the United States does not absolve him of the cold-blooded murder of a woman physician in this county.... It does not make him immune to prosecution for a felony committed under the laws of the State of New York.... The State of New York shares sovereignty on this soil with the United States of America...each sovereign in its own sphere.... Neither is the superior of the other...."

"Mr Morrison...what if the President resists arrest...?

He's quite capable of doing that...."

"We'll cross that bridge...when we come to it...."

Needless to say, about two hundred miles south of Manhattan, the President was holding a hastily called televised press conference in Washington to vehemently deny the allegations.

"Do you intend to submit to arrest...Mr President...?"

"Of course not.... I have no intention of being any part of this circus.... I have the business of the nation to run...and I am not going to let some kid try to make a big name for himself...at my expense...."

"Then you'll be resisting arrest...under an arrest warrant issued under the laws of New York.... I couldn't do that...Mr President.... Why can you...? Are you above the law...?"

"No man is above the law...if the law is being validly executed.... It is not being validly executed in this case...."

"Why not...Mr President...?" asked another reporter. "A New York County grand jury indicted you for first-degree murder...for a crime committed several years ago.... An arrest warrant was issued against you...by the chief judge of the County Court of New York County...based on that indictment.... I understand that the chief investigator...of the Manhattan DA's office...will attempt to execute that warrant...here in Washington...."

"I'm sorry...ladies and gentlemen...but I have some very urgent matters to take care of...dealing with our foreign affairs...much more important that the script written by Mr Morrison...," and with that final statement, President Lancaster left the podium as the senior White House reporter uttered the traditional "Thank you...Mr President...."

Vice President Sally Campbell was distressed by the situation, and like any woman still in love with her man, and thinking that he still loved her, she believed him to be totally innocent. But the very next day, Joan Lancaster made an appointment to see her, which caught Sally quite by surprise. She agreed to see Joan in her official residence on Observatory Circle the same afternoon.

"I'm very glad to see you...Joan...," she tried to keep her composure. "What terrible things they're saying about James...."

"And I'm sorry to say...Sally...that they are very probably all true...." Sally was stunned, but Joan continued, "All during his public career...James was portrayed to be a family man...but he never was.... Right after I first became pregnant...and even before the birth of our first child...he become a womanizer...without any limit to his appetite...and I can readily surmise what he said to you...and did to you...to cause you to throw away your own chance to live in the White House...rather than here.... Has he recognized your existence...even officially...since the inauguration...?"

Sally said nothing, but shook her head laterally in the negative.

"I assumed that was the case.... I feel very sorry for you...Sally...but if James told you he intends to marry you once I divorce him...only one part of that statement is true.... I do intend to divorce him...as soon as he gets through this situation...one way or the other...but he never intended to marry you...or anyone else.... I have no doubt that James murdered that woman.... I've known Mark Rosenblueth for many years...and he has always been a man of the greatest integrity.... If he says there's conclusive evidence...that my husband killed Dr Dinah Steinberg...then there is conclusive evidence.... James will obviously play hardball...and use all the powers of his office to get out of this.... I don't know what the eventual end will be...."

The Vice President of the United States began to sob. Joan got up from her chair, placed her arm around Sally's shoulders, and tried to comfort her, saying over and over again, "It's alright Sally.... You'll be alright.... You're a very fine woman...a very capable person...and I'll be very proud when you become the next President.... There's no question in my mind that James will not succeed in getting out of this mess...."

"I don't know why I fell for that line of his...," Sally lamented.

"Don't feel too badly about it...Sally.... After all...I did...a long time ago...and I've been paying for it ever since...."

NINE

One of the biggest news story of the century was still unfolding, and it was now Governor Rosenblueth's turn to hold a press conference, a press conference forced on him by the clamoring of the press.

"No...this indictment is not politically motivated...," he exclaimed in answer to a question. "Mr Lancaster...Mr Morrison...and I...are all of the same political party...and we ran together in the last election.... Mr Lancaster even acknowledged...publicly...that he owed his election to me...for swinging the New York electoral vote behind him...."

"Then why was the indictment brought...?" asked a reporter.

"I hate to call anyone stupid...but that is really a stupid question...and a very insulting one.... When I was the Manhattan DA...a terrible crime was committed against a woman...a physician...in Manhattan.... My office and the police tried very hard...since that time...to find the murderer.... We had his fingerprints...from the neck of the victim...but we could never find out whose fingerprints they were...until now.... They were James Lancaster's fingerprints that were embedded in the neck of that strangled woman...and the sovereign State of New York will bring her killer to justice.... We are not interested in criminalizing any policy differences...between the sovereign State of New York and the sovereign United States of America...New York as a sovereign state represented by me...its Governor...and the second sovereign represented by the President.... We are interested in prosecuting an individual for murder...first-degree murder...."

"Governor...what do you expect will now actually happen...?"

"Mr Lancaster will play hardball...as it has never been played before.... I'll bet...as we are gathered here...that a federal grand jury in the Southern District of New York...which means the island of Manhattan...is about to return an indictment against me...and against the Manhattan DA...Roger Morrison...among others...accusing us of conspiring against the life of the President of the United States...or some other conjured-up federal crime...and that will set the stage for the greatest constitutional crisis since the civil war...."

"Can you possibly hope to win...?" asked another reporter, this one not stupid at all.

"I feel we shall.... Most people...and that includes most lawyers and politicians...and even some judges...they don't realize that our country is still a federation of sovereign States...States that delegated some of their sovereignty to the federal government in very specific areas...for their common good...all the remaining areas of jurisdiction the States retaining for themselves.... In the ultimate...the States are supreme...if the States wish to constitutionally exercise that supremacy.... It has to be done according to the federal constitution...the compact the original States entered into with each other...and which the other thirty-seven States subsequently adhered to.... It cannot be done...other than according to that compact...."

Many hands shot up, asking to be recognized, and one of them asked the next question.

"But it's my understanding that federal law is the supreme law of the land...."

"I have John Paulsen standing beside me...a noted expert on federalism.... I'm going to ask him to answer your question.... Ladies and gentlemen...Mr Paulsen...."

"First of all...," said John Paulsen, "...the federal law you speak of are Acts of Congress and treaties.... It does not include the decisions of the federal courts...or the decisions of the President...meaning that even the decisions of the federal supreme court are not the law of the land.... If you read the last article of the original constitution...there is provision for amending the federal constitution.... It is not necessary that a federal constitutional amendment originate in the federal legislature...the Congress.... It can originate in a convention called by two-thirds of the States...and then each such proposed amendment would take effect when ratified by three-quarters of the States.... The States...standing together...can lawfully change the federal constitution...by themselves...and they can...if they so desire... completely recast the federal government...or even constitutionally abolish it...." John Paulsen returned the podium to Governor Rosenblueth.

"It's all a question as to whether the States wish to continue to abdicate their sovereignty...or to assert it.... What I intend to do is call a meeting of all the State governors.... This is not a partisan battle.... Either the States are sovereign in their sphere...or they are nothing but historically quaint administrative units of an all-encompassing central government.... The States have for too long been hit over their collective heads by a federal supreme court using the fourteenth amendment...specifically the so-called privileges and immunities clause.... As the three greatest jurists of this century...Chief Justice Stone...Justice Brandeis...Justice Cardozo...all of the United States Supreme Court...pointed out many years ago...that clause deals only with the privileges and immunities of citizens of the United States...not with the privileges and immunities of citizens of each State.... Very few of our people even realize they have dual citizenship.... Each is a citizen of his State as well as of the United States...."

"What will you do...if your prediction does come true...that there's an indictment in the federal court in Manhattan...to harass and intimidate you...and the Manhattan DA...."

Mark Rosenblueth laughed. "We'll resist arrest...on

the trumped-up charges...and I'll take the issue to the other forty-nine States...and settle it there.... I don't think we should even try to enforce that valid arrest warrant of ours against James Lancaster.... It's obvious what will happen to the man...or woman...who tries to execute such a warrant...and I have...and Mr Morrison has...no intention of going through a procedure that will obviously lead to naught...a procedure that would place any man or woman in jeopardy...."

The senior reporter thanked the Governor, and as Mark walked with John Paulsen back to his office, both protected by a large detail of the state police, a small group of men in civilian clothes approached them, identifying themselves to be agents of the Federal Bureau of Investigation, and that they were there to arrest both the Governor and John Paulsen on federal criminal charges. The state police then proceeded to arrest the FBI agents, and at the same time in New York City, the New York City police detail assigned to the office of the Manhattan DA arrested the FBI agents sent to arrest Roger Morrison and Robert Ginsburg. The confrontation between James Monroe Lancaster and the People of the State of New York had begun!

A politician is a statesman if he acts on principle, but his principles must of necessity be realistic. By this definition, and it is a good one, Mark Rosenblueth was a statesman. The question that now arose in everyone's mind: Were the Governors of the other States also statesmen and stateswomen?

When he finally got back to his office, Mark placed calls to all the other forty-nine Governors. Not one of them was in to answer the call, even though they were all in, each in close conference with his advisors deciding what to do when the Governor of New York called. In his press conference, the Governor of New York publicly put them on the spot, that they either defend the sovereignty of their States or allow the final demise of the American States as sovereign entities.

Mark's phone call was for a meeting of all the Governors to be held in New York City at Governor Rosenblueth's office, to be held in three days, and his second call was returned by all the Governors, who all agreed to come, Governor Rosenblueth not knowing whether they were all coming to support him, or whether some of them were coming to urge Mark Rosenblueth to back down, to surrender.

Two days before the meeting of the Governors, Mark Rosenblueth had an emergency meeting with Major General Cornwall, the adjutant general of the New York Army National Guard, who pledged to support the Governor of New York, that he would refuse to obey any order calling the state militia into federal service. When this decision became known to James Lancaster, he announced to the nation that he had ordered units of the regular army and of the Marine Corps to stand by, to be ready to move into New York State, to arrest the Governor. Mark countered by calling up the state militia to defend New York against an illegal invasion.

On the day appointed for the meeting of the Governors of all the States in the nation's financial capital, the President of the United States issued a proclamation declaring the State of New York to be in a state of insurrection against the United States of America, for having arrested the FBI agents. Despite the announced intention of General Cornwall not to obey such an order, the murderer of Dinah Miriam Steinberg followed the proclamation with an order calling the New York State militia into federal service to suppress the insurrection, an order that was not obeyed. The news of the proclamation astounded the assembled Governors, and all of them realized that this was indeed the most serious constitutional crisis since the American War Between the States.

At that meeting of the Governors, Mark Rosenblueth presented to them conclusive proof that James Lancaster was a murderer.

"I ask each one of you...ladies and gentlemen...what you would do if the murder had taken place in your State.... Is the President above the law...? Is he above the law of murder...?" asked the Governor of New York. "Would any of you...under a constitutional duty to your State to enforce its laws...decline to enforce the law against murder just because the murderer happens to now be the President of the United States...? And what if a person...even while occupying that august office...commits a murder...within the boundaries of one of our sovereign States...? The States have slowly abdicated their sovereignty...all these many years.... If they continue to do so...there will be no States...and we might as well all resign...and let a central government in Washington appoint administrative heads in our stead.... Ladies and gentlemen...please remember that the States hold the ultimate power under the federal constitution.... This nation is a federation of States.... We created the federal government.... The federal government did not create us...."

"What do you propose we do...Mark...?" asked Governor Lester of New Jersey.

"First of all...we must all stand together.... Lancaster is grossly abusing the powers of the Presidency...for his own personal purposes...and that's the beginning of tyranny...of dictatorship.... If he can force New York to back down...he can force any State to do what he wishes.... For the time being...the commanding general of the New York State militia voluntarily remains under my authority.... He refuses to obey the orders of the President.... But we...the Governors of the States...must move...legally...and constitutionally.... The New York delegation...in the House of Representatives...in Washington...this morning introduced a bill of impeachment against President Lancaster.... Assuming impeachment is voted...each of us must convince the two Senators from his State to vote to remove Lancaster from office unless he resigns...to submit himself to the criminal due process of a State.... If the House does vote a bill of impeachment...then we'll ask the House managers to try Lancaster in the Senate for the crime of murder...under the other high crimes clause.... We'll turn all our evidence over to the House.... The most the Senate can do is remove him from office...but then we shall arrest the man...bring him to New York County...in the State of New York...and try him for first-degree murder.... There will be no double jeopardy...since the first trial...before the Senate...could result only in removal from office...and can't in any way possibly put Lancaster in jeopardy of life or liberty or property...."

The assembled Governors felt that Governor Rosenblueth was presenting a sensible course of action, and each one did promise to pressure the members of the House and of the Senate from his State to remove the President from office on the issue of murder. They also unanimously signed a statement addressed to President Lancaster demanding that he stop his obvious harassment and intimidation of the Governor of New York and of other elected officials in New York.

In response, James Lancaster publicly threatened to send units of the Navy into New York harbor to bombard the island of Manhattan unless Mark Rosenblueth and Roger Morrison personally surrendered to agents of the Secret Service. To back up this threat, he called to his office Allen Redmond, Secretary of Defense, and General John Wrightson, Chairman of the Joint Chiefs of Staff.

"Are you mad...James...? Are you stark raving mad...?" asked his friend of many years. "Everyone knows this action by Mark Rosenblueth is not politically motivated...and all the Governors have signed a statement backing him.... You can't use the armed forces of the United States as your own private military organization...."

"May I speak...Mr Secretary...?" rhetorically asked

General Wrightson. "Mr President...the army units you ordered to stand by...will not stand by...and the naval units you ordered to enter New York harbor to shell the city will mutiny...if your order is repeated.... Mr President...you are denigrating your high office by using the awesome powers of the presidency to protect yourself against personal charges...charges directed at you...not as President...but as citizen James Lancaster.... You must not refuse to defend yourself against this most serious charge...this charge of murder.... We all realize that any State could bring such a charge...in order to harass you...but I'm told by many...privately...in and out of the government...that Mark Rosenblueth is a man of great honor...a rarity nowadays...and his action against you is being regarded by everyone as that of an honorable man...."

"Gentlemen...I am innocent...and Mark Rosenblueth isn't as honorable as you think.... He wants to sweep me away...so he can inherit the leadership of my party.... What else can you expect of a Jew...?"

"Mr President...," exclaimed Allen Redmond, "...how dare you say such a thing...!"

"I'll say what is so...and I expect the resignation of each of you...in writing...by four o'clock this afternoon.... If you will not serve the President of the United States...duly elected by the people...then I'll find those who will.... Good day...gentlemen.... Your resignations by four o'clock...."

The Secretary of Defense and the Chairman of the Joint Chiefs walked out of the Oval Office without saying a word and without so such as a "by your leave," and as they arrived in their limousine at the White House west gate on Pennsylvania Avenue, the White House police stopped them.

"I'm sorry...Mr Redmond...but we just got a telephone message from the Secret Service...to arrest you...for threatening the life of the President...."

With that, the sergeant driving the motor car, and his companion, drew pistols from the glove compartment, and quickly opened their doors and stepped out of the limousine. This unexpected action took the several White House police officers completely by surprise. They were disarmed, the phone in their sentry house was ripped from the wall, and the two sergeants drove away, with their two grateful charges in the back seat.

"That was very good thinking...Sergeant.... You are to be commended...."

"What in the hell is going on...sir...?"

"A very serious problem...Sergeant...."

The brief confrontation at the White House gate did not escape the notice of the several reporters who habitually monitor the goings and comings of people in and out of the executive mansion, especially at that gate. The incident was on the front page throughout the entire country the next day, together with wire photos. It was difficult to tell, however, whether the news accounts were criticizing the President or criticizing Allen Redmond and John Wrightson.

Redmond and Wrightson returned the same day directly to the Pentagon to jointly inform their colleagues of what happened, and were told that the President himself had just called the Provost Marshal General of the Army to arrest them both, but no one at the Pentagon obeyed the order. Redmond called all the service secretaries and subcabinet officers into an emergency meeting with the members of the Joint Chiefs of Staff.

"Ladies and gentlemen...strictly speaking...I'm no longer Secretary of Defense...and General Wrightson is no longer the Chairman of the Joint Chiefs.... It's obvious that the President plans to use his high office for his own personal interest.... He is therefore violating his constitutional oath of office...and we would too if we were to obey any order by James Lancaster to fire upon our own people...on Americans...just because James Lancaster is unwilling to defend himself against a most serious criminal charge.... I intend to go from this meeting to see the Vice President and urge her to call a meeting of the Cabinet.... As many of you know...the Vice President can become acting President...if the Cabinet agrees that the President is incapable of exercising his office.... I feel that James Lancaster is irrational...and General Wrightson is of the same opinion.... We just came from a meeting with him at the White House.... He demanded our resignations...which we will send to him later this afternoon...because we refused to back his personal use of the armed forces...and on our way out...he tried to have us both arrested on the ground of conspiring against his life.... He is indeed irrational...and General Wrightson and I must now be on our way to see Vice President Campbell...."

When Sally Campbell received Allen Redmond's phone call for an urgent meeting with her, she sensed its purpose, and phoned Joan Lancaster to join the meeting. Joan was waiting with Sally as Redmond and General Wrightson were shown into the Vice President's office. They were surprised, at first, that the First Lady was there, but then realized why she was.

"Mrs Campbell...we met with the President this morning...and he is adamant about using the armed forces for his own personal gain...to defeat any attempt to have him submit to the judicial process of the State of New York.... He asked for my resignation...and General Wrightson's...because we refused to back him in this folly...and on our way out of the White House gate...the White House police tried to arrest us...on the ground of conspiring against his life.... If James Lancaster is not stopped...we shall have a dictatorship...if the armed forces support him...and even worse...we may even have a civil war.... This entire situation has gotten out of hand...and I am strongly suggesting that you convene the Cabinet...to declare you acting President...on the ground that James Lancaster is irrational...that he is unable to discharge his responsibilities under the constitution...."

"I thank you both very much for coming here...and I fully intend to do what you are recommending.... Indeed...I have already asked the members of the Cabinet to meet here later this afternoon...to place the matter before them...but I have no illusions about the result.... They're all appointees of James Lancaster...and I feel that at least two of them will refuse to go along.... If they don't go along...then there's nothing further that I can do...as Vice President...and indeed if they don't go along...then I think the wisest course for all of us would be to go to New York for safety...until we learn what the armed forces will do...not only what the top leaders will do...but also what the lower-level officers and enlisted personnel will do.... We're all in personal danger if the Cabinet does not act...but in the final analysis it's all up to the armed forces.... If they're willing to back James Lancaster...then he could even arrest members of Congress and federal judges...on one trumped up charge or another...."

"What is your opinion...General Wrightson...?" asked Joan Lancaster. "I agree with what you say...Allen...and that's why I'm here.... Sally feels that I ought to address the Cabinet...and urge them to make Sally the acting President.... I don't feel that's a wise thing for me to do.... It would be much better if I were not involved...as far as my husband would know about it.... In that way...I could continue to more or less monitor what's going on at the White House...but I urge both of you to address the Cabinet and make them understand the seriousness of the situation.... And if the Cabinet refuses to constitutionally act...then I agree with Mrs Campbell that we all ought to leave Washington...to go to any State...."

"Well...Mrs Lancaster...," the General replied, "...I feel that the armed forces in general will not obey the President in this matter...although some units might.... Governor Rosenblueth has convinced all the Governors of your husband's guilt...by showing them the conclusive evidence.... They have all been in contact with the units of the armed forces located within their boundaries...and each has called up the militia of his State...each militia greatly augmented by new volunteers who apparently do not take kindly to any attack against their State.... I would assume that...by and large...the armed forces of the nation will remain neutral...and let the President and the Governors fight it out constitutionally.... That's what I think...."

"General Wrightson...I certainly hope you are correct...," responded the First Lady.

TEN

The Cabinet met in the conference room of the Vice President's mansion on Massachusetts Avenue, on the grounds of the Naval Observatory. Allen Redmond, a full-blooded native American of the Cherokee tribe, forcefully urged his Cabinet colleagues to act responsibly. Mrs Campbell, presiding, then called on General Wrightson, he not a member of the Cabinet but there as a guest of the Vice President.

"Ladies and gentlemen...there will be much strife in this country...even more than we already have...if James Lancaster is not stopped at this point.... He is prepared to use the armed forces of this nation against American citizens because he will not defend himself...in any way...against a legitimate charge of murder.... He has not even suggested that he be tried in a different State...to avoid what he insists is the malice of the Governor of New York against him.... But no...he will not respond to any allegations except to threaten to literally destroy New York City...."

"Just a minute...General Wrightson...," interrupted John Everett Rainey, of Houston, the Secretary of the Interior. "I think the President might have a point.... Mark Rosenblueth is a Jew...and you know how Jews are...."

Sally Campbell exploded, and so did most of those present in that conference room. When she recovered, she said, "John...I think you're completely out of order.... We all know your disgusting views.... I was truly surprised when James Lancaster appointed you...although from what I had been told just before this meeting...I can now understand why.... Let's be very responsible about this.... We're all of Lancaster's party...and so in Mark Rosenblueth.... Indeed...if it were not for Mark Rosenblueth...Lancaster would not be in the White House...and you would not be members of the Cabinet.... As Allen and General Wrightson have pointed out...this situation is getting out of hand...and something has to be done until the matter is settled.... Now...constitutionally...we can declare the President temporarily incapable of performing his duties because he's irrational...but I realize that under that same constitutional amendment...he can recover the presidency by simply addressing a letter to us that he is capable once again.... So that might not be the course to take.... Do any of you have a suggestion...?"

"I apologize for my intemperate statement...Madame Vice President...," said John Everett Rainey, "...and you have presented the dilemma very well.... I don't think there's anything we can do....

The constitution hoped to avoid military dictatorships by placing the military under civilian control...but the founding fathers apparently didn't reckon with a President who would be able to use the armed forces to effect a dictatorship.... I know that Texas will fight...and so will others.... What's your opinion of the attitudes in the armed forces...General Wrightson...? And I'm glad you invited General Wrightson to this meeting...Mrs Campbell.... In a way...he's the key to the whole shebang...."

"To answer your question...Mr Rainey...I don't think the armed forces will take sides...but they're not the only organized body of armed men in this country.... The FBI has over twenty-five thousand agents...and most are very loyal to their director...and their director is very loyal to James Lancaster...but the really difficult problem are the armed antisemites who will rally to James Lancaster if he makes an issue of the Christian knight James Lancaster against the Jewish evil dragon Mark Rosenblueth.... That's really what frightens me...and if you think more about...Mr Rainey...it should also frighten you...."

"I've just thought about it...and it does...and I again apologize for what I said...."

"Then what shall we do...?" asked Sally Campbell.

After much further discussion, the meeting ended inconclusively. Mrs Campbell thanked everyone for attending, and after they all left the vice presidential mansion, she packed a bag and drove her own personal car out of the garage. She picked up her daughter at school, and then drove out Massachusetts Avenue extended to the Capital Beltway in suburban Maryland, from there over the Cabin John Bridge into Virginia, continuing on to Interstate 95, and then to Richmond, arriving only several hours later unannounced, but most welcome, at the well-guarded home of Naomi Steinberg, well-guarded by the Virginia State Police and the Virginia state militia. Naomi herself answered the door chimes, was surprised to see the Vice President, but immediately invited her to come in.

"I'm sorry to intrude on you...Dr Steinberg...but this was the best place I could think of when I zoomed out of that garage back in Washington.... If Lamcaster had any intention of trying to arrest me...he would probably assume I would go to New York...."

"I'm glad you came...Mrs Campbell...and I fully understand why you left Washington...and please call me Naomi...and please stay with us as long as you like.... My mother and grandmother are out to a fund-raising dinner...but they should be back shortly.... Let me have one of our guest rooms made ready for you...and Julia.... Do you want to call your son at his college...to make sure he's alright...?"

"You're very kind...Naomi...and please call me Sally.... I intend to call Kenneth Strong...the Attorney General of Virginia...first thing in the morning.... I knew him well when I was the Attorney General of New York...and I always admired his grasp of federalism and constitutional law.... Perhaps both of us can come up with some constitutional way of stopping Lancaster...very quickly...before he seduces enough of the armed forces into following him...." She hesitated, for the time being, to relate to Naomi the concern voiced back at her official residence of a possible antisemitic upheaval, a possible American Kristallnacht.

The following day, Sally had her meeting with Kenneth Strong, he at seventy-five still one of the best and most active legal minds in the country. His white hair and white goatee beard, and especially his courtly manners, placed him right in the middle of antebellum Richmond.

"I am most honored that you came to see me about this problem...Sally...."

"I could think of no one better...and to be frank...I came to Richmond also to see Naomi Steinberg...."

"Ah...yes...that fine and cultured family.... I hope that the murderer of Dr Steinberg's sister is properly punished.... From what I read in the press...the Governor of New York has convinced all the other Governors of Lancaster's guilt.... I do not doubt that to be so.... Mark Rosenblueth is a man to be completely trusted...."

"James Lancaster plans to use what he can of the armed forces to protect himself...and he plans to rouse all the latent antisemitism in this country...and there is plenty of it...against Mark Rosenblueth.... We have to stop him before he's really able to do anything...and we must do it constitutionally.... So...," Sally smiled for the first time since her arrival, "...I came to see the expert...."

Mr Strong laughed. "You know...Sally...one of these days when this is all over...I am going to court you...in the old-fashioned way...."

"That's the best way...Kenneth...."

"Well...let me see.... I am sure you considered the disability amendment...but that will not work.... Let me see...," and he again fell into deep thought. Sally just looked at this handsome courtly gentleman, and waited very patiently and very quietly. "I know a way...but it would require the House of Representatives to do it.... The majority is of his party...but so are a majority of the Governors...and all the Governors have publicly announced for the Governor of New York...who is also of Lancaster's party...so this is not a political matter...but a constitutional one.... The members of the House certainly cannot ignore the Governors of their States.... After all they are the representatives of their States...."

"Please Kenneth...on with it...."

"Do not rush me...Sally.... I shall compose this as I go along...but I must say that it a very clever approach...."

In a terrible situation of this kind, in a free democracy, the ultimate resolution depends on public opinion. The press, both printed and electronic, as the ultimate formulators of public opinion, sprang very heavily into action to mold that public opinion. Editorials were written, news articles were typically slanted, and the television "talk shows" were more than alive with constitutional experts of all kinds. Although the fundamental issue was whether an incumbent President was immune to criminal charges that he committed a common-law felony, which immunity would apply to no other American, most of the self-appointed experts, in and out of the universities, sufficiently muddied the issue so as to make it hardly recognizable. Although Mark Rosenblueth admitted at his next press conference that a State could present fabricated charges of a common-law felony against a President, and by doing so harassing him in the performance of his very important duties, he did say that "The issue must be resolved by the federal House impeaching the President...and the federal Senate removing him from office...essentially a trial on the criminal charges of a State.... That solves the problem of possible State harassment...."

"But what if thirty-four Senators hold firm for the President...come what may...?"

"Then I would propose that the States amend the federal constitution...to alternatively provide for the removal of the President by a vote of two-thirds of the Governors...following a bill of impeachment brought by the legislatures of a majority of the States...if the issue is one of committing a common-law felony.... The removal would of course be followed by an actual trial in the State courts...."

Kenneth Strong made an appointment for him and Sally Campbell to see Governor Garry of Virginia, to discuss Kenneth's plan with him, and all three then asked the Virginia and New York delegations in Washington to come to Richmond to meet with the Attorney General of Virginia. The New York delegation went, but only after informing Mark Rosenblueth, and Mark immediately called Kenneth to discuss what he intended to propose to the representatives.

"Mark...I am not at all sure that our phone lines are

not tapped...but if you wish to fly down in your official plane...and if you feel you are safe in doing so...then by all means I would be delighted to have you here when I meet with your New Yorkers as well as my Virginians...and you can bring that Manhattan DA with you if you wish...but I frankly do not think it is safe.... We have a very serious and difficult problem on our hands...and I think the House might constitutionally be the key...."

"Do you mean impeachment...Kenneth...? The bill has already been introduced...and we expect it to be enacted in a few days...."

"I mean beyond impeachment...and before trial...."

"I'm very curious...but I trust your judgment completely...Kenneth.... Just let know...or I suppose I can wait...most impatiently...until the House does what you will propose they do...."

Most of the Virginia and New York delegations arrived the following day, and several floors of the Commonwealth Park Hotel were reserved for their use. They met after dinner with the Attorney General and the Vice President.

"Ladies and gentlemen...we need not relate to each other the seriousness of the crisis in Washington.... We all know how serious it is.... The important thing...as I see it...is to neutralize James Lancaster...and to do it quickly and above all constitutionally...before the situation gets completely out of hand.... When the thirteen States each obtained its independence about two centuries ago...the common law of England became the law of each State...and the legislature of each State succeeded to the inherent powers of the House of Commons...except that the legislatures by the constitution of each State could not enact a bill of attainder.... When the States formed the Union of States...the federal constitution provided for a House of Representatives holding the power of the federal purse much as the House of Commons held it in England...and in effect the House of Representatives succeeded to all the powers of the British House...but only in the area of sovereignty delegated by the States to the federal government...again except for the constitutional prohibition against bills of attainder...." He paused, and took a sip of water from the filled drinking glass in front of him. "Ladies and gentlemen...the House not only has the power to impeach...but it also has the power to declare and punish contempt of the House.... I see no reason why this power cannot extend to the President.... It is true that he is a chief of state...as well as a chief of government...but this nation is a republic...and the President is not a monarch.... I strongly suggest that the President is vulnerable to the power of the House to punish for contempt as any person is...."

"Excuse me...Mr Strong...," interrupted Simon Branchley of New York, "...but aren't all contempts of the House tried by the courts...?"

"But only because that is the way it is provided for...by Act of Congress...as a delegation to the courts...but in the early history of our republic...each house of the Congress did arrest people for contempt...bring them before the bar of either the House or the Senate...and then summarily punish the offender.... This was an inherent power of the House of Commons to which each house of the Congress succeeded.... I would therefore suggest that you sponsor a resolution that the President not leave the seat of government before he must appear before the Senate for trial on your bill of impeachment.... Assuming that the House will adopt such a resolution...I would wager that he will refuse...and deliberately show that he can disobey the resolution...whereby the House will proceed to arrest the President...and bring him before the bar of the House to be adjudged by the House...."

"And how does the House of Representatives possibly arrest the President...?" asked Mrs Georgia Worthington of Virginia.

"The House has a sergeant-at-arms...and he can appoint as many deputies as the House will authorize and pay for.... I would suggest he appoint say a hundred deputies...or several thousand...to go to the White House with him to arrest the President.... It is all very constitutional...and once Lancaster is brought before the House of Representatives...he can be placed under restraint at his official residence...the White House...until the trial before the Senate.... The conditions of the restraint could be that he communicate with no one except his lawyers...and that would then give Mrs Campbell a reason to exercise the disability amendment...."

"It's a very clever approach...Mr Strong...," commented Ralph Unger of New York, a member of the New York bar. "I hope it works.... I'm sure everyone here will try to make it work...."

ELEVEN

Realizing that the armed forces would not fully back him because of John Wrightson's influence, and facing a bill of impeachment, President Lancaster did back down, for the time being. He called off the awesome raw power of the federal government, at least the power that he could still command despite the negative public opinion beginning to develop against him, a power the founders of the nation did not intend the federal government to have, certainly not against the States that formed that government and not against the States that ratified the Fourteenth Amendment. He put very heavy pressure on the thirty-eight United States Senators who were very loyal to him, strongly urging them to remain loyal to him in any impeachment trial, but seven of those thirty-eight informed him that they would vote for his removal if the trial were on the issue of murder and if the evidence were conclusive. Thirty-one votes in his favor would not prevent Lancaster's removal from the Oval Office.

"We are sorry...Mr President...," said Senator Symonds, speaking for the group of seven at lunch with President Lancaster in the White House, "...but we have to live with our consciences...and with our families...."

Naomi found herself in the center of the storm, and if the press ever victimized anyone in this entire affair, Naomi was that victim. Her home was surrounded day and night by reporters, under constant surveillance by TV cameras, and it was only because of a very sympathetic Mayor of Richmond and a cooperative Governor of Virginia that her home and person were well protected as she went between hospital and home. She was besieged by questions, one after the other, continually, without respite, until she was on the verge of a nervous breakdown. On top of this, the crank phone calls and crank letters were in the worst taste, and had to be filtered by the police officers on guard inside and around her home. It was all enough to bring the human insects out of the woodwork.

She wanted to contact Roger, to find out what New York was doing, but she was afraid the phone lines were tapped, either by the press or by federal agents. As for the mail, despite its purported sanctity, there was really nothing that could be done to prevent federal agents from intercepting a letter. So she decided to ask a first cousin of her mother's, Mrs Judith Benjamin, to go to New York bearing a letter to Roger, and to bring back any reply he might wish to send. To prevent her cousin from being tailed, which would be the fate of anyone visiting her or her family at home, Naomi had her cousin come to her office at the hospital, as though she were a patient, and Mrs Benjamin left there with the letter safely in her purse, directly for the airport.

It was not a love letter, for Naomi was not in love with Roger, but it was very friendly. She expressed her great appreciation for all that he and the others were going through to bring her sister's killer to justice, and she asked that he let her know what she could do to help. She asked about his health and well-being, and that he send back his reply, if any, in the hands of her cousin. The reply was a love letter, very constrained, but the emotionalism seeped through despite the constraint, ending with an expression of hope that someday he might be able to see her again, personally not professionally.

On the very day that Judith Benjamin returned for her next "appointment" with Dr Steinberg, a very large number of FBI agents, in charge of an agent Joseph Angstrom, appeared at the hospital, and went directly to the hospital administrator's office, there to show Dr Rawlings a warrant, issued by the federal magistrate for the Northern District of Virginia, a warrant for the arrest of Dr Naomi Anna Steinberg on the fabricated charge of conspiring to assassinate the President.

"I would strongly suggest you accompany us...Dr Rawlings...to her office...to make sure there are no incidents...," said Mr Angstrom. "I would not want to have to arrest you too...for aiding someone resisting arrest...."

"But her office is heavily guarded by the Virginia State Police...and by the Richmond police.... I can't have a forceful confrontation in this hospital...."

"Then...if you are concerned about the welfare of your patients...and you should be...pick up your telephone...and ask Dr Steinberg to come to your office...."

"She will be accompanied in the hall...by some of the police officers...."

"Not too many.... I'm sure my agents can neutralize them...."

Naomi was arrested and handcuffed as she innocently walked alone into Dr Rawlings's office. The three police officers waiting outside were quickly disarmed by the FBI agents who appeared to be just standing about waiting, and Naomi was taken away. Dr Rawlings immediately called a special number at the Governor's mansion in Richmond to let the state police know what had just happened, and very apologetically explained why he had to betray Dr Steinberg for the sake of the patients in the hospital and its staff.

"The FBI agents seemed very determined...and I could under no circumstances...tolerate any gunplay...."

The state police immediately placed a road block on all main roads leading out of Richmond, but did not count on the FBI using a helicopter from one of the small private airports about the city, for that is how the federal agents got Naomi to Washington, the helicopter landing on the pad at the White House.

"I'm not a lawyer...but I do know that if I'm arrested by federal officers...I'm supposed to be taken before a federal magistrate...to be arraigned...not to that monster you work for.... This is not an arrest.... It's a kidnapping...."

"I suggest you shut up...or you won't survive long enough...to be able to complain.... We're going into the White House.... The President wants to see you...to talk to you...to try to straighten things out...."

"You had no right using an arrest warrant for that purpose.... This is not a Nazi state...not yet...."

"We're now going to leave this helicopter...and go into the White House.... I strongly suggest you keep absolutely quiet.... Otherwise...I'll shoot you...and say that you tried to break into the White House...to avenge yourself against the man you falsely accuse of killing your sister.... So you see...Dr Steinberg...you are in considerable jeopardy...if you make any sound...or commotion.... I'm now going to remove your handcuffs...and I expect you to behave yourself...."

Despite her very muted protests, Angstrom hustled Naomi into the executive wing of the White House, and from there into the main part of the executive mansion, all the way to the President's private apartment, to the President's bedroom, skillfully not encountering anyone as Angstrom pushed her along, and both waited in the bedroom until President Lancaster arrived.

He was heavier than he seemed in public, his face still good-looking, but somewhat dissipated at close range, and this time his body was clad only in a bathrobe.

"Thank you...Joe.... I think I can handle things from now on....," and Joseph Angstrom left Naomi with the President in his bedroom. Naomi walked over to one of the corners and stood there facing outward toward him.

"I'm not interested in what you have to say.... You are a murderer...and now also a kidnapper.... What is your next crime...Mr Lancaster...?"

Lancaster moved toward her as she edged herself out of the corner toward the door.

"If you come any closer...I'll scream.... How will this all look on the front pages of the newspapers...?"

"No one will hear you.... You're in the President's private apartment.... My wife is out...shopping...and my children are at school...." He lunged forward and grabbed her left arm as she tried to elude him. His hand firmly encircling her left forearm, he threw her toward the bed, and violently pushed her down on top of it. He then removed his bathrobe, revealing a body covered by drooping skin, a sign of a man aging all too soon, much before his time.

"I'm going to do with you...what I wanted to do with your sister.... She repulsed me...me.... I could have any woman...anytime.... What is it with you Jewish women...? Can't you recognize an attractive man when you see one...? If you make one sound...so help me...I'll kill you...," and he then placed his unclothed body directly on her clothed body as she lay there, momentarily paralyzed by fright.

As he lay on top of her, pinning her to the bed, he

reached down with one hand to try to lift her dress and lower her panties, all the while holding her face with the other hand under her jaw, but Naomi managed to roll out from under him and off the bed. Despite his flab, he moved too quickly for her and grabbed her again to throw her back on the bed with the entire weight of his body thrown on top of her. He tried to kiss her, again using his heavy weight fully on top of her to pin her down, but Naomi got her head loose from his forced kiss, only for a moment, and during that moment screamed as loudly as she possibly could despite the more than two hundred pounds on top of her body.

Lancaster's reaction to the scream was to seize her throat in his two hands, and to slowly but surely begin to strangle her, just as he had strangled her sister. But this time there was another reaction to the scream. It was heard by Joan Lancaster, the First Lady, as she returned earlier than planned from her shopping tour.

Mrs Lancaster ran toward the bedroom door, and quickly opened it to see the horror lying there on the bed. She knew she was not strong enough to pull her husband away from his victim, and rushed out through the door she had left open, to find someone to help her. She found two of the cleaning women who were about to go off duty, and strongly ordered them to follow her. When the three women arrived, President Lancaster had almost succeeded in killing Naomi. Horrified, the two household servants did not have to be told to pull him off his victim as Joan Lancaster hit him over the head with one of the heavy vases on the fireplace mantle. Before James Lancaster even partially recovered from the blow, all four women fled the bedroom.

"Roberta...Audrey...you had better leave the White House right away...or else go to my bedroom...and pretend to be cleaning there...if the President shows up...," then turning to Naomi, "...and you must be Naomi Steinberg.... I recognize you from your picture in the papers.... How can I possibly apologize for all of this...? But that can wait till later.... Right now...let's get out of this horrible place...downstairs to the White House garage...to my personal car.... Come with me.... I'll make sure you're alright...."

The two cleaning women suddenly became very industrious cleaning the First Lady's clean bedroom, and Joan Lancaster and Naomi Steinberg left the White House in Joan's personal car, unchallenged when the regular White House police recognized the First Lady.

"I'm going to pick my children up at school...and then we'll all go to Richmond.... I'm leaving that monster...right now.... I'm going to divorce the bastard...."

"You saved my life...Mrs Lancaster.... I'm very grateful...but why Richmond...?"

"Oh...we have a lot in common.... I'm from one of the First Families of Virginia...born and bred in Richmond...as you were.... I must apologize for what you've been through...and please call me Joan.... I think we'll be seeing a great deal of each other.... I knew he was a womanizer...all these years...but I kept quiet...and played the dutiful wife...for his political career...which I never really cared for...but I never thought he would be a murderer.... He tried to murder you...as he must have murdered your sister...."

"To his crime of murder...he just added...kidnapping... attempted rape...and attempted murder.... We had better get your children...before he realizes what you might be up to...before he prevents you from picking them up.... It's amazing how power can be so terribly abused...."

TWELVE

Joan Custis Lancaster was a very attractive woman in her mid-forties, slender, well-dressed and well-groomed, very much like the more mature sophisticated women of Europe. She was born in Richmond, as she said, actually in the same enclave about the state capitol where Naomi was born and bred and now lived. Mrs Lancaster was a research professor of educational policy at The George Washington University, one of the better private research institutions on the eastern seaboard, especially in those areas of studies that closely related to the many activities of the federal government, the university law school itself being only four blocks from the White House. She specialized in the role of the federal government in educational matters, and was very critical of that role, for the constitutional power to maintain and regulate schools and colleges and universities lay with the States, not the federal government, and the only reason the federal government was able to worm its way into the important educational process was through the power of the purse. The federal government essentially bribed the States to do what the federal government wanted, and interestingly it was the wife of then Senator Lancaster who advocated the abolition of the Department of Education in Washington, although she then muted her position during the presidential campaign for the sake of her husband.

Amongst many other things, Joan was also very critical of the percentage of the educational dollar that supported an educational bureaucracy rather than the teachers themselves. As for the teachers, Professor Lancaster could not reconcile the concept of professionalism with the idea of teachers going out on strike. All in all, she was not particularly liked by the educational establishment.

Joan picked up her son and daughter at Western High School and then her younger daughter at a private elementary school in Montgomery County in suburban Maryland, and none too soon, for instructions were already going out from the White House to the secret service agents at those schools to not allow Mrs Lancaster to pick up her children, but the messages arrived too late.

The secret service assumed she would then go out the George Washington Memorial Highway to the Capital Beltway, and then turn south to cross the Cabin John bridge over the Potomac into Virginia, continue on the Beltway to interstate route I-95 and then on I-95 southbound all the way to Richmond. Several helicopters and cars were sent to the interchange points to intercept her, but anticipating this, Naomi convinced her to instead head north on the Beltway, and get away from the Washington area by taking I-270 to Frederick, Maryland and then I-70 eastbound to the Baltimore Beltway.

"We can pick up I-95 on the Baltimore Beltway...north of Baltimore...to the Delaware Memorial Bridge...and cross over to get the New Jersey Turnpike.... If we stay on I-95...we would go through Pennsylvania...but I understand the attorney general there is a very good friend of your husband's... He's been giving his Governor a very hard time...because the Governor is supporting Mark Rosenblueth.... Roger Morrison once told me how an unscrupulous prosecutor can really give elected officials in high places a hard time by charging corruption...the magic word.... Now let me see...about half-way from the bridge to New York City...we should run into the interchange with the Garden State Parkway.... We'll take the parkway...instead of continuing on the turnpike...until it enters New York State.... We should be safe there.... I'll contact Roger Morrison...and Governor Rosenblueth ...once we get across the state line into New York...about fifty miles north of New York City...on the west side of the Hudson...."

"I think we ought to assume their lines are tapped...," suggested the First Lady, "...by the FBI...or the CIA...although the CIA is not supposed to play a domestic role...but then again there are a lot of things that are not supposed to be.... The President is not supposed to be a murderer...or the other way round...a murderer is not supposed to become President.... I suppose that's what it says in some textbook or other...."

"I'll be as cryptic as I can when I call them...and then we'll have to find a safe place to stay...preferably not in New York City...."

The Lancaster younger son, John Custis Lancaster, 17, was in the back seat along with his two sisters, Abigail, 15, and Gabrielle, 12. A much younger physical version of his father, he finally began to speak. "Would someone please tell us what's going on...Mom.... You pulled us out of school...without any explanation...and we've been listening to something I don't understand...."

"I'm sorry...John.... I owe you all an explanation.... First of all...I want you three to meet Dr Naomi Steinberg...who lives in Richmond...." Gabrielle very cordially said Hi, but John and Abigail acknowledged the introduction in an ill-mannered way, but under the tense circumstances, Joan chose to ignore their unpleasant behavior. "There's every indication that your father murdered Dr Steinberg's sister in New York City...several years ago...and earlier today...I personally witnessed him trying to kill Dr Steinberg.... Your father's an evil man...and is in much trouble because of it...."

"I don't believe it...," retorted John, not very respectfully.

"The evidence that he murdered Dinah Steinberg is very strong...and I myself witnessed his crime against Dr Steinberg...."

"You're lying...," exclaimed Abigail. "Dad never really liked you...and you're trying to get back at him.... He told me many times you were very bad to him...and I was very good to him...," and then very proudly, "I'm going to have his child...."

"You are what...!" screamed her mother.

"I think you had better pull over...Joan...," said Naomi very quickly, "...and let me drive.... You're too upset to drive...and I would be too...."

Joan pulled over on the shoulder, and exchanged positions with Naomi, who then drove off, leaving Joan now able to turn around and face her children from her front-row passenger seat. A little more calm, she asked, "And what month are you in...my darling daughter...?"

"Third...," answered Abigail, now a bit sheepish.

"Is it really true...?" asked John, who now lost himself in doubt. "I don't know what to believe.... Who would do such a thing...to his own daughter...?"

"I believe Mom...and Dr Steinberg...," insisted little Gabrielle.

"We're on our way to New York State...and when we get there...we'll have to sort everything out.... In the meanwhile...your father has much power...to harm me...and Dr Steinberg...and you.... We'll have to be very careful.... Your brother James Jr is at Princeton...more or less on our way...but your father might assume we'll stop there to get him...as I got you.... We won't fall into any trap...which means we'll see your brother at a later time.... The important thing is for us to get to New York safely...."

"I can drive...if you get tired...Dr Steinberg...,"

John offered, now considerably more friendly.

"I'd appreciate that...when I need to rest...."

They were now in Delaware, on the Delaware Turnpike, before it finally occurred to Joan to turn on the radio, to try to pick up the news, and there was nothing but news, news about how a deranged Naomi Steinberg broke into the White House, assaulted the President with a heavy blow to the head, kidnapped the First Lady, and then forced her to drive to pick up her children, all except James Jr at Princeton.

"Their whereabouts are unknown...although the FBI feels they are on their way to Richmond...where both the First Lady and Dr Steinberg were born and raised.... If you'll tune to your TV set...you will see pictures of all five.... If anyone sees any of them...please contact the local office of the FBI...and if you're in the Washington area...contact the Secret Service...." And for those not tuning to TV sets, the radio gave verbal physical descriptions of the two women and three children, and a description and the tag number of the First Lady's private Lincoln sedan.

"What a crock of lies...," exclaimed Joan Lancaster. "That's going to make things very difficult for us.... We dare not stop...."

"There's a tollbooth...in a few miles...," said Naomi. "We'll have to get off the pike...and avoid it...," but just then a small helicopter appeared, unnoticed until now because of all the excitement, showing a tail sign reading: Pick up your mobile phone when it rings.

"This is the Delaware State Police.... Please remain

on the turnpike.... Several of our police cars will be waiting at the tollbooth...to escort you to the New Jersey Turnpike...where the New Jersey State Police will escort you further.... You are safe...."

About four hours into the trip, they reached the New York Thruway spur that connected that toll road with the northern terminus of the Garden State Parkway, where six New York State Police cars were waiting for them, and with the police officers were Roger Morrison and William Salinger. That hello kiss between Naomi and Roger was friendly, and then everyone was introduced all around. John Lancaster was trying his best to be grown-up.

Roger explained. "Everyone was listening to that pack of lies from the White House...and I immediately contacted Mark...Governor Rosenblueth...in Albany.... He assumed...and rightly...that you would try to get to New York...rather than Richmond.... He then arranged with the Governors of Maryland...Delaware...and New Jersey...to protect you all the way.... As soon as we all get to Albany...Mrs Lancaster...the Governor will hold a televised press conference...for you to tell the true story...of what happened at the White House.... The crime of abduction was committed in Henrico County...Virginia...and I assume something will unfold there.... It's been a very long day...for all of you...and it's now almost sundown.... We'll stay the night at a good motor inn several miles from here...where we'll all be protected.... The Governor has already neutralized the FBI in this State.... He met this morning with all the federal judges in the State...and was pledged their complete cooperation...after he presented the evidence of the murder.... He and the chief judges...of the four federal judicial districts in New York...and of the federal circuit covering New York...will meet tomorrow morning with all the commanders of those units of the armed forces stationed in New York State.... His goal is to neutralize the awesome retaliatory power of the President...before his most certain removal from office by the House and Senate.... The same things are taking place in every State...."

"And then what will happen...after he's removed from office...?" asked Mrs Lancaster.

"Your husband will be tried in New York County for the murder of Dinah Steinberg...and I assume also in Henrico County for the kidnapping of Naomi Steinberg...but first things first...."

Abigail began to cry bitterly, and was very maternally consoled by the woman she had tried to replace in the love-life of her father. "She's going to need an abortion...the sooner the better...," thought Dr Naomi Steinberg. "Poor girl...."

THIRTEEN

At about 11 o'clock the following morning, everyone arrived safely in four police helicopters at the Executive Mansion in Albany, where Mary Rosenblueth, Mark's wife, was waiting for them, to greet them, and to make them all feel welcome in her home. While everyone had a good lunch, Mark was still meeting with the military commanders in his office at the Capitol, and did not return until well after lunch, but he did return with a look of complete satisfaction on his face.

Naomi and all the Lancaster children were introduced to him, and then Mark told Joan Lancaster and Naomi Steinberg that a televised press conference was scheduled for three o'clock in the Governor's press room.

"What shall I say...?" asked the First Lady with some trepidation.

"Just tell the world what actually happened...."

The television anchorman announced: "We now take you to Albany...the capital of New York State...for a press conference by the First Lady of the Land.... It surprised everyone...when it was learned only this morning that she is in Albany...as the guest of Governor Rosenblueth of New York...the former Manhattan DA.... Mrs Lancaster is now entering...escorted by the Governor...and walking behind her is Dr Naomi Steinberg...escorted by the new Manhattan DA...Roger Morrison...the man who intends to prosecute James Lancaster for the murder several years ago of Dr Steinberg's sister.... Ladies and gentlemen...Mrs Lancaster...."

Dressed in a trim business suit, Joan Lancaster looked very proper but was obviously very nervous. She had to grab and hold on to the podium before she could even speak, but it took only a few moments for her to compose herself, and then she did speak.

"It is always very difficult for a wife to publicly say...even what should be said...about her husband.... But because my husband is the President of the United States...it is most important that I relate to you...the people of the United States...what happened at the White House...only yesterday.... Dr Naomi Steinberg...standing beside me...was arrested by FBI agents at her hospital in Richmond...using an arrest warrant issued by a federal magistrate in Alexandria...under the sham pretext that she was conspiring with the Governor of New York...the District Attorney of New York County...and other important people too numerous to mention...to assassinate the President of the United States.... It was all a sham...a fraud.... Were the arrest legitimate...then Dr Steinberg would have been immediately brought before the federal magistrate...to be arraigned...after she had the opportunity to get her lawyer...but instead...Dr Steinberg was taken directly to my husband's private bedroom at the White House...there left alone in his presence...he dressed only in his bathrobe...." Joan's nervousness quickly returned, but once again she successfully fought to compose herself. "I returned from a shopping trip much earlier than expected...and heard loud screams...and then an ominous quiet...almost as loud as the screams...all coming from my husband's bedroom.... I quickly rushed to the door...it was fortunately unlocked...and I opened it...to see my husband forcibly lying on top of Dr Steinberg on his bed...his two hands around her neck...choking her to death.... I rushed out of his bedroom to find some people...somewhere in the White House...to help me...and when I got back with two women on the White House staff I broke a vase over his head...to knock him out...as the two women helped me pull him off Dr Steinberg...barely gasping for breath.... Dr Steinberg...still hardly able to breathe...and I left the room in a hurry...rushed down to the White House garage...and together left in my personal car...picking up the younger three of my four children...at their schools...on our way to New York.... Here we are...safe...thanks to the Governors of Maryland...Delaware...New Jersey...and New York...."

The assembled reporters were much more subdued

than it was usual for them to be at a press conference, and the first question came from a woman reporter.

"What do you intend to do now...Mrs Lancaster...?"

"I intend to file for divorce...in my home state of Virginia...where Governor Garry has done his best to protect Dr Steinberg...against harassment and intimidation by FBI agents...and other federal agents beholden to my husband.... James Lancaster was always a womanizer...but I chose to overlook it...because of his political career...but this time I actually witnessed his committing two serious crimes...attempted rape and attempted murder...and it is obvious that he is implicated in the abduction of his intended victim in Richmond.... If I had not arrived back in the White House earlier than I had planned...the attempted rape and attempted murder would have been actual rape and actual murder...."

"Do you feel he killed Dinah Steinberg...Dr Steinberg's sister...several years ago in Manhattan...."

"Yes...I do.... As I said...my husband was a womanizer...and as a Senator he would go to New York at least one day each week...during the week.... I have been told by the Manhattan district attorney...Mr Morrison...that his office has conclusive proof that my husband had obtained an apartment in Manhattan...in the same co-op building in which the two Steinberg sisters lived...and that he used it under an assumed name...apparently to play around to his heart's content.... What happened at the White House must have been a repetition of what happened in Dinah Steinberg's apartment when she was murdered...and the

Manhattan district attorney has well-documented proof that Mr Lancaster's fingerprints were found on Dinah's neck...although they did not know whose fingerprints they were...until recently...."

Everyone in the United States must have been watching that press conference, for within the hour the House of Representatives met to pass the pending bill of impeachment against James Monroe Lancaster for the high crimes of murder, abduction, attempted rape and attempted murder. The House then appointed a committee of its members to prosecute the impeachment in the Senate, and it instructed its sergeant-at-arms to arrest James Monroe Lancaster, residing at 1600 Pennsylvania Avenue, Northwest, to bring him before the Bar of the House to determine what constraints were to be placed on his movements, and authorizing the use of whatever force might be necessary to effect his arrest.

And when Joan Lancaster felt it was safe, two days later, she left with her children in a private executive jet, to return home to Richmond, to the Benjamin house on Richard Henry Lee Drive.

As the House was taking its action, Governor Elbridge Garry of Virginia was meeting with Lieutenant General Alfred Seymour, commander of the Military District of Washington, at his headquarters at Fort Myers, in northern Virginia.

"General...the House had acted.... I have no doubt that the President will be removed from office.... All fifty Governors support this action...against a man who has committed horrible crimes...including the crime of abduction in Virginia.... I expect that Vice President Sally Campbell will soon call a meeting of the Cabinet...if she has not already done so...to formally declare James Lancaster unable to discharge the office of President...and she will then assume the office temporarily as Acting President.... As you know...that is provided for in one of the amendments to the federal constitution...."

"What is it that you want me to do...Governor...?"

"Nothing...exactly nothing...except to obey the lawful orders of the Acting President...if the Vice President succeeds in convincing the Cabinet to make her Acting President.... I am asking you to remain neutral.... The last thing this country needs is military intervention...in a political matter...and in the criminal justice process.... I feel that Lancaster may try to use the military to take absolute power by a coup d'etat... something that has never happened in our history...and I fervently hope never will...."

"You can rest assured...Governor...that I'll be faithful to my oath under the Constitution.... I took it to the Constitution...not to James Lancaster.... This is not Nazi Germany...where the military took their oaths to Adolf Hitler...rather than to Germany...."

"We are all grateful to you...General Seymour.... Please keep in touch with me in Richmond...."

"I shall...Governor...but please keep in mind that Lancaster is still the President...and if there is a national emergency of any kind...the military will obey the orders of the commander-in chief...."

"I realize that...General...and that is what really

bothers me...that he might concoct some emergency for that very purpose...."

As the Governor of Virginia was meeting at Fort Myers, the Governors of all the States were meeting once again with the commanding officers of all the units of the armed forces located within their States, and also with all the federal judges within their States, asking them all to remain neutral. It was for the House and Senate to decide this matter, and then for the criminal justice systems of New York and Virginia, and also of the District of Columbia, to follow once James Lancaster was removed from office. But each military leader reminded the Governor what General Seymour was reminding Governor Garry.

Vice President Campbell, now back in Washington, once again called an extraordinary meeting of the Cabinet at her residence on Observatory Circle in northwest Washington. The House having acted so resolutely against the President, the members of the Cabinet realized all the more that the country was in a constitutional crisis because of the personal misbehavior of one man. Acting under the federal constitution, they formally declared James Monroe Lancaster to be temporarily unable to discharge the office of President until the Senate made its decision on his removal.

The House sergeant-at-arms, John Patrick Ryan, a physically small but very determined-looking man, appeared at the front entrance of the White House in the company of six of his deputies, each of them considerably more imposing physically than he was. About two hundred deputies were in position around the perimeter of the White House, and the White House police at the sentry houses were quickly neutralized. Mr Ryan informed the chief of the White House police, and also the agent-in-charge of the White House secret service detail, that he had a House warrant for the arrest of James Monroe Lancaster, Mr Lancaster to be brought before the Bar of the House of Representative to answer charges of high crimes.

"I'm not at all sure I can permit you to execute this warrant...Mr Ryan.... I shall have to consult the President's legal counsel...Mr Joel Seligman....

"I must have your response within one hour.... If he resists arrest...I'm sure that the House will hold Mr Lancaster in contempt of the House...and punish him accordingly...."

While Mr Ryan and his officers waited inside the White House, the President and his legal counsel held a rather urgent meeting.

"But that sounds archaic...like the English House of Commons...," exclaimed the President.

"It does sound archaic...but it's perfectly within the inherent powers of the House of Representatives to do what it's doing...," responded Joel Seligman.

"I don't agree.... That power never extended to the sovereign...to the chief of state...and I'm the American chief of state...."

"The President is the chief of state...but in a republic...it is the republic that is sovereign...not the President...."

"I don't agree...and as for the Cabinet declaring Sally Campbell Acting President...I'm sending a letter to her by special courier...and to each member of the Cabinet...that I'm not disabled...and that under the constitution...I'm still the President...but Jesus Christ...I must be out of my mind.... Why am I discussing these matters with a Jew...? Get out of here...Seligman...right now...and I'll get a real American lawyer...."

"As you wish...Mr Lancaster...," said Mr Seligman, and out of the White House went Joel Seligman, young man of thirty-five, good-looking, brilliant lawyer, and a bachelor.

On his way out, Joel Seligman encountered John Ryan in the lobby of the White House, and explained what happened, suggesting that Lancaster might refuse to accept arrest. "There are many secret service agents about...and also many White House police.... The President has a military command and control center right here in the White House...to call for military help.... How many men do you have...Mr Ryan...?"

"About two hundred...Mr Seligman...but we don't want any trouble.... If Mr Lancaster will not accompany me...then we shall all return to the Capitol...and report to the House that Mr Lancaster resists arrest...."

"Yes...and then the House can hold him in contempt...a very clever way for the House to proceed.... I wonder who thought of that...."

"I don't know...but it was presented to the House by the New York and Virginia delegations...."

"The House must realize that Lancaster is still very much the President.... He is sending letters to the Vice President...and members of the Cabinet...that he's quite capable of exercising his responsibilities...and will do so...until such time as he is removed by the impeachment process...."

"Thank you for informing me...Mr Seligman.... Tell me...Mr Seligman...why do you continue to act as White House counsel...?"

"I no longer do...Mr Ryan...," and Joel left the White House to return to his apartment on Connecticut Avenue.

It was about eleven in the morning when Mr Ryan and his deputies all returned to the Capitol, and the sergeant-at-arms then reported to the Speaker that Mr Lancaster had refused to obey the order of the House. The Speaker, George Creighton, presented the matter to the House at its afternoon session, and the House almost unanimously voted to hold one James Monroe Lancaster in contempt of the House, and authorized the issuance of another arrest warrant, this time for contempt, to bring him before the Bar of the House.

FOURTEEN

Although General Wrightson did not realize at the time that it would be used for its real purpose, President Lancaster had arranged during the early weeks of his administration for the organization of a special army division to quickly defend the White House in the event of a severe civil disturbance in the City of Washington, or so he said, and Lancaster carefully had the division staffed only with officers whom he felt he could completely trust and with enlisted personnel who would obey any order. It was nicknamed the President's Division, and was stationed right in the District of Columbia, at an expanded Fort McNair in the southwestern quadrant of the District, at the site of the Army War College, in newly constructed housing for officers and enlisted personnel. It was now Lancaster's time to make use of what he had prepared.

President Lancaster called Major General Luke

Martins, commander of the President's Division, to have him place the entire division on full alert, and he told the general to immediately send a battalion, equipped with armored vehicles, to the White House.

"I fully understand...Mr President...and I'm very glad you at least have us.... I never really liked that nigger John Wrightson.... Too high and mighty for a black...."

"Alright...Luke...never mind the speeches.... Have your men here within the hour...and have them take up positions about the entire perimeter of the White House...."

He then called Jefferson Smith, head of a rabidly antisemitic organization called Cleanse America, and asked him to come to the White House as soon as possible. "Let me know where you are...and I'll send an executive jet for you...."

Mr Lancaster then moved quickly to consolidate his control over the armed forces of the United States while diverting the attention of the people from the issue of his crimes. And what better way to accomplish both than to act as though an international crisis suddenly developed, a crisis that could result in nuclear war. After all, he was the constitutional commander-in-chief. Using the national military command system, he ordered all land, sea and air forces of the United State placed on full alert, and the intercontinental ballistic missiles made ready in their silos. And he then summoned Rupert Matthews, Director of the Federal Bureau of Investigation, and Arnold Boswell, Director of Central Intelligence, both long-term friends of Lancaster, whom he felt he could completely trust.

"Rupert...Arnold...I'm going on national TV this evening to report to the American people that this nation is on the brink of nuclear war...that we are in the midst of secret negotiations to try to prevent it...that these Jews are doing their best to divert my attention from this awesome task by concocting a tale that I killed a woman in New York.... And the fact that my wife has thrown in with them only indicates how much she has abused my trust in her as my wife...."

"Unless you have information we do not...Mr President...," said Arnold Boswell, "...the CIA has no information to indicate an impending international emergency suggesting nuclear war...."

"Of course it doesn't...because there isn't any.... Arnold...this is my way of getting rid of my domestic enemies...."

"Very clever...Mr President...," exclaimed Rupert Matthews. "I never did like those people...and this might be a good chance to put them in their place.... I'm surprised that the Christian governors are supporting a Jewish governor...."

"Exactly what I've been thinking.... As a matter of fact...I'm going to name Israel as our potential nuclear adversary...and proceed to round-up all American Jews...just as we rounded up all Japanese-Americans in the Second World War...and that will include Mark Rosenblueth...."

"Although...in all honesty...Mr President...," commented Arnold Boswell, "...there was indeed a potential problem in that war which warranted the detention of the Japanese...but I very much doubt the American Jews would not behave as Americans...even against Israel...if Israel were indeed a real threat to America...."

"You know that...and I know that...Arnold...but there are a lot of hardcore antisemites out there...and a much larger number of latent antisemites...and I intend to tell them what they will completely swallow.... Now...I want both of you to be standing alongside me while I address the nation tonight...."

"What are you going to do about Wrightson...and Redmond...?"

"I've alrady fired them...and I'll make that announcement this evening..... I'm also replacing the entire Cabinet...and any member of the Joint Chiefs who does not give me a letter stating his loyalty to me...."

"That was Hitler's approach...," exclaimed Rupert Matthews.

"Hitler was an outstanding leader...," said President Lancaster, "...and a very great man...."

That same evening, James Monroe Lancaster went on network television, on all major networks, to report to the American people, to say, "My fellow Americans...my fellow Christians.... You have heard many stories...all of them lies...that I killed a Jewish woman in New York City.... I've been so busy tending to an international crisis...a crisis threatening each of you with a nuclear holocaust...a crisis pitting us against the Jews...that this has been my first opportunity to report to you.... And now you can understand why that Jew...Mark Rosenblueth...made up a story about some killing in Jew-town to try to divert my attention from what his country...Israel...not America...was planning to do.... You see standing beside me...Rupert Matthews...Director of the FBI...and Arnold Boswell...Director of the CIA...both patriotic Christians.... They uncovered an effort by the Israelis...in concert with Jews living in America...to install a nuclear bomb in their embassy in Washington...a bomb large enough to destroy the White House...the Capitol...the Washington Monument...all those buildings in our nation's capital that are so dear to us.... You will note...my fellow Christians...that I do not say American Jews.... No Jew can be an American in Christian America.... This effort by the Jews also resulted in bombs installed in their various consulates around the country...each bomb capable of destroying most of the city in which each consulate is located.... The FBI...and with my authorization the CIA...are both busy trying to contain this problem of the planted bombs...all while I threaten the State of Israel with total annihilation...and the severe punishment of their six million people living amongst us...if any of the bombs is detonated.... I have placed the armed forces of the United States on alert...fearing that other nations who are our enemies may take advantage of this terrible problem the Jews have presented to us.... General Wrightson has been discharged as Chairman of the Joint Chiefs of Staff...and Allen Redmond as the Secretary of Defense...for outright insubordination.... I have also discharged the entire Cabinet...for trying to stab me in the back...and I'll send nominations to the Senate of good Christians to replace them all.... And if the Senate does not co-operate...then I shall take measures to ensure the safety of this nation against any effort by petty politicians in Congress to do the work of the Jews.... I shall...over the next few days...replace any officer of the armed forces who is not loyal to this country.... I am the commander-in-chief...elected by the people...and the measure of their loyalty will be the measure of their loyalty to constitutional authority...to the President.... I shall also not permit any radio or television station...or any newspaper or magazine...to present any material to the people that would tend to undermine the security of this beloved land of ours.... If all of us cannot conduct ourselves as Americans...then I shall have no choice but to declare martial law...and suspend the writ of habeas corpus...."

"My God...!" Sally's thoughts exclaimed when the broadcast was followed by the playing of the national anthem and the film clip showing the American flag being planted on the hilltop of Iwo Jima. "That awful man has just loosened the whirlwind.... And for a man who never served in time of war...to exploit those symbols of American sacrifices.... How awful on both counts...but especially on the first...."

But even before any censorship could possibly go into effect, one of the networks immediately switched via a satellite link to its chief correspondent in Jerusalem, who had a linkup through Israel Television with the prime minister in Jerusalem, to interview him.

The Israeli prime minister vehemently denied that his country had taken any hostile measures against the United States.

"We have been close friends since our beginning.... There can be no possible reason we would threaten our only true friend with nuclear bombs.... I am most saddened by this latter-day Hitler sitting in the seat of great power...threatening us...and the American Jews...just as Hitler did.... I am authorizing our embassy in Washington...and our consulates throughout America...to open their doors to responsible members of the American press...and to whatever friends we still have in America...to see for themselves that these buildings do not contain nuclear bombs...." The broadcast from Jerusalem suddenly stopped as the main power switch at the Washington broadcasting station was turned off.

The President's Division surrounded the Israeli Embassy in Washington, and General Martins himself led a full company of his troops to invade Israeli territory on Embassy Row. The ambassador and his entire staff, and their families, were taken into custody, and the general then came out of the building announcing that, "We found the bomb.... We found the bomb...."

"Then show it to us...," shouted a reporter.

"Can't do that.... National security...."

"But why would our seeing the object of all this activity compromise national security...?" asked a woman reporter.

"Arrest that woman...," the general ordered, and the reporter was led away, her colleagues stunned by the advent of a presidential dictatorship.

"I have gathered you all together...," said Umberto Rossi, the Italian ambassador, to several other European ambassadors meeting in the Italian Embassy, "...to discuss this terrible...and sudden...turn of events in America.... If one of the embassies can be invaded and the ambassador taken into custody...a complete violation of international law...then each of us is equally vulnerable.... I very much doubt that Israel would do what Lancaster said it is doing...and it is obvious to me that Lancaster is taking these measures to protect himself against those criminal charges against him.... He is putting millions of people in jeopardy...to save himself.... If we do not protest the treatment of Samuel Alvarez...then we are not honorable men...."

"We tried to contact our government in Copenhagen...," said Niels Bohr, "...but all the communication lines have been cut...."

"We tried our high-powered radio transmitter to reach Amsterdam...," said Pieter van der Vere, "...but the Americans are using jammers to prevent us from getting through.... It seems that we are all prisoners...of one kind or another...."

"I fully expect my embassy to be surrounded...when I return this evening...," lamented Jaime de Cristobal. "What will our governments do...if anything...? The world can do without superpower states...especially countries that allow one man to do what Lancaster is doing...."

Even before army troops arrived at the Israeli consulate in Boston, the consul went to see Governor Bradley, to beg him to officially investigate his consulate to see that there were no nuclear bombs in the building.

"The country is in a state of panic...Mr Schmuel.... I know you too well to doubt your word...but there'a nothing I can do...."

"Governor Bradley...you can at least go on a local radio and television station to say that the Massachusetts militia thoroughly searched our building and found nothing...."

"Alright...I'll do that...," responded the Governor as the commotion grew outside his inner office. In burst several agents of the FBI to arrest the Governor on charges of aiding and abetting the enemy, and to also arrest the consul. But now the commotion was caused by a much larger group, of the state police, entering the building to protect the Governor. They disarmed the federal agents and escorted the Governor very openly to the Israel consulate, but were there met by an even larger force of marines sent from the Boston Navy Yard.

During the stand-off at the Boston consulate, several reporters managed to get through the military cordon into the consulate building, and once inside were taken on a thorough tour of the building, every nook and cranny included, but no bomb could be found. They then managed to elude arrest as the superior force of marines took everyone into custody inside and outside the building. At their newspaper, they told their managing editor what they had not found, but were told in return that the paper could not print anything to contradict the President.

"The country has gone mad...," exclaimed Joseph Durham, the managing editor. "I was a young reporter in Berlin in 1934 when Hitler legally became Chancellor...just as Lancaster legally became the President...but then he immediately began to do what Lancaster is now doing.... How easy it is for a highly civilized nation to suddenly become uncivilized.... How easy it is to abuse power...if there is a suitable bogeyman.... If any of you is Jewish...I would strongly suggest you take your family and immediately leave for Canada....

The next morning, Ambassador Rossi lead a delegation of ambassadors to the White House to see President Lancaster, to protest the measures he had taken against the diplomatic corps. Lancaster refused to see them, insisting that he was too busy ridding America of its domestic enemies, but the Secretary of State was at the White House to talk to them.

"I am here to inform you...Mr Secretary...that our governments take a dim view of what is going on...and we formally protest...."

"I do not know how your government learned what is going on...Mr Rossi...but they did refuse any further port facilities for our Mediterranean Fleet until you and your staff were allowed to leave us to return to Italy.... Our ambassador in Rome warned them that their refusal...under a treaty...would be considered an act of war...."

"Does American intend to fight the entire world...just because Mr Lancaster will not answer the criminal charges brought against him personally...? I am proud of my government for standing up to his bullying...."

"I suggest you watch your tongue...Mr Ambassador...."

"I shall say what I have to say...no more...no less...."

"What is the American fleet planning to do in the Mediterranean...?" asked Mr van der Vere.

"The entire fleet is steaming toward Israel...and once within carrier range...it will attack...as a punishment for threatening America with nuclear bombs...."

"I hope the Israelis sink your whole damn fleet...," exclaimed Mr Rossi. "I always thought that America was the greatest nation ever conceived...but then so was Germany once a civilized country...but at least Germany was in a very serious economic depression...to possibly warrant surrendering itself to a madman...but what is America's excuse....?"

"You dare to compare President Lancaster to that odious Hitler...."

"It is my understanding that Mr Lancaster does not regard Hitler as having been an odious man...and the comparison must be very acceptable to him...Mr Secretary...if not to you...."

FIFTEEN

Those American Jews in the armed forces were placed under house arrest, and massive arrests of all known Jews began to take place. The arrests of judges, legislators, prominent lawyers and doctors, and high-level civilian officials of the federal government were all officially well publicized, but Naomi Steinberg and her mother and grandmother, and also Joan Lancaster and her family, all proclaimed by Lancaster to be vicious enemies of the American people, they were all flown out of Richmond to Canada just in time by the official airplane of the Governor of Virginia.

The following evening, Lancaster returned to the airways to further inform the American people what their savior had done for them since he had last addressed them twenty-four hours ago, that he had uncovered a plot by the Jews living in this Christian land, the Jews led by that Jew in Albany, a plot by the Jews to assassinate the President and to kill every Christian clergyman they could lay their hands on, these accusations among many others that came into Lancaster's mind as he spoke somewhat incoherently to the American people. The antisemites of the land, at least those sufficiently rabid and armed, continued to take to the streets to attack Jewish homes, synagogues and businesses, shouting over and over again, "In the name of our new savior...James Lancaster...."

But strongly urged by clerical and lay leaders of a coalition of Christian organizations, with the Cardinal Archbishops of Boston and Chicago especially adding their voices, the citizens and police of many communities responded to protect American Jewish families, aided by the militia of many of the States, but things were beginning to get out of hand as James Lancaster sat in the comfort of the White House and contemplated what he had wrought to far, and he was very satisfied with what he was doing and continuing to do.

"We cannot allow the destruction of the Jewish state...," proclaimed Reverend Silas Weatherby of the Evangelical Church on several of the clandestine stations of the Christian radio network. "The Second Coming of our Lord depends on the existence of the Jewish state.... There is no threat from Israel...or from the people of Israel.... It is all a hoax...!" And then the stations fell silent from a power outage.

In Leghorn, at the southern tip of the Italian peninsula, Admiral Joseph Meridan, Commander-in-

Chief of the United States Mediterranean Fleet received orders from the President to move the entire fleet to the eastern end of the great inland sea, to destroy the Jewish state for having threatened to destroy the great cities of America. The Italian liaison officer attached to Admiral Meridan's command, Rear Admiral Lorenzo Rossi, a brother of the Italian ambassador in Washington, finally managed to meet Admiral Meridan before the American ships sailed.

"We are old friends...Joseph.... Please remember what happened to the Nazis who claimed they were innocent of atrocities because they were acting under orders.... Lancaster must be mad...to order you to do what I hope you will not do.... You cannot possibly believe what he says.... We still have a small remnant of the very illustrious Italian Jewish families...most of them dating back to the days before Jesus was born...and they have been the most honorable of people.... Why would they do what your Lancaster says they have done...? And when our ambassador in Washington tried to verify the accusation...neither he nor anyone else was permitted to...."

"I share your concern...my friend...but the only thing I can possibly do is delay our departure.... I cannot stop it.... I cannot specifically disobey an order of the President of the United States...."

"Even if it is an illegal order...? Your Congress has taken no action...no action of any kind...that could possibly authorize this massive aggression against a tiny state.... Its population is half that of New York City.... If you do obey this criminal order...you will be tried once Lancaster is brought down...and sooner or later...he will be brought down.... There is too much opposition to him...for him to ultimately prevail...."

"Congress has not taken action because its members are being held on charges of conspiracy...."

"The American equivalent of the Reichstag fire...."

"The what...?"

"Never mind...Joseph...." Admiral Rossi paused. "My government has already informed the Israeli government of your intentions...assuming you do intend to go through with this criminal action.... As I said...Israel is a tiny country...but a valiant one.... They will defend themselves...."

"I realize that...Lorenzo...but we do have a rather large number of officers who are very anxious to attack Israel in retaliation for their sinking of our LIBERTY...."

"Oh yes...the LIBERTY.... You sent a ship into a belligerent war zone in 1967...and expected it to remain untouched...."

"But it was flying the American flag...."

"And how did the Israelis...fighting for their survival against the Arab countries...fighting for the second time in the short life of their state...how did they know it was not an Egyptian ship out of Alexandria flying the American flag...? Flying a false flag is one of the oldest tricks in naval warfare...but you Americans are always so naive about these matters...and assume that everyone...including the Arabs...will always act honorably.... If I had been in a position to give the order to sink your ship...I would have done so under the circumstances...."

"Alright...Lorenzo.... If you'll excuse me...I have much work to do...to move this entire fleet to the eastern Med...."

"Then you are actually going to do it...."

"Yes...I am...."

"And what of your Jewish officers and enlisted personnel...?"

"They have divided loyalties...and will remain here...at our base...all under guard...."

"They do not have divided loyalties...except in favor of doing the right thing...and you are doing the wrong thing.... This base is an Italian naval base...not an American one...and we shall insist that your Jewish personnel be placed ashore in our care.... We cannot prevent your ships from leaving this port...but we can make it very difficult for you to return...."

"Do you voice these threats on behalf of your government...?"

"Yes...I do.... We were never antisemitic...like the Nazis...and always valued our Jewish countrymen...which is something your latter-day American Führer does not seem to understand.... Heil Lancaster...!" Admiral Rossi clicked his heels together as he gave the Nazi salute.

In Jerusalem, the ambassadors of all the countries friendly to Israel, not a large number and not now including the United States, were all asked to meet with the prime minister, and to bring their military, naval and air attaches with them. All seated in a small auditorium, the prime minister announced, "We have received word from Rome that the entire American fleet is moving toward our coastline...to attack us.... We shall take whatever measures to defend ourselves...as though ancient pagan Rome were attacking.... You may have time to leave our country...if you wish...or you may come with me into our command center...and watch us take whatever action we can to defend ourselves...."

"I think I speak for all of us...," said Count Wallenberg of Sweden, "...when I say that I would prefer that we remain here...and watch David defeat Goliath...." There was no dissent.

"Thank you...gentlemen.... We shall now move into our command center...but before we do...you shall have ample opportunity to inform your families by telephone that you will be indisposed for some time...."

All Jewish naval personnel were placed ashore at Leghorn in the care of the Italian naval authorities, and the following day the entire American fleet in the Mediterranean, some ships nuclear-powered and the remainder by bunker fuel, the entire fleet set sail for the Israeli coast without maintaining a combat air patrol, Admiral Meridan deciding it would not be necessary until the fleet arrived within striking distance of the Jewish state. After all, he felt, Israel was not a formidable adversary against a superpower, and the Jewish state had no navy to speak of.

When about two hundred miles from Haifa, the fleet was suddenly attacked by long-range dive-bombers, of Israeli design and manufacture, their initial target the steam-powered launching catapults of the aircraft carriers, the Israeli aircraft coming down almost vertically from a very great altitude and coming down too suddenly to enable the fleet to take evasive action or launch defending fighter planes, the vertical trajectory of the attacking dive-bombers not showing on the radar PPI (plan position indicator) screens in the CIC (combat information centers) of the American warships. The high-penetration bombs found their targets, and very soon another wave of dive-bombers attacked the carrier flight decks, destroying the planes on them and making them also inoperative. With the carriers operationally disabled, a third wave attacked all the conventionally powered warships, one of them a carrier and the others missile-launching cruisers, by accurately dropping low-intensity bombs down their stacks, deliberately to destroy the boilers with a minimal loss of life, all of the action reported on-line to the war room in Jerusalem. About a quarter of the attacking planes were shot down by antiaircraft missiles launched from the escorting destroyers, but shot down only after each of the aircraft had pulled out of its vertical dive, their bombs finding their mark. Many ships were sunk, but most of their officers and crew were able to jump into the water before the ships actually went down. The fleet was so badly damaged that it could manage to fire only several rounds of surface-to-surface missiles, the first round falling short into the Mediterranean Sea about a mile off Haifa, the second round overshooting their mark and hitting the Jordanian capital of Amman, and the third round successfully intercepted about fifty miles from the Israeli coast by antiaircraft missiles of the new Israel-developed Arrow system, a system developed to be used against Israel's enemies, not against a nation once Israel's best friend. There was no cheering in the war room in Jerusalem, but instead a pervading mixture of gratitude and dismay, gratitude that Israel was spared the wrath of the most deadly armada since the sixteenth century, and dismay that America had sent that armada against its most steadfast friend. The military attaches present made mental notes to discuss with their governments the procurement of the Arrow system from Israel for their own protection.

Admiral Meridan, now brought to his senses and actually grateful that he had failed in his mission, he ordered the surviving Israeli pilots to be fished from the sea and treated as though prisoners of war. The many survivors of the sunken American ships were also fished from the sea, and all those needing medical attention received what they needed as the entire fleet turned about to limp back to Leghorn and to other Mediterranean naval bases for extensive repairs.

Reports of the successful defensive action against the offensive American fleet in the Mediterranean reached the New England states, the Pacific northwest and the remaining American states of the northern tier, all through the Canadian radio and television stations, the news greeted by Americans with a mixture of admiration for David and chagrin that their own Goliath had proved inadequate. But it did not take more than several days for the massive reaction to set in, to raise questions about the tales spun by James Lancaster, and more and more of the press, both electronic and print, began to crawl out of their hiding places.

To keep the pot boiling in the face of the naval fiasco, President Lancaster now ordered an invasion of Canada for harboring the American Jews conspiring against him, the order placed through the National Military Communications System, and it was not until the invasion actually began that anyone in Canada was aware of it. Alarmed, the Canadians fought back as best they could, holding the not-too-eager American land force at bay, but American warplanes attacked Montreal, Toronto and Vancouver. When news of the invasion reached London and Paris, the British and French ambassadors, both of them accompanied at the last minute by the German ambassador acting on his own volition, all three European ambassadors joined the Canadian in a vehement protest before the American Secretary of State, and threatened to take retaliatory action if the Americans did not stop their aggression against Canada. The Secretary of State strongly advised the President to withdraw, which Lancaster refused to do. But much doubt began to reach even the armed forces, and in the face of widespread mutinies, the new Joint Chiefs ordered the cessation of all hostilities against Canada and against other Americans.

From the very beginning of this monstrous hoax perpetrated by James Lancaster, Sally Campbell tried her best to counteract him, and for her trouble she was abducted and brought to the White House, all the while that the President's Division had surrounded the Capitol and started to take those members of Congress into custody who had opposed the President.

Sally was confined to her bedroom suite, her protests ignored by all the secret service agents who stood guard to keep her confined. But after the disaster in the Mediterranean and the aborted invasion of Canada, it now seemed that everyone, everyone except James Lancaster and his close friends, finally did realize that the man in the White House had perpetrated a monstrous hoax. The Joint Chiefs began to take matters into their own hands. They arrested the Secretaries of Defense, Army, Navy and Air Force, and ordered the commander of the President's Division to release all persons under house arrest, and to return to barracks. General Wrightson was asked to resume his position as their chairman, which he did, and Allen Redmond was asked to resume his position as Secretary of Defense, which he did, and both men, accompanied by the Joint Chiefs and a large contingent of the Maryland and Virginia state militias, appeared at the White House to arrest James Lancaster on behalf of the House of Representatives.

Informed by the chief of the White House police of the arrival of Mr Redmond and of General Wrightson, James Lancaster immediately went to Sally's bedroom suite, dismissed the secret service agents guarding her, and entered the suite. Without saying anything, he moved quickly toward her, she beginning to scream and grabbing a heavy flower vase on one of the tables.

"Don't you dare come any further...!" she exclaimed.

"Is that the way to talk to the man you once

loved...?"

"I never loved you.... I was seduced by you...."

"It really doesn't matter.... What does matter is that you and I are going into the bedroom...into bed...to make love...just as we used to...."

"Over my dead body...and I'm warning you again...I won't hesitate to hit you...."

James Lancaster lunged, but Sally Campbell quickly moved out of his way, and as his body hurled passed her, she did strike him with that vase, the blow knocking him unconscious to the floor. Eluding anyone in the hall, she managed to get out of the White House, running into Allen Redmond and John Wrightson as she left the building.

"Mrs Campbell...what happened...?" asked a most concerned Mr Redmond as he saw her disheveled clothes and perspiring face.

"I'm so glad to see you.... I hope you're not prisoners of that monster...as I have been...."

"No...we no longer are...," Allen Redmond replied. "Everyone...almost everyone...has finally come to his senses.... It's all over for Lancaster...."

"He's still constitutionally the President until removed by the Senate on impeachment...," said General Wrightson, "...but under the circumstances...he will be rendered disabled...and you will become the Acting President...."

"Under the circumstances...," said Mr Redmond, "...I don't think we have to follow the letter of the constitution in this case.... There must be some way to disable a President who's acting as a madman...."

"Lancaster is lying unconscious on the floor of the

bedroom suite I was confined to.... I had to hit him...to avoid being raped...."

"Well...Mrs Campbell...," suggested Allen Redmond, "...let's go upstairs...and make sure that he's truly disabled for the time being...until at least Congress has the opportunity to freely act...."

General Wrightson used the Maryland and Virginia militias to protect the Members of Congress as they reconvened in their two chambers. By unanimous vote, the Senate and the House declared James Lancaster disabled and the Vice President to be the Acting President. Sally now called in army units from Fort Myer, and Marine units from Quantico, to further protect members of the Congress, and they did arrive in time to thoroughly neutralize the President's Division. It was temporarily a military standoff as the House of Representatives voted once again to hold James Monroe Lancaster in contempt of the House, and formally sent Mr Ryan and a large number of deputies to arrest James Lancaster in the White House, he now fully recovered from the blow by that vase, Lancaster to be kept confined to his bedroom suite by Mr Ryan's deputies. In this and in related matters, Mr Ryan and Mrs Campbell were aided by the presence of several armored brigades flown into Andrews Air Force Base from army bases throughout the eastern States.

SIXTEEN

At her very first opportunity, Sally Abigail Adams Campbell addressed the nation as Acting President, especially giving thanks to all the Christian clergy and lay religious leaders who had been steadfast in their opposition to Lancaster's effort to complete the Holocaust, the Holocaust begun many years before by another madman, and to also profusely thank those members of the Washington diplomatic corps who had displayed the epitome of civilized behavior. Many of the Jews who had fled to Canada decided to remain in Canada, to transfer their businesses and professions there, especially to the maritime provinces where they were notably welcomed for what they could do for the economy, but the others returned to the United States much as many German Jews returned to Germany after the destruction of the Nazi regime.

The Acting President appointed a new Cabinet, each

nominated member quickly confirmed by the Senate, and the business of the general government in Washington began to return to normal. Naomi Steinberg and Joan Lancaster both returned to Richmond, Joan with her three younger children, and Naomi with her mother and grandmother.

Even the arrest of the President by officers of the restored House of Representatives and the national address by the Acting President did not completely stop the prolonged American Kristallnacht, and the very next day after that address, a mammoth cavalcade of pick-up trucks, vans, sedans, 18-wheelers, and almost every kind of motor vehicle converged on Albany to get that Jew, that Jew who had remained in Albany with his family during the worst of Lancaster's offensive against the American Jews. Most of those trying to cross the New York line on the main roads were stopped by the New York militia aided by the militias of New York's neighboring States, but those hoodlums born and bred in New York State itself continued their quest for the head of Mark Rosenblueth especially now that their latter-day savior was no longer in any position to save them. And what were they supposed to be saved from?

Realizing that the rabble could not all be stopped before they reached the Executive Mansion, the superintendent of the state police urged Governor Rosenblueth and his family to get away to safety. Mark insisted to his wife Mary that she and their children leave.

"Darling...I can't run away.... I'm the

Governor...and must remain to stand fast.... I'll be alright...and well-protected...but you and the children should leave right now.... You should have left when this nightmare all began...but this looks even worse than before.... The police have a helicopter ready on the grounds...to take you and the children to safety.... I'll join you as soon as this agony is over...."

Mary, his wife of twenty years, now in her early forties and still looking much like the college student Mark fell in love with, and whom he still loved most dearly, Mary protested. "I'm only going for the children's sake.... Please be careful.... You may be the Governor...but that's no license to die...."

Mark kissed his wife and children so-long, and they then boarded the large passenger helicopter waiting to take off. The vehicle quickly rose into the sky and began to move away from the Governor's house at three o'clock in the afternoon.

Several miles away, an advance contingent of hoodlums, personally lead by Jefferson Smith and overly armed with heavy-duty weapons and easily stolen manual missile launchers, saw the helicopter rise into the air and assumed the Governor was aboard.

"Just like a Jew...to run away from a good fight...," exclaimed the savior's first disciple. "Roy...you have the missile launcher we got from that last armory.... Let's see how good your aim is...."

Roy Carpenter took aim, fired the missile, and hit his target, the helicopter immediately falling in a ball of flame. A great shout of accomplishment arose among the motley gang, but there were no shouts of triumph from the Executive Mansion as Mark, beside himself in anguish, saw his world go down in flames.

Mark, the police and the militiamen were not the only ones to see the tragedy. It was also seen by many ordinarily law-abiding people who had stood by on the sidelines, trying to be neutral in this conflict, but now realizing that on fundamental issues sides must be taken. Many of the men, and women too, were armed with sporting rifles and protective pistols, and those that physically could now took to the streets to stop this gang of murderers moving ever closer to the Executive Mansion.

The tide was finally turned, and Jefferson Smith and the entire gang in his immediate entourage were encircled by police, militia and armed citizens. Smith decided not to fight his way out, and surrendered, assuming that his latter-day savior would somehow save him. The police took him and all three hundred and seventeen of his immediate henchmen into custody, and charged every one of them with first-degree felony murder.

"It's not our fault...," shouted the first disciple. "We were just following the teachings of the President...." And after all the three hundred and eighteen were taken away to the county jails in the Albany region, an arrest warrant was issued by a local magistrate for the arrest of James Monroe Lancaster for conspiracy and incitement to commit murder.

News of the murder of Mary Rosenblueth and her children, and of the two pilots, fell as a monstrous explosion on the conscience of the nation, and all the commotion stirred up by the President now finally simmered down to nothingness, at least for the time being. Roger Morrison rushed up to Albany to console his good friend and benefactor, driving the entire distance with William Salinger accompanying him, and using the vehicle's siren only when absolutely necessary, but on the way up he suddenly felt strongly compelled for some reason to stop off at Veritas to very cruelly ask his parents whether it was a sin to kill a Jew, or was it only a sin to marry a Jew.

Sally Campbell once again addressed the nation over all networks from her office in the vice presidential mansion, and expressed her deepest regret for what had happened in Albany. She voiced the hope that the man still residing in the White House, but under constraint by order of the House of Representatives, would receive the full punishment he deserved for all the crimes he had committed, now including the crime of inciting the murder of Mary Rosenblueth. If Henry II took full responsibility for the murder of Thomas a Becket, then James Lancaster ought to bear an even heavier responsibility for his latest heinous crime.

Immediately following her broadcast, Sally boarded an army helicopter and escorted by army helicopter gunships flew directly to Albany, to the Executive Mansion, and there landed on the grounds close to the house about two hours later.

Mark was still in a state of shock, lying in bed under a strong sedative. Dr Jonas permitted only the Acting

President to see him, once he was conscious, and Sally went in alone, sat down on the bed beside him, took his hand and leaned over to kiss him lightly on his cheek. Mark did not respond, but he did not withdraw from the comfort of her hand.

"I'm so sorry for what happened...Mark.... Everyone knew how much you loved her...and your children...but life must go on.... We still have to take care of that bastard in the White House...."

Sally remained in Albany for the funeral the following day for Mary Rosenblueth and her children, and the day after that for a memorial service in the Rosenblueths' conservative synagogue, doing her best all the time to console Mark. Mark was reasonably recovered physically by then, but his face seemed to have aged a hundred years, and it was only Sally's presence that sustained him. He grabbed her hand as they stood side-by-side at the gravesite and then when they sat side-by-side in the synagogue, and would not let go even though Sally felt it was unseemly for the Acting President and the Governor of New York to be holding hands in public. After the memorial service, Mark returned very despondently to the Executive Mansion, and Sally returned to the vice presidential mansion in Washington with a promise to see him again as soon as possible.

The House of Representatives once again voted a citation of contempt against James Monroe Lancaster, and sent their sergeant-at-arms once again to the White House, this time to bring him in custody before the Bar of the House. Mr Ryan agreed to avoid a public spectacle of the arrest of the President in the presence of the massive crowds in the blocks of streets enveloping the White House, the crowds spilling over into the adjoining streets and Lafayette Park, into Pennsylvania Avenue, well beyond 18th street on the northwest side and beyond 14th street on the southeast side. Realizing he actually had very little choice in the matter, Lancaster finally agreed to voluntarily leave with John Ryan in one of the White House limousines directly for the Capitol, but driven by one of Mr Ryan's officers. The other deputies followed in the motor cars they had used to go the rather short distance from the Capitol to the White House.

On arrival at the Capitol grounds, the limousine and escorting cars parked in the underground garage of one of the House office buildings, again to avoid the press, and James Monroe Lancaster was escorted to the Capitol using one of the tracked vehicles between the Capitol and each of the office buildings for Senators and Members of the House. Once they reached the Capitol itself, Mr Ryan and his officers escorted the President and his new legal counsel to the well of the House, there to stand at the Bar of the House, and to listen to the charges, first of impeachment and second of contempt, against him by the House of Representatives, read to him by the Speaker of the House, a member of his own political party. The visitors gallery was empty, no visitors being permitted during that meeting of the House, but the press gallery was filled to capacity. It was only some months ago that President Lancaster gave his triumphant State of the Union address in this very chamber before an enthusiastic joint session of the Senate and the House, with the Justices of the Supreme Court as honored guests, and with all the galleries filled to overflowing. How the mighty have fallen!

"What do you say to these charges...Mr Lancaster...?" asked Speaker George Creighton.

"I shall fully defend myself before the Senate...against the charges of high crimes while in office...but I do not accept the charge of a common-law crime allegedly committed by me before I assumed the office of President...."

"You are nevertheless also charged in the bill of impeachment with the common-law crime of murder...committed before you took the oath of office as President...as well as the charges of abduction...attempted murder...attempted rape...and conspiracy and incitement to riot...murder...and pillage...while in office.... You are also charged with making war against a friendly foreign state without any declaration of war by the Congress...and with making domestic war against innocent citizens of the United States.... It shall be for the Senate to decide on what count or counts...in the specification of the charges...it wishes to remove you from the office of President of the United States...."

"Mr Speaker...," responded the President, "...my wife has publicly announced that she intends to divorce me...in Virginia.... I intend to contest that divorce for the sake of my children...and I must have the freedom...to go to Richmond...to do so.... I'm still the

President...even though we now have an Acting President...and I'm entitled to the liberty I need...to contest that divorce action...and to do whatever is necessary and proper...for me to defend myself...against the conspiracy closing in on me....."

"The House of Representatives will decide...once you have returned to the White House...whether or not to permit you that liberty...until your trial before the Senate.... In the meanwhile...the sergeant-at-arms will escort you back to your official residence.... In confining you to the White House...until the trial...we in no way prevent you from fully consulting with your legal counsel...but the divorce proceedings in Virginia are another matter.... We shall inform you once the House decides...."

The President was continued in the custody of the House sergeant-at-arms, to return him to the White House, there Mr Ryan planning to post dozens of armed deputies around the clock to keep Lancaster confined to his apartment. The sergeant-at-arms escorted the President out of the House chamber, back to their limousine, and then back to the White House in the company of several dozen deputies. All telephone lines connecting the apartment to the remainder of the White House were disconnected, and a substantial guard of deputies of the House sergeant-at-arms was posted in the White House to ensure that James Lancaster met only with his counsel. The secret service agents assigned to guard the President, and the White House police assigned to guard the presidential mansion, were transferred elsewhere.

At Lancaster's request, approved by Ryan, a courier was sent to Joel Seligman carrying a message from James Lancaster apologizing for what he had said and done, and asking Joel to defend him in the Senate trial. Joel obviously hated Lancaster's guts, but decided it was his duty as a lawyer to provide legal counsel to any person in need regardless of whether he liked that person or not.

By the time that Governor Garry had returned to Richmond from a meeting with all the other Governors in Albany, the state's attorney for Henrico County, the county containing Richmond, had already obtained a warrant for the arrest of Joseph Angstrom for the crime of abduction, and proceeded to have the warrant executed at the home of Mr Angstrom in Falls Church, a residential suburb of Washington in northern Virginia. Joseph Angstrom was taken into custody, brought to Henrico County, and in the presence of his lawyer, proceeded to make a statement that he "arrested" Dr Naomi Steinberg, and brought her to President Lancaster's bedroom, under the direct orders of the President.

"Did you do this sort of thing...with other women...for the President...?"

"Yes...but all of the others came most willingly...and did not have to be forced in any way.... Lancaster knew that Dr Steinberg would not come willingly...and had me arrange a sham arrest.... I realize I was actually perpetrating a fraud on the federal magistrate...who issued the warrant based on my affidavit...."

"A gross abuse of power...."

"Yes sir...but he was the President...and it's very hard for a federal employee to say no to the President...to his face...."

SEVENTEEN

A major constitutional crisis was finally eased when the good sense of the American people once again asserted itself, but it would not have been possible had not the Governors of the united States under the leadership of the Governor of New York, and the coalition of Christian organizations, all taken a firm stand against the President of the United States. The functioning of the federal government returned within a few days to normal under Acting President Sally Campbell, who acted with dispatch and soon began to demonstrate that she would be an able President if the Senate were to remove James Monroe Lancaster from office.

As the world awaited the Senate trial of President Lancaster, his daughter was going through a much more personal trial. Once Mark Rosenblueth recovered, Naomi and Joan returned to Albany to see him, and while there they asked for a private meeting with Mark and Roger Morrison, to discuss the problem of Abigail's pregnancy which the young lady wished now very much to abort. The two women said nothing to the two men as to the identity of the father, and the two men did not ask them.

"Why do you want to see us about it...," asked Mark. "It's legal to have an abortion...in this State...without question...in the first trimester...."

"That's the problem...Mark...," replied Naomi. "I've examined her...and she's well into her second trimester.... It's still safe...medically...to abort the pregnancy...but I understand that New York law requires some legal procedure if the pregnancy is in the second or third trimester...and if we follow that procedure...it might mean a leak to the press...and as things are going right now...Abi's in considerable psychological danger...if a leak does occur...."

"Then you want to operate...with some kind of legal immunity...."

"Exactly...."

"You have it.... I'll give you a letter...taking care of it...and if you want to operate in Manhattan...I'm sure our good friend here would give you immunity...in a most quiet way...."

"I'd do anything...for you...Naomi...," as Naomi blushed, and Joan and Mark knowingly smiled at each other.

"I'm going to call my sister Cathy...my half-sister...," Joan suggested, "...to ask her to come here...to keep Abi company.... Catherine's twenty-eight...never married...vivacious...and just the right companion for her niece...especially at this time...."

"That would be very good for Abi...," Naomi commented. "Where does you sister live...and can she get away from what she does...for a few weeks....?"

"She's been living in London...for the past few years...on her share of the income from the trust fund our father set up for both of us...writing a more modern version of The Forsythe Saga...."

"She can always bring her typewriter...or word processor...with her...," suggested Roger, trying to interject some humor, "...and if she forgets...I'm sure we have a spare somewhere...in good working condition...we can let her use...."

Abigail Lancaster was admitted to a small private hospital in Albany with the official diagnosis of pains in the pelvic region, and Naomi was given hospital privileges to treat her. One of Dr Steinberg's trusted nurses was flown up from Richmond at Joan's expense, simply using some of the considerable income from that considerable Custis trust fund, and the surgical procedure to abort a four-month old fetus went smoothly. "I hope he burns in hell!" was the first thing Joan said when Naomi told her that everything was alright.

A few days later, Joan chartered a plane to carry herself, her family and Naomi nonstop back to Richmond, avoiding the terrible invasion of privacy they would all suffer were they to take a regular commercial flight. Roger asked to go along, explaining that his case against James Lancaster was prepared, but that he would not be able to do anything until James Lancaster was removed from office, that there were no other important cases for the moment, that he had inherited a well-organized and functioning office from Mark, and so on and so forth.

"Alright...Roger...I would also like to spend some time with you...but remember that nothing has basically changed...between us...."

Catherine Custis flew in from London's Heathrow, two days after Joan called her, nonstop to Washington's Dulles International Airport. Roger offered to drive up from Richmond to Washington to pick her up, and John Lancaster, now feeling considerably more grown-up, went along to keep him company. Joan was too busy tending to Abigail, and Naomi had too much to catch up at the hospital of the Medical College of Virginia.

Catherine Custis was attractive in personality and temperament, rather than in the geometric dimensionality and configuration of her body and face. She was about five feet six, somewhat overweight but still reasonably well-proportioned, with dark brown hair and brown eyes. Her mother Rachel was her father's second wife who married him about a year after the death of his first wife. Rachel was an observing orthodox Jew and an outstanding lawyer, while Henry Custis was a practising high Episcopalian and comparably outstanding lawyer. Indeed, while they were still alive, Catherine's mother and father, Joan's stepmother and father, were partners in a very successful law practice. Both Joan and Catherine were brought up in their father's faith, even though Rachel Custis continued to remain an observant Jew, but the family did participate in the ceremony performed by Rachel each Friday at sundown opening the Jewish sabbath meal. As Catherine grew older, she began to realize what a burden this interfaith marriage had placed on her mother because both she and Joan were being systematically taught in their Sunday school classes to hate the Jews. When she was old enough, Catherine just dropped out of Christianity, but for some psychological reasons she could never explain, even to herself, she did not convert to her mother's religion. Perhaps, subconsciously, the Sunday school classes were effective, even in her case. In any event, Catherine promised herself that she would never cross religious lines in marriage, if she ever did marry, feeling as she did that it would not be fair to the children of such a marriage.

"Then you're a half-Jew...," commented Roger as Catherine related her family background while they drove down I-95 to Richmond.

"You sound like a Nazi...," she laughed, a bit nervously. "Is the child of a Baptist mother and Catholic father...a half-Baptist...or a half-Catholic...?"

"Of course not.... I see your point...and I must apologize...."

"Oh that's alright.... It's very difficult to break the Christian mind-set.... I think I should have followed my mother's religion...even as a child.... It has much more warmth.... That very brief Sabbath ceremony...by the mother of the family...was so beautiful...so strengthening of the family...of the home...that I miss it...miss it very much...now that my mother is dead.... You have no idea what it's like to have a real Jewish mother...." No, Roger did not know.

The remainder of the trip turned to other less emotional topics, and despite the rather pointed criticism, Roger, without feeling any sense of disloyalty to Naomi, was rather taken by her as they drove down I-95 to the capital city of the Confederacy, and John tried not to interfere too much as Mr Morrison and Ms Custis conversed all the way from Dulles International Airport to Richard Henry Lee Drive.

Joan finally became settled with her family in Richmond, where the Lancasters had maintained their legal residence during their political absence in Washington, and very soon after her arrival she filed a suit for divorce from her husband of twenty-two years. Given the liberty by the House of Representatives to leave Washington for Richmond, but in the company of two of Mr Ryan's deputies, James Lancaster did make a personal appearance in the initial court hearing, in the company of his personal lawyer, not of his White House counsel Joel Seligman, there to contest the divorce action, and it became a matter of waiting until the case of Lancaster v. Lancaster would come up on the docket of the court. It was expected that the issue of his common-law crimes in New York, Virginia and the District of Columbia would come up in both the Senate impeachment trial and divorce trial, but it seemed that the Senate trial would occur first. As to whether the Virginia court would accept the findings of the Senate in a proceeding based on that body's own rules of procedure and evidence, everyone would have to wait. The three younger children were in favor of the divorce, and Abigail was especially angry at her father, saying many times that she never wanted to see him again. "I wish he was dead...!" she said over and over again.

In the meanwhile, the press was obsessed with the criminal issues common to the trials, wondering how the Senate would handle the charges against Lancaster of making unauthorized war, both foreign and domestic, and the obsession reached a peak when the Senate trial opened two weeks after the House's amended bill of impeachment was formally presented to the Senate. Fortunately, most of the urgent legislative business of both houses of the Congress was already settled for that session, especially the appropriation bills to keep the federal government in cash.

Under the United States Constitution, the Chief Justice of the United States, rather than the Vice President, presides over the Senate when the Senate holds a trial for the removal of the President. The purpose of our founding fathers was to deny the Vice President an opportunity to prejudice the outcome, for the removal of the President would make the Vice President the President thus giving the Vice President a stake in the removal. But the Constitution did not consider that the Chief Justice might be someone very close to the President and appointed by him to that high judicial office, resulting in a Chief Justice perhaps more than willing to prejudice the outcome in favor of the President.

Chief Justice Askins was a former law partner of James Lancaster, sponsored by Senator Lancaster for a federal district court judgeship in northern Virginia, and then for a seat on the United States Court of Appeals for the District of Columbia Circuit, and he briefly served on both courts without having written any opinions at all. Within only a few days of the Lancaster inauguration, the chief justice who had administered the oath of office to President-elect Lancaster died of a massive heart attack at age seventy-seven, and the very next day the new President Lancaster sent to the Senate the nomination of Judge Askins to be Chief Justice of the United States. Wilberforce Askins had no record of scholarly writings to pick over, and his confirmation hearings were over in only a few days, but he was confirmed by a majority of only fifty-one senators out of one hundred, those voting in the negative complaining about Askins' lack of legal scholarship and very limited judicial experience. Regardless, Askins was now Chief Justice Askins, the person who would preside over the Senate in the trial of his very good friend and former law partner.

A few days after the House had enacted the bill of impeachment, the House selected a committee of its members as managers to prosecute the impeachment before the Senate, and Representative Jeremiah Carlssen was chosen by the House to be the chairman of that committee and in effect the chief prosecutor against James Lancaster. He had been elected to the House six years previously after many years as the elected chief public prosecutor of his home county, and had then subsequently engaged in the private practice of criminal law to defend clients against the prosecutor who succeeded him.

This was only the second time in the history of the United States that a President was to be tried before the Senate, the first President being Andrew Johnston, the Vice President in Abraham Lincoln's second term, who had succeeded President Lincoln upon the President's murder. A select Senate committee was now appointed to review the rules of procedure and evidence used in that trial and to recommend any changes. The committee recommended to the Senate that Rule 110 not be followed, but that instead the trial be held before the entire Senate. Rule 110 provided for a special committee of Senators to hear all the evidence in an impeachment trial, and to then make a recommendation to the full Senate, but in the case of the trial of a President, the Senate felt that the entire Senate ought to hear all the evidence directly.

The only question before the Senate was whether President Lancaster ought to be removed from office, for under the Constitution there could be no further punishment awarded by the Senate. Bills of attainder, where a legislative body may by legislative act deprive a person of life, liberty or property, were forbidden to the Congress by the Constitution. The Senate was to act as jury, and a vote of two-thirds of all Senators present would be required to find the President guilty of the charges brought by the House of Representatives.

Furthermore, the Senate in effect would also act as the judge, for any decision of the presiding officer, the chief justice, could be overruled by the Senate on appeal by the party aggrieved by the ruling, either the House or the President.

Understanding that delaying tactics might be employed by the presiding officer, Senator Ronald Mays, the majority leader of the Senate, warned Chief Justice Askins openly from the floor of the Senate, on the very first day of the trial, even before the proceedings began, that the Senate would not tolerate any attempt by the presiding officer to delay the trial or to try to prejudice the outcome. Senator Mays reminded Chief Justice Askins very pointedly, perhaps too pointedly, that he too could be removed in the same manner as the President. A great hush fell over the chamber when Senator Mays spoke this warning to the presiding officer, but the Senator felt it had to be made, for otherwise all the effort to constitutionally remove this President might be for naught.

On that first day, and on all the days to come, the public, diplomatic, VIP and press galleries were crowded to capacity, but the gallery reserved for the President and his family was noticeably empty. The sergeant-at-arms of the Senate posted extra deputy sergeants-at-arms and extra officers of the Capitol Police about all the galleries and in the lobby of the Senate and on the floor of the Senate, to quickly restrain and expel anyone who might try to disturb the proceedings.

Two tables were placed in the well of the Senate chamber between the front row of senatorial desks and the desks of the secretary of the Senate and his assistants. One table was for the House prosecutors and the other for the President's legal counsel Joel Seligman and his associates, all defense counsel in this matter to be paid by the taxpayer. To the left of the presiding officer was a raised witness chair, and a qualified court reporter, there to supplement the regular Senate reporter, sat to the right of the Chief Justice. Microphones were installed for the presiding officer, the witnesses and for counsel on both sides.

Roger Morrison, District Attorney of New York County, and Donald Carter, State's Attorney for Henrico County, Virginia, sat at the prosecution table at the invitation of the House committee of managers, alongside Mr Carlssen, to emphasize that the prosecution charges of murder and abduction would be pursued in these removal proceedings in addition to the charges of making unauthorized war. Although it was not required that the President be present at a trial of this kind, James Lancaster was indeed present, not leaving it to his legal counsel alone to manage his defense.

It would not be very difficult to say to what extent Senator Mays's admonition to Chief Justice Askins failed to prevent the presiding officer from being partial to the President. Once everyone was in his place, the Chief Justice of the United States opened the proceedings.

"This is not a trial...in the judicial sense.... It is an

adversarial hearing before the Senate of the United States.... The power to impeach lies solely with the House of Representatives...and the power to remove lies solely with the Senate...both powers enunciated in Article I of the Constitution...the legislative article.... There is no mention of impeachment and removal in Article III...the judicial article...and the only other mention in the Constitution of impeachment and removal is in Article II...the executive article...which denies the President the power to pardon those removed by the Senate upon impeachment by the House...and which also states in Section 4 that the President may be removed from office for treason...bribery...or other high crimes and misdemeanors.... Thus the proceedings we are entering upon are purely legislative...not judicial...and the Senate has the power to hear whatever evidence it wishes in order for this august body to made its decision as to whether to remove James Monroe Lancaster from the office of President of the United States...." The Chief Justice paused to clear his throat, total quiet prevailing during the brief pause, and he then continued.

"There has been in our history a running controversy...as to whether the other high crimes phrase in the Constitution refers only to indictable offenses.... That controversy does not apply here.... The charges levied by the House against the President are that he committed first-degree murder in New York County...in the State of New York...that he committed the felony of abduction in Henrico County...in the Commonwealth of Virginia....and that he committed the felonies of attempted rape...and attempted murder...in the District of Columbia...that he committed felonies in Albany County in New York State.... All of these are indictable offenses under the common law...and if the President is removed from office...New York...Virginia...and the District of Columbia would be readily able to bring him to trial for these indictable offenses.... It is my understanding that James Monroe Lancaster is already under indictment in New York for murder...in two of its counties...and under indictment in Virginia for abduction...."

The Chief Justice paused again, and again he continued.

"The select committee of the Senate has informed me of the rules to be followed.... The House will present its case...including documentary and testimentary evidence...and then the President will present his case...also including documentary and testimentary evidence.... Each side may cross-examine the witnesses of the other side...but counsel are reminded that...although this is not a court of law...as presiding officer of the Senate in these proceedings...I shall insist that the questioning of the witnesses be to the point.... Any ruling I make...of any kind...in any matter...may of course be appealed to the Senate...which has the final power...to decide all matters.... My role here is as presiding officer...not as judge.... The Senate is the judge and jury in this matter...but the basic rules of fairness of a judicial trial will have to be followed...and if they are not then anyone aggrieved by the violation of the commonly accepted rules of procedure would have a controversy that can be decided in the federal courts.... Mr Carlssen...do you wish to open the case for the House...?"

Senator Mays immediately jumped to his feet. "Just a minute...Mr Carlssen.... I think it is important...before we proceed...that the Chief Justice be forcefully corrected as to his last point.... There is no appeal from any action of the Senate...to remove a President...or even...," and he paused for effect, "...a Chief Justice.... That gratuitous remark...Mr Chief Justice...about a justiciable controversy...is not correct...and I am afraid shows considerable bias by you in favor of Mr Lancaster...."

"You are out of order...Senator.... I did not recognize you...."

Senator Mays turned to the Senate, ignoring Chief Justice Askins, and moved to recess the trial to permit the Senate to go into executive session, "...and for the purpose of this motion...it would be most appropriate that our presiding officer be the President of the Senate...but she now being the Acting President...then the President pro tempore of the Senate.... Senator Abbott...would you be so kind as to preside over us...while we consider my motion...?"

Senator Abbott left his chair to mount the podium, the Chief Justice refusing to leave, whereupon the Senator cupped his hands at his mouth, and very loudly asked for the assistance of the Senate sergeant-at-arms. Mr Cantrell hurried down the aisle with two deputies, and stood before the Chief Justice, saying "I'm sorry...sir...but you will have to leave.... The issue at hand is a motion by the Senate to temporarily recess...not a motion dealing with the issue of impeachment and removal...."

"I realize that...," responded the Chief Justice, rather testily, "...but the issue pertains to the larger issue of the President's removal...."

"You have no authority here...Mr Chief Justice...," insisted Mr Cantrell, "...and if you do not give way to Senator Abbott...I shall have to forcibly evict you from the chamber...."

Rather nonplused by being spoken to in this manner, Chief Justice Wilberforce Askins left the podium with as much dignity as he could manage, and while escorted by deputy sergeants-at-arms he quietly left the chamber to go to the Capitol office of the President of the Senate.

EIGHTEEN

After Wilberforce Askins left the Senate chamber, Senator Abbott took his chair as President pro tempore of the Senate, and struck his gravel many times to try to quiet down a Senate chamber consumed in turmoil. Again, Senator Mays raised his hand, and this time was formally recognized.

"The Senator from Illinois...," said Senator Abbott as he recognized Senator Mays.

"Mr President...I wish to present a resolution to the Senate...as follows...," and then he paused, "...that the Senate requests the House of Representatives to consider the adoption of a bill of impeachment against Wilberforce Askins...Chief Justice of the United States...for attempting to cause the judicial branch to usurp the sole constitutional power of the Senate to try impeachments...," causing a burst of commotion as reporters scurried to leave the press gallery to transmit this stunning development, and it required much pounding of the gavel to quiet the galleries.

"Is there a second...?" asked Senator Abbott.

"I second the motion...," shouted several other Senators.

"Is there debate...? The Senator from Illinois...."

"Mr President...too long has this nation witnessed the encroachment by the judicial branch on the legislative...slowly but surely.... We have watched over many decades as the federal courts...courts which the Congress constitutionally authorized...and can at any time de-authorize...as the federal courts took a role in the governance of this nation that has been far beyond what was contemplated by our Constitution.... Today...Mr Askins went too far.... As far as I am concerned it was the last straw.... Under the Constitution...the House of Representatives has the sole power to impeach...and the Senate has the sole power to try impeachments brought by the House.... There is no review.... We are governed by the elected representatives of the people...not by some non-elected committee of nine lawyers.... They and all the other judges in the judicial branch are there to hear cases and controversies...not to govern the nation.... Thank you...Mr President...," and he sat down. There was total quiet in the Senate chamber, and then a swift crescendo of very loud applause.

"Is there further debate...?" Senator Abbott paused for an entire moment. No other Senator wished to debate, and the question was called. Eighty-nine senators voted for the Mays motion, and the remaining eleven against. The President pro tempore of the Senate again recognized Senator Mays, who placed another motion before the Senate.

"I move the following bill...that in the event of a vacancy in the office of Chief Justice of the United States...that the senior associate justice become the acting chief justice...with all the duties and responsibilities of Chief Justice of the United States...," all to provide for the continuation of the Senate trial even if Wilberforce Askins were removed from office. And this too caused much commotion. The Senate unanimously agreed to limit debate, and after several speeches from the Senate floor the motion carried with only three dissenting votes. Senator Abbott again recognized the Majority Leader of the Senate, and this time Senator Mays moved that the Senate recess for no more than three days to await the actions of the House of Representatives, actions to adopt a bill of impeachment against Chief Justice Askins and to concur in the legislation to make the senior associate justice the acting chief justice in the event the Chief Justice were removed from office.

These unforeseen developments obviously caught everyone by total surprise, although the events should not have been completely unforeseen. It was well-known that Askins was Lancaster's old friend, and that something would probably happen because of that, but what actually did happen was of course the surprise.

As everyone, including James Monroe Lancaster, left the floor of the Senate chamber, the leaving was not very orderly or quiet. Mr Lancaster tried to physically reach Roger to strike him, but the Manhattan DA was well protected by several deputy sergeants-at-arms and also by the prosecutors. Defense counsel were finally able to fully restrain the President and to lead him in a more dignified manner out of the chamber through the front door ordinarily reserved for the President of the Senate.

More history was rapidly made during the next few days. The House later that very afternoon adopted a bill of impeachment against Wilberforce Askins on the charge of attempting to usurp the constitutional authority of the Senate, and indirectly of the House, for if the Senate's power to try impeachments were in any way abridged, then so was the power of the House to impeach. The House also enacted the bill proposed by Senator Mays, which was then sent by special messenger to the vice presidential mansion, and there Sally Campbell, joining in the outrage of the Congress, quickly signed the legislation that very evening without ceremony. Early the next morning, Mrs Campbell received another important document, Wilberforce Askin's letter of resignation, and at ten o'clock the following morning, the Senate reconvened under a new presiding officer, to continue with the impeachment trial of James Monroe Lancaster.

All one hundred Senators were present, and so too were all the parties and their legal counsel. The galleries were once again filled to overflowing, and Mr Justice Benjamin, the acting chief justice, was in the presiding officer's chair, no one in the Senate chamber aware that Mr Justice Benjamin was a grand-uncle of Naomi Steinberg, her grandmother's brother. After a few introductory remarks, very carefully worded to avoid offending the Senate at all costs, Mr Benjamin called the chief prosecutor for the House.

"Are you ready...Mr Carlssen...?"

"Yes...Mr Chief Justice...."

Jeremiah Carlssen stood up, and turned around to face the Senate. He was in his early sixties, over six feet tall, and slim, but he had developed a forward curvature of the spine which made him appear much shorter than he really was. A soft-spoken man, Mr Carlssen would have to depend on the excellent pick-up qualities of the microphones at this desk.

"Senators of our United States...!" Mr Carlssen began. "The House of Representatives by overwhelming vote has impeached the President of the United States for other high crimes...for having committed the heinous crimes of murder...abduction... attempted rape...attempted murder.... These are indictable crimes under the common law...and in the case of murder and others there are no applicable statutes of limitations.... James Monroe Lancaster is under indictment in New York County...in the State of New York...for the first-degree murder of Dr Dinah Miriam Steinberg...a physician then at Presbyterian Hospital...of the Columbia-Presbyterian Medical Center in New York City.... We will present conclusive evidence before the Senate that James Monroe Lancaster committed that crime...and to assist the House in its presentation of that evidence...we have Roger Morrison...assistant district attorney of New York County at the time of the murder...and now the elected District Attorney of New York County....

"Senators...! James Monroe Lancaster is also under indictment in Henrico County...in the Commonwealth of Virginia...for the abduction of Dr Naomi Anna Steinberg...the younger sister of the murdered Dr Dinah Steinberg...and to assist the House in its case against James Monroe Lancaster...we have Donald Carter...State's Attorney for Henrico County.... Two more heinous crimes were committed...both of them in the District of Columbia...at 1600 Pennsylvania Avenue Northwest...in the White House itself...in the residence occupied in trust by the President for the people of the United States.... We will show that James Monroe Lancaster committed the felonies of attempted rape and attempted murder against Dr Naomi Anna Steinberg.... I shall present the evidence on behalf of the House for the crimes committed in the nation's capital city....

"Mr Lancaster is also charged by the House with having made war against a friendly foreign state...without a constitutional declaration of war...and having committed domestic violence against citizens of the United States...causing the deaths of citizens of the United States.... These are not crimes under the common law but they are serious crimes against humanity...and I shall personally prosecute these counts of the bill of impeachment....

"Senators...! There is nothing partisan in these proceedings against James Monroe Lancaster.... Everyone sitting at this table who will actually present the case for the House is a member of the same political party as he is.... The majority of the membership of the House is of the same political party.... This is not a political question.... It is a question of justice...for the victims of these crimes...but even more importantly for the people of the nation...! Shall we permit a murderer to continue to be the President of the United States...?"

Jeremiah Carlssen stopped, turned about to momentarily face the acting chief justice, and then sat down. A loud murmur swept, as though a tidal wave, through the entire chamber. The presiding officer brought his gavel down to restore quiet, and then asked, "Mr Seligman...do you wish to make your opening statement for the President...?"

"Yes...Mr Chief Justice...." And Joel Seligman stood up, stepped out into the aisle alongside the table, and turned about to face the Senate. As related before, he was a very good-looking young man in his mid-thirties, a brilliant lawyer despite his limited years of experience, but with experience of very high quality, and he stood about as tall as Mr Carlssen would if Jeremiah Carlssen were more careful about his posture. Roger turned about to look at him, and suddenly had the ominous feeling that this American Jew might be too much competition for this American Methodist were Joel Seligman to become interested in Naomi, and what single man in his right mind would not be interested in her? For the moment, all that Roger could hope for was that Joel Seligman was married, but Roger would have to put all these thoughts aside when it was his turn to stand before the Senate.

"Members of the Senate...! As legal counsel for the President...I shall show that the evidence to be presented by the House will be too questionable to warrant the awesome act of removing a President of the United States from office...an office to which he was elected by the will of the people of the United States...the same people who elected the Members of the House...and who elected you...the Members of the Senate.... I have no documentary evidence...nor do we have testimentary evidence...to disprove the allegations against the President.... One does not ordinarily have evidence of not committing a crime.... We shall assume...for the sake of elemental fairness...that it is the House that has the burden of proof.... It shall be my task to show the weakness of the proof presented by the House.... We are fully confident that these proceedings will result in the President of United States remaining in the office to which he was elected...." Joel Seligman turned around, said "Thank you..." to the acting chief justice, and sat down.

A very good opening statement, under the circumstances, thought Roger, still concerned about his own personal future, and the only two possible futures he could think of was the one with Naomi and the one without her. Was there a third possible future, somewhere deep down, with Catherine Custis? Catherine had put him at his ease during that long drive from Dulles to Richmond, and he had enjoyed her company on the trip. But now it was necessary to get his thoughts quickly back to the matter at hand.

"With the permission of the Senate...," intoned the presiding officer, "...I shall declare a recess...until two o'clock this afternoon...."

Naomi and Joan were not in the Senate chamber

during that opening morning session, but Catherine Custis was, in the visitors' gallery. Instead, they were in the office suite of the Vice President of the United States and President of the Senate, an office suite not now being used because Sally Campbell was too busy being Acting President in the White House offices, and the suite was being used instead by the House committee of managers and its witnesses, which were quite a few in number. Besides Naomi and Joan, there were Mark Rosenblueth, John Paulsen, Robert Ginsburg, William Salinger, Thomas Malloy, Juan Ramos, and the two White House cleaning women Roberta Albertson and Audrey Galinsky. Also, fingerprint experts from the New York City Police Department, the New York State Police, the New Jersey State Police, the Delaware State Police, the Maryland State Police, the Virginia State Police, and the FBI. Since Joseph Angstrom was under indictment in Virginia, he was kept under guard in the offices of the Senate sergeant-at-arms.

Everyone had two hours for lunch, and a special table was made available in the Senate restaurant for the House managers and associated counsel and for the witnesses for the House. During lunch, Senator Mays and several other Senators came over to Mr Carlssen to congratulate him on his opening statement to the Senate. They having met Joan Lancaster on many previous occasions, it was she who introduced them to Naomi Steinberg, and Roger thought he saw more than one handshake much too prolonged by the Senators.

NINETEEN

The House managers and associated counsel returned to the Senate chamber, and the House witnesses to the Vice President's office, by two o'clock. The acting chief justice declared the opening of the second session of that day. "Mr Carlssen...will you present the case for the House...."

"Mr Chief Justice...the House will first present conclusive evidence that James Monroe Lancaster...when a Senator...murdered Dr Dinah Miriam Steinberg.... For this purpose...Mr Morrison will actually present our case...." Jeremiah Carlssen sat down, and Roger Morrison stood up.

"Mr Chief Justice...," said Roger in a firm voice despite his nervousness, "...the House calls as its first witness...Joan Custis Lancaster...."

"I object...," shouted Joel Seligman as he jumped to his feet. "You cannot call a wife to testify against her husband...."

"That was so under the common law...Mr Seligman...," responded Mr Justice Benjamin, "...but the current rule in many States is that you cannot compel a spouse to testify against his or her spouse...for to do so would jeopardize the marriage...an institution still of considerable sanctity in the law.... Mrs Lancaster...I have been informed...wishes to testify.... She is not being compelled to testify.... As I said...many of our States have modified the common-law rule to permit the voluntary testimony of a spouse...on the ground that if the testimony is voluntary...the marriage is already on its way to oblivion.... Besides...Mr Seligman...the ordinary judicial rules do not apply here.... I shall rule that Mrs Lancaster may testify...and you may appeal my ruling to the Senate...if you wish...."

"I do wish...."

"Senators...," said Mr Justice Benjamin to the assembled United States Senate, "...the question before you is whether Joan Custis Lancaster...who has filed for divorce from her husband in Virginia...may voluntarily testify on behalf of the House.... How say you all...? The secretary of the Senate will please call the roll...."

Roger was concerned that this might be a close vote by a predominantly male Senate, which might not like the idea of permitting a wife to testify against her husband, under any circumstances. Roger silently breathed a sigh of relief when the Senate voted 95 to 2, with 3 abstentions, to allow the testimony.

A deputy sergeant-at-arms went to the Vice President's office to escort Joan Lancaster to the Senate chamber, then down to the witness chair, where she was sworn in. Roger walked to a position in front of the tables so that the witness would be on his right and the Senate on his left, positioning himself so as not to block James Lancaster's and Joel Seligman's view of the witness.

"Please state your full name and address....," Roger opened the questioning.

"My name is Joan Alice Custis Lancaster...," began Joan in her very pleasant Virginia accent. "Custis is my maiden name...which I use professionally.... I now live at 35 Richard Henry Lee Drive...in Richmond...with three of my four children.... That is the residence of the family of Dr Naomi Steinberg...which they have very kindly asked us to share with them until my own house...the one I had inherited from my father...is put back in order.... My fourth child is a student at Princeton University...in New Jersey...."

"And would you state your profession...."

"Mother...housewife...and incidentally research professor of educational policy...at the George Washington University...my profession to a great extent chosen so as to give me the flexibility of time to devote to my two more important roles...as wife and mother...."

"Would you state your relationship to the President...."

"I have been his wife...for twenty-two years...but I have filed for divorce...in our home state of Virginia...."

"Can you tell us why you are seeking a divorce from your husband...?"

"He has been a womanizer...for almost all of those years...and has committed adultery...even with women with whom I have been acquainted...some very well.... I knew he continued his philandering ways...even when he entered the White House...but I kept quiet about it all...for almost twenty-two years...to avoid a scandal that would involve my family...and his legal career...and then political career.... Women were even surreptitiously brought into the White House...all voluntarily...except for Dr Steinberg...."

"Please tell us what you know of his activities in New York City...."

"About five years ago...he began to go out of town...usually for two days at a time...and always during the week...without telling me where he was going...but saying it was on the business of the Senate.... After about a year...I became rather curious...but I could not hire a private investigator...because I was concerned that the man or woman might prove to be not too reliable...as far as confidentiality was concerned.... And so one day...I kept the children out of school for two days...canceled a graduate seminar...and took a trip...just for the fun of it...or so I told my children.... I rented a sedan...on the pretext that my personal car needed routine service...and followed him...to where he was driving...and it was all the way to New York... It was very difficult keeping my children in line for that long a trip...but I did not want to lose sight of his car.... And obviously he did not recognize my rented car...which was the whole idea of renting one.... I followed him directly to this modern high-rise apartment building in the West

Seventies...in Manhattan...saw him use a hand-held radio device...to open the garage door to the underground garage...drive in...and I could only assume that he had an apartment in that building...or he was regularly seeing some woman...who had an apartment in that building...."

"With the permission of the Senate...," said Roger, "...we are going to set up a large projection screen suspended to the presiding officer's right...just behind the reporter.... We are then going to project two images...side by side.... One is a press photograph of Mr Lancaster...which will remain on the screen...and the other will be a sequence of video-camera photographs taken of certain people...on other occasions.... As we go through the sequence...would you...Mrs Lancaster...please let us know if you recognize any of those in the sequence.... Because of the nature of the projection screen...there will be no need to dim the lighting in the Senate chamber...."

The projection screen was set up very efficiently and quickly, and the photograph of the President's head, showing his face straight-on and taken by a press photographer at one time or other, was projected onto the left half of the screen. Then another photograph was shown, projected alongside the President's, one after the other in sequence, but not too quickly, until one of them bore an extremely close resemblance to the other photograph once they were viewed side-by-side. The Senate chamber became astir, and Joan shouted, "That's James Lancaster...."

"What we have done is present to you...Mrs Lancaster...and to the Senate...security photographs taken by the video cameras that were part of the security system for that apartment building.... Photographs were routinely taken of everyone entering or leaving the building...either through the lobby...or through the garage.... Quickly obtaining a warrant...the New York City police seized the video cassettes...as evidence...for the day of the murder...and for the several days before and after...and placed them in the police file...for this murder case.... The guards were able to identify that video-photograph as that of an occupant...known to them as Maxwell Randolph...who owned an apartment in the building...and occupied it one or more days a week.... We are therefore able to prove that James Lancaster...did have an apartment...under an alias...in the same building...in which I had an apartment...and in which the Steinberg sisters also had an apartment.... None of the security photographs taken after the day of the murder show the image of James Lancaster...but those before that day...and specifically on the day of the murder...do show his security photograph.... We shall also present...as a witness...Mr Justice Berger...of the New York Supreme Court...in and for New York County...who will testify that the man with whom he briefly discussed matters of law...in the lobby...or elevator...or halls...is the man sitting next to Mr Seligman...at the President's table.... I have no further questions of this witness...for the time being...."

"Mr Seligman.... Do you wish to cross-examine...?" asked the presiding officer.

"No...Mr Chief Justice...we have no questions to ask of this witness...," and the President engaged in a private argument with his counsel, apparently over that reply. The President immediately stood up, and said in a very loud voice, "My counsel may not have questions of this witness...but I have...."

"Then you may ask them...Mr Lancaster...."

"Mrs Lancaster...can you tell the Senate why I became a womanizer...."

The acting chief justice very quickly interrupted. "You need not answer that question...Mrs Lancaster.... Mr Lancaster...that is not a pertinent question.... The issue as to whether or not you were...to use the term...a womanizer...is not pertinent to this hearing.... The witness introduced it to express her opinion as to why you were in New York City...under an alias...and in an apartment you bought and occupied under that alias.... There is inherently nothing illegal about using an alias...or even being a womanizer...unless it is for the purpose of committing a criminal offense or a fraud or a tort.... If you wish to appeal my ruling...you are free to do so...."

"I do wish to appeal...."

The presiding officer put the appeal to the Senate, and the appeal lost by the vote of 95 against and only 5 for.

"Do you have any further questions...Mr Lancaster...."

"None at this time...Mr Chief Justice...."

"Mrs Lancaster...the Senate thanks you for your testimony.... You are excused...and Mr Morrison...you may call your next witness...."

"The House calls Mr Justice Berger...."

In repetition of the previous procedure, a deputy sergeant-at-arms escorted Justice Berger to the witness chair. The judge took the oath, and sat down.

"Mr Justice Berger.... You have previously stated to the police that you occasionally ran into a tall man...in his late forties...in the lobby...halls...and elevator...of your apartment building...whom you did not see regularly...."

"Yes...Mr Morrison.... Whenever I did run into him...we briefly talked about some matter of law.... He must have known that I was on the bench...and from my conversation with him...I assumed he was a lawyer...."

"Do you see that man in this chamber...Mr Justice Berger...?"

"Yes... That man is now the President...seated next to his counsel...Mr Seligman...."

"Thank you...Justice Berger.... I have no further questions of Justice Berger...."

"Do you have any questions...Mr Seligman...?" asked the Acting Chief Justice of the United States.

"Yes...I do.... Mr Justice Berger...if you are able to identify the President now...why could you not state his identity...at the time of the murder...when the police asked you about this man whom you only occasionally spoke to...."

"For the same reason that the police have live line-ups.... I had never seen Mr Lancaster in person before that time.... I saw many photographs of him in the newspapers...and on television...subsequent to that time...but it is not the same...as seeing the person in the flesh...so to speak...and that is why I never before connected Maxwell Randolph and James Lancaster.... And that is why the police and Mr Morrison could not identify the video photographs...and the security guards merely identified them as those of Maxwell Randolph...an occupant of the apartment building.... He bought his apartment under that name...."

"That is all...Mr Chief Justice.... I have no further questions of Justice Berger...."

"But I have...," shouted James Lancaster.

"Then you may ask your questions...Mr Lancaster...," responded the presiding officer.

"Judge Berger...I have never seen you before in my life.... How old are you...Judge Berger...?"

"I'm now seventy-two...but if you're implying that my eyesight is faulty...you are sadly mistaken.... My vision is corrected to...20...30...and I always wear my glasses...and I have no eye ailments.... If you're implying that eyewitness evidence is not very reliable...this particular witness you're examining is very reliable...."

"I said...I never saw you before in my life.... When did you and the others decide to conspire against me...?"

"We never conspired against you...Mr Lancaster.... I have reviewed all the evidence...as though I were a judge trying you without a jury...and I am firmly convinced...beyond a reasonable doubt...that you killed Dinah Steinberg...," generating another tidal wave in the Senate chamber.

"It's a lie...all lies...," the President shouted, and began to move toward the witness, but his counsel Joel Seligman stopped him before he could move more than a step.

The Acting Chief Justice of the United States pounded his gavel, and ordered the President of the United States to sit down, or else be removed from the Senate chamber.

"The Senate thanks you for your testimony...Mr Justice Berger.... You are now excused.... With the approval of the Senate...I shall now declare this trial in recess until ten o'clock tomorrow morning...."

TWENTY

All witnesses at the Senate trial on behalf of the House were staying at the Washington Hilton, and moved between the Capitol and the hotel in chauffeured limousines provided by the House sergeant-at-arms. Catherine Custis shared a suite with her sister Joan after spending several days in Richmond with Abigail, the three younger Lancaster children remaining back in Richmond with Naomi's mother and grandmother. In the evening of the first day of the trial, and of all subsequent days, they all had their dinner together in a private dining room. All the witnesses from New York and Richmond, with the exception of Naomi, were married and had brought their spouses with them, with the obvious exception of Joan Lancaster, but the presence of the spouses made the dinners a social rather than a shop-talk experience. Joan found this a welcome relief, and so did Naomi and Roger, and Naomi took each occasion to become better acquainted with Catherine and to try to steer her and Roger closer to each other. Although she tried to do it very casually, Roger was well aware of it, and had mixed feelings about it.

The Senate reconvened promptly at ten o'clock the next morning, with the galleries again filled to overflowing, Catherine and all the spouses in the visitors galleries, and all the witnesses for the House present in the Vice President's office.

"Do you wish to call your next witness...Mr Morrison...?"

"Yes...Mr Chief Justice.... The House calls William Salinger...," and Inspector Salinger was escorted to the witness chair.

"Mr Salinger...would you state your full name...your position now...and your involvement in the investigation of the murder of Dr Dinah Steinberg..."

"My name is William Benson Salinger... I am an inspector in the New York City Police Department...promoted from the rank of captain about six months ago...and now assigned to the office of the District Attorney of New York County...as its chief investigator.... At the time of the murder...I was a police detective lieutenant in the homicide division...in the Borough of Manhattan.... Dr Dinah Steinberg shared an apartment with her younger sister...Dr Naomi Steinberg...in a cooperative apartment building just west of Central Park.... Both were physicians at the Columbia-Presbyterian Medical Center.... Dr Naomi Steinberg was at a medical symposium in Stockholm when her sister was murdered in the apartment they shared....

Dr Dinah Steinberg...being overly absent from the hospital without notification to the hospital...an assistant hospital administrator had gone to see her...to make sure she was alright...and got the building security guards to unlock the apartment door when there was no response.... They found her dead...lying on her bed.... I was called in as a homicide detective...together with my two sergeants...Thomas Malloy...and Juan Ramos.... The medical examiner found that her death was by strangulation...using two powerful hands...the death occurring within twenty-four hours of the discovery.... You could see the bruise marks on her neck...as the outline of two hands...."

"Please continue...Inspector Salinger...."

"Roger Morrison...an assistant district attorney in New York County at the time...the gentleman now examining me...lived in the same building...and was informed of the death when he arrived home.... He went to the Steinberg apartment with me...then asked Sergeant Ramos to accompany him to his own apartment...to get his camera...and to load it with a fresh roll of film in the presence of Mr Ramos.... Mr Morrison was a very avid photographer...had fine equipment...and his own darkroom.... He also has a college degree in computer science.... Both he and Sergeant Ramos returned...the sergeant carrying the camera...and Mr Morrison very carefully took close-up photographs of the neck of the victim...using special lenses.... Another occupant of the apartment building was Justice Berger of the New York Supreme Court...and Mr Morrison asked us to fetch Justice Berger...to ask him to come to Mr Morrison's apartment.... Justice Berger and I and both my sergeants witnessed the removal of the film from the camera...and the processing of it in Mr Morrison's darkroom...and saw discernible thumb prints on the front of Dr Steinberg's neck...and fingerprints of the other fingers of the killer...on the back of the neck.... All of this procedure was carefully documented in signed statements...and verified by Justice Berger himself.... Conformal copies of the prints and statements were deposited with the clerk of the court of the New York Supreme Court...in and for New York County...with the clerk of the court of the County Court of New York County...in the official files of the New York City Police Department...in the official files of the District Attorney of New York County.... We had the fingerprints of the killer...and it was now a question of finding out whose prints they were...."

"And did you find out who belonged to the fingerprints...? And would you tell the Senate how the identity of the killer was finally ascertained...?"

"At first...we went through the usual routine of sending the prints to the FBI...and asked them also to check their civil collection...which would include law enforcement officers...those having held government security clearances...commissioned officers of the armed forces...fingerprints held purely for identification purposes.... There was no match.... Justice Berger had mentioned to me that he briefly talked of several occasions...either in the lobby...or in the elevator...with a man called Maxwell Randolph...who had only a few months previously bought an apartment in the same building.... Justice Berger felt that the man must have been a lawyer...for it seemed he was very knowledgeable about certain very technical aspects of the law.... On this assumption...John Paulsen...chairman of the committee on admissions...of the New York Court of Appeals...was approached as to whether the top pages...just the top pages...of the New York bar examination applications...could be examined for fingerprints...for thumb prints.... At first...Mr Paulsen felt that he was in no position to cooperate...but then realizing that this was a murder investigation...he agreed.... Mr Morrison worked out a computerized method of scanning and photographing the top pages for any fingerprints on them.... We assumed a bar-examination applicant would not ordinarily use gloves to fill out...and handle...his application form...." (some laughter in the Senate chamber)

"Did you find fingerprints in the Randolph apartment...?"

"Not a one.... It was as though it had been very thoroughly wiped clean...and even if we had found his fingerprints...they still would not have necessarily identified who the fingerprints actually belonged to.... Maxwell Randolph could have been an alias...and as it turned out...it was an alias for James Monroe Lancaster...under which alias he bought the apartment...."

"Returning to the New York bar examination papers.... Was a match found with the fingerprints from the murdered woman's neck...?"

"None.... It then occurred to us that the killer might have been practicing law in Washington...and was in New York City weekly...for certain extramarital activities.... We obtained a court order in the District of Columbia leading to the cooperation of the committee on admissions of the District of Columbia Court of Appeals...and repeated the same procedure as in New York...."

"And what was the result...Inspector Salinger...?"

"A perfect match...with the fingerprints of James Monroe Lancaster...." A very loud murmur swept the chamber.

"And then what happened...?"

"Mark Rosenblueth...now Governor of New York...at the time of the murder was the District Attorney of New York County...and was elected Governor when Mr Lancaster was elected President.... Governor Rosenblueth was stunned...and decided that he would obtain fresh fingerprints of James Monroe Lancaster...just to be very sure.... Mr Rosenblueth visited Mr Lancaster at the White House...and left with Mr Lancaster's drinking glass... purportedly as a souvenir.... The fingerprint experts of the New York City Police Department readily lifted the prints from the glass...and made a positive identification of the prints on the neck of Dr Dinah Steinberg as those of James Lancaster...."

"Have these matches been confirmed by others...?"

"Yes...by the New York State Police...by the New Jersey State Police...the Delaware State Police...the Maryland State Police...by the Virginia State Police...and by the FBI...."

"Thank you...Inspector.... Mr Chief Justice...I have no further questions of this witness...for the time being...."

"Do you wish to examine this witness...Mr Seligman...?"

"Yes...I most certainly do...," and as Roger resumed his seat, Joel Seligman took his position in the well of the chamber with the witness on his left, and the Senate on his right.

"Inspector Salinger...is it possible that the fingerprints experts could have made a mistake...? After all...there are millions and millions of sets of fingerprints...in the FBI files alone...."

"The probability of half a dozen different experts...from that many different organizations...all making a mistake...is zero.... The modern techniques for identifying fingerprints...for discriminating between one set and another...make a mistake by even one expert almost impossible...but for all of them to make a mistake...that is definitely impossible...."

"The House provided us with a copy of the prints taken from the murder victim's neck.... We had a fingerprint expert compare them to the President's prints...and he can testify that they do not match...."

"May I ask...Mr Seligman...the name of his organization...?"

"His own private investigation firm.... He was retired from the FBI...and set up his own company...about ten years ago...."

"Was he a fingerprint expert...or a special agent...?"

Joel Seligman swallowed hard, realizing he had just been caught. "He was a special agent...."

"I wouldn't call a special agent a fingerprint expert...just as I am not a fingerprint expert...despite my many years in law-enforcement...."

"Inspector Salinger...is it possible for someone to

use someone else's fingerprints...? Can someone else paste plastic tape to his fingers...the tape simulating the fingerprints of another...? If he could that...then the killer could pass the blame on to someone else...."

"It is easy to do that if the purpose of the false fingerprints is to fool an optical scanning device for security purposes...as in physical access control...but to do what you are suggesting...would require that the tape be embossed...not printed...with the fingerprints not his own.... If a person were to be so prepared...by going to all that trouble...it would be much easier for the killer to simply use gloves...and leave no fingerprints at all.... And if the killer meant to frame someone else...there are easier ways to do that.... We suspect...because of the absence of any evidence of a break-in...that Dr Dinah Steinberg was acquainted with Mr Lancaster...invited him into her apartment...or that he seized her in the hall as she was opening the door...and pushed her in as he closed the entry door behind them.... The absence of gloves would indicate that the murder was decided upon then and there...because the opportunity presented itself...but the premeditation...required for the murder to be one in the first-degree...could be over a short period of time.... I have been told by legal experts that the premeditation need not take place over a long period of time...."

"But what would the killer's motivation be...?"

"I understand that Mrs Lancaster will testify concerning the crimes in the White House...that she will testify...or has already testified...that her husband was a womanizer...over many years.... Dr Dinah Steinberg...an extremely attractive woman...undoubtedly spurned his advances...probably the only woman...other than her younger sister...who ever has...and he killed her...."

"Mr Chief Justice...I am finished with this witness...."

During the lunch recess, Roger and Jeremiah Carlssen met with Mark Rosenblueth and the police witnesses from New York and the other States, telling them that their testimony would not be needed. Mark said he would return that same afternoon to Albany, and congratulated Roger and Jeremiah on their handling of the case.

"Joel Seligman is also doing rather well...," Mark commented, "...considering the very difficult position he's in.... I wouldn't want to be in his professional shoes...but everyone has the right to defense counsel.... I wonder whether he'll take Lancaster's criminal case in New York...or Virginia...or the District...."

Roger thanked Mark for remaining in Washington, just in case he were needed, and then asked Salinger, Malloy and Ramos to remain until the Senate votes. The fingerprint experts from New York and the other States also decided to leave that afternoon, they too no longer needed.

TWENTY-ONE

When the Senate reconvened at two o'clock, the acting chief justice asked Jeremiah Carlssen whether he had more evidence to present to the Senate.

"Yes...I have...Mr Chief Justice...and for this purpose...Mr Donald Carter will present it...."

Donald Carter, State's Attorney for Henrico County in Virginia, stood up and took his place at the same location that Roger had, with the witness chair on his right and the Senate on his left. He was in his mid-fifties, of medium height and medium build, with greying hair and a small grey beard that gave him a considerable air of dignity, and the air of dignity was much reinforced by his general manner of great civility.

"Mr Chief Justice...the House calls Joseph Angstrom...."

This startled James Lancaster, who jumped to his feet to protest the calling of this particular witness.

"On what grounds do you object to the calling of

this witness...?" asked the acting chief justice.

"He is under indictment in Virginia...and will obviously lie...if necessary...to implicate me...to get more lenient treatment from the Virginia authorities...."

"This kind of witness is not unusual in criminal matters...," responded Mr Justice Benjamin. "His status will be made known to the Senate...and it is up to the Senate to take his status into account...as to his credibility.... Mr Carter...you may call your witness for the House...."

The sergeant-at-arms himself returned shortly with Joseph Angstrom, who then took the oath of a witness.

"Please state your name...and residence...."

"My name is Joseph Angstrom...and I am being held without bail at the Henrico County Jail in Richmond...."

"On what charge...?"

"Abducting Naomi Steinberg...but I was only following the instructions of the President...," causing another tidal wave of murmurs through the Senate chamber. He then related in full detail how he obtained an arrest warrant from a federal magistrate in northern Virginia on a false affidavit, arrested Dr Naomi Steinberg at her hospital in Richmond in the company of several other FBI agents, and then how he brought her against her will to the bedroom of the President in the White House rather than before a federal magistrate. "I realized it was all a sham to abduct Dr Steinberg for the pleasure of the President...."

"Did you bring other women to Mr Lancaster's bedroom...either before or since...?"

"Many times...but all the others went most willingly.... We certainly did not need to use a false arrest as a subterfuge...as was necessary to bring Dr Steinberg to his bedroom...."

"Mr Angstrom...did you receive any promise from me...or from anyone else...in exchange for your testimony here...?"

"No sir...I did not.... I would like to say I realized I was doing the wrong thing...but he was the President...and I was a government employee...and the President wields great power.... As I said to the Virginia police...when I was arrested at my home in Falls Church...it's very hard to say no to the President...."

"Mr Chief Justice...that concludes my presentation on behalf of the House...."

"Mr Seligman...do you have any questions of this witness...assuming you are still representing the President in this matter?"

"Yes...I do...and yes...your assumption is correct...sir...." Then taking his standing place, Joel Seligman asked, "What reason did the President give you...to arrest Dr Steinberg...and bring her to the White House...?"

"He said he wanted to talk to her...."

"Did he say about what...?"

"About the malicious rumors that he had killed her sister...."

"Did he tell you to bring her directly to his bedroom...?"

"No...he did not...but I assumed that is where he would want to see her...and my assumption turned out to be correct.... He did say to use an arrest procedure to bring her to the White House.... He told me he did not expect her to come voluntarily...."

"Did he say why he expected her to refuse to go to the White House...? Most people would jump at an invitation from the President...."

"He didn't say why she would refuse...but he did say that she would refuse...."

"Could it be...Mr Angstrom...that you completely misunderstood the President's instructions...? Were you the only one present when he gave you these alleged instructions...?"

"Yes...I was...but I did not misunderstand his instructions...Mr Seligman.... They were very clear...to obtain an arrest warrant...to arrest her...and bring her to the White House...."

Joel turned to the President, James Lancaster still seated, and leaned over the table to ask in a very low voice whether he wished to question Mr Angstrom. Lancaster slowly moved his head laterally, back and forth, several times, and Joel then turned back to the Mr Justice Benjamin and said, "We have no further questions...Mr Chief Justice...," and then returned to his seat.

Jeremiah Carlssen then stood up, and said, "Mr Chief Justice...the House once again calls Joan Lancaster...." Joan was once again escorted to the witness chair, and was reminded by the presiding officer that she was still under oath. It was now Jeremiah Carlssen who presented the case for the House.

"Mrs Lancaster...would you relate to the Senate what happened at the White House on May 3rd of this year...."

"I had returned...earlier than expected...from a shopping trip to buy clothes for my two younger children.... Mr Lancaster and I have occupied separate bedrooms for many years.... When I passed by his bedroom...I heard a very loud scream coming from it...as though someone were in great pain...or peril.... I rushed to the closed door...found it unlocked...opened it...and rushed into the room.... The sight horrified me.... Mr Lancaster...completely naked...was lying with his full weight on top of Dr Naomi Steinberg...still dressed...but there were indications that he had tried...unsuccessfully it turned out...to pull her panties down her legs.... She was struggling to get out from under him...and he had both his hands around her neck...strangling her.... He was too heavy for me to pull him off her...and too strong for me to release that death grip around her neck.... I rushed out of the room...to find some help...and encountered two cleaning women...who came back with me to the bedroom.... I reached for a heavy vase on the mantle...which I should have done when I first saw him...and hit him over the head as Roberta and Audrey pulled his body off Dr Steinberg...who by this time was almost dead...but thank God...not quite.... We left Mr Lancaster on the floor.... I told my helpers to leave the White House...or else go to my bedroom and stay there pretending to clean it...and Dr Steinberg and I rushed...my pulling her by the hand...down to the White House garage.... We got into my personal Lincoln...and the White House police officers...recognizing me...and not knowing what had occurred upstairs...let me pass...."

"Lies...all lies...," shouted the President, as he quickly stood up. Joel Seligman quieted him down, and he returned to his seat.

"If you do not behave yourself...Mr Lancaster.... I shall have the sergeant-at-arms escort you to his office...to confine you there.... You have no authority in the Capitol...."

"The President is under great strain...Mr Chief Justice.... I'm sure this will not happen again...," Joel Seligman assured Mr Justice Benjamin.

"Mr Chief Justice...I have no further questions of this witness...."

"Do you...Mr Seligman...?"

"Not at this time...but we reserve the right to cross-examine this witness...at a later time...."

"Then you may call your next witness...Mr Carlssen...."

"The House calls Dr Naomi Steinberg....," the simple statement causing a loud murmur in the Senate chamber. Naomi was escorted from the Vice President's office to the witness chair, and took the oath. As beautiful as ever, Roger thought, and apparently from Joel Seligman's reaction, chief defense counsel must have thought so too.

Naomi related how she was kidnapped, taken against her will to the President's bedroom, that he removed his robe after the FBI agent left her there, how he threatened her with bodily harm if she screamed. "He said that if I screamed...despite his warning...and if that brought someone to the bedroom...he would simply say that I had broken into the White House...to kill him...for having killed my sister.... He had a very plausible story ready to use against me...and I did keep quiet...until he began to try to rape me...and then I did scream...which brought Joan Lancaster to my rescue...and then Roberta and Audrey.... If it were not for those three women...I would have joined my sister...as another murdered victim of James Lancaster...."

"Lies...all lies...," James Lancaster shouted again, but this time he jumped out into the space alongside the table, drew a small pistol from his inside jacket pocket, and pointed it at Naomi. Joel Seligman, intently watching his client, quickly jumped up and over the table to literally come face to face with Lancaster, blocking the pistol. He very skillfully seized his arm and deflected it so that the bullet hit the ceiling rather than the witness. While Joel was physically struggling with James Lancaster, Naomi rushed from the witness chair, up the aisle and out into the Senate lobby. Joel continued to fight with his client, a rather big man in height and weight, but managed to knock him to the floor with a skilled punch to his jaw. All the while, several deputies of the sergeant-at-arms ran to help subdue the President, but after that blow from his own lawyer, he was lying half-unconscious on the floor when they reached him. One of the deputies handcuffed the President, pulled him to his feet, and led him out of the chamber to the office of the Senate sergeant-at-arms.

The Senate chamber was in turmoil, but once James Lancaster was subdued and taken from the chamber, the noise and movement began to quiet down. The acting chief justice used his gavel more than a few times to bring the chamber to total quiet. Senator Mays then rose, and was recognized by the presiding officer.

"Mr Chief Justice...I move that the evidentiary hearing phase of this proceeding be terminated...and that we recess until tomorrow...and if my motion is adopted...then I shall move at our session tomorrow that James Monroe Lancaster be removed from the office of President of the United States on impeachment of the House of Representatives...."

The motion was seconded, and the acting chief justice called for a roll-call vote. The vote was unanimous to conclude the hearing and to take a vote the following day. James Lancaster was returned to the White House by Mr Ryan and a dozen of his deputies, and there placed under guard until the next day.

Rupert Matthews was still the Director of the FBI and Arnold Boswell the Director of the CIA, but only because of their long professional acquaintanceship with the Acting President, even though they were not very successful in explaining away their involvement with James Lancaster during the President's war against the Jews. And in the turmoil during the transfer of power from the President to the Acting President, it was very easy to allow some things to fall through the cracks. The Director of the FBI had fallen through the cracks, and so had the Director of the CIA.

On the eve of the Senate vote, Rupert Matthews

and Arnold Boswell decided to act, to implement the plan they had developed to rescue James Lancaster, to act in view of the Senate's certain removal of the President from his august office the next day, both of them realizing that their own official days were also numbered.

The CIA, using a budget without scrutiny by any committee of the Congress, had properly formed many companies to surreptitiously further its statutory role of gathering intelligence data and engaging in needed covert operations on behalf of the United States. But the use of a budget supervised only by the President could be abused, and James Lancaster did abuse it. Funds were illegally spent directly by Lancaster and Boswell through one of those many business organizations to purchase a luxurious estate overlooking the ocean directly on the Pacific seacoast of Colombia, the grounds containing a private airport with a paved airstrip able to handle a Boeing 707 or a McDonnell-Douglas DC10, and part of that airport was one plane of each manufacture, both aircraft fully updated with the latest technology and each equipped to carry both cargo and passengers. The entire area was enclosed in a sophisticated security fence, and well-guarded by well-paid mercenaries.

Carrying the markings of the company that owned it, the Boeing flew into Dulles International Airport, arriving about an hour before the last scheduled commercial flight was due to arrive for that day. But earlier that evening, both directors arrived at the White

House, both recognized by the White House police, the purpose of their arrival questioned by the Ryan deputies although the deputies did not question their identities. The sedan was driven by an FBI agent with a CIA agent sitting next to him, and another agent sitting in the back between the two directors, all five showing their identity cards.

"We have a letter from President Campbell...," said Arnold Boswell to one of Ryan's deputies, "...instructing us to obtain certain information from Mr Lancaster as to a foreign policy matter...a matter that cannot wait until tomorrow...." The Director of the CIA showed the letter carrying a well-forged signature of Mrs Campbell, and the car and its passengers were passed through and driven into the White House underground garage.

It did not take very long inside the White House for the five men to overcome the unsuspecting Ryan deputies, and to then leave the White House grounds about fifteen minutes later with Lancaster himself occupying the seat between the two directors, his face hardly showing at night despite the artificial lights, and the third agent who gave up his seat for James Lancaster left the White House grounds in the trunk of the sedan, to be released once the sedan stopped at CIA headquarters in Langley, Virginia. The sedan continued on to Dulles, where the two directors and the president boarded the aircraft, it now receiving permission to take off about a half-hour before the airport closed for the day for non-governmental aircraft, and this plane was not a government plane, certainly not with the markings of the Global Transportation Company painted on it.

The United States Senate reconvened the next morning at ten o'clock to vote on the question of removing James Monroe Lancaster as President of the United States, it being fully expected that the vote would be overwhelming in favor of removal. Joel Seligman was present, but his official client was not, he announcing before the vote that Lancaster had fled the White House and presumably had left the country. The Senate chamber was in an uproar, which the acting chief justice finally brought down to silence.

"This does not affect the action to be taken by the Senate...," announced Mr Justice Benjamin. "It is not necessary that the President be present for a vote to be taken.... If Mr Lancaster is removed from office...then the matter of apprehending him would fall to the new President...if he has indeed fled the country...."

"Mr Chief Justice...," Senator Mays asked to be recognized, which he was. "You have stated the matter very succinctly.... One thing has nothing to do with the other.... I now move to convict James Monroe Lancaster of high crimes...and to remove said James Monroe Lancaster from the office of President of the United States of America...," those momentous words bearing down on a hushed chamber.

"I second the motion...," shouted Senator Manning of Virginia. And the president officer asked the secretary of the Senate to call the roll, both he and the secretary to record each vote, although almost every Senator planned to do the very same thing. All one hundred Senators were present, and all voted in favor of the motion. When the roll-call vote was completed, a thunderous applause struck the chamber like a thunderclap, which the presiding officer made no effort to stop. And when it did finally settle down of its own accord, the acting chief justice intoned in a very clear voice, "I now declare Sally Abigail Adams Campbell...heretofore Acting President...to be President of the United States of America.... I shall formally notify her...and arrange for her to take the President's oath...for until the constitutional oath of office is taken...she is still Acting President...." More applause and cheers, even from the usually staid Senators, fully joined in by the galleries.

Senator Mays and other Senators rushed down to the well to congratulate Jeremiah Carlssen and his associated counsel, and also to thank Joel Seligman for saving Dr Steinberg's life. When things began to quiet down, Mr Justice Benjamin brought the chamber to total quiet, as he had done many times before, and then addressed the Senate from the chair.

"Ladies and gentlemen...I have presided over this impeachment trial fully aware of its immediate and historical importance.... I am a member of the judicial branch...not of the legislative branch...and have been so for many years...but I do agree with Senator Mays's comments concerning judicial usurpation.... I myself have striven to exercise judicial restraint...but it cannot be left up to each judge to do so.... There must be some mechanism...one I cannot yet devise...that would insist that judicial restraint be observed...." He paused for almost a minute without a sound in the Senate chamber, and then he said in a very firm voice, "I shall now go to the White House to swear in our new President...Sally Campbell.... May Almighty God bless her and keep her...."

With those remarks and with the opening phrases of the ancient Jewish blessing, Samuel Mordecai Benjamin arose from his chair and left the podium, to return to the office of the President of the Senate, now the office of the President pro tempore of the Senate, and as he did so a very loud burst of applause and shouting bid him a fond farewell from the Capitol. Senator Abbott, the president pro tempore, quickly assumed the chair to recognize Senator Mays once the noise died down and it became apparent that the Senate was still in session.

"Mr President...I wish to offer another motion to this august body...this time directed to the new President of the United States.... We join in Justice Benjamin's earnest prayer...and we constitutionally advise her to appoint Mr Justice Samuel Benjamin as the next Chief Justice of the United States...."

There were many shouts of "Second...," and when the presiding office asked for debate, and there was none, the question was called. Eighty-nine senators voted aye and eleven voted nay.

President Campbell's first action following her taking the constitutional oath of office was to formally nominate Samuel Mordecai Benjamin to be the Chief Justice of the United States, and the Senate without committee hearings consented to his appointment the very next day on the votes of the same number of

Senators who had previously concurred in advising the new President to nominate him. The nation now had a Chief Justice in the intellectual mold of Benjamin Nathan Cardozo, but the nation wondered what had happened to James Monroe Lancaster.

President Campbell next planned to nominate Mark Rosenblueth to be the next Vice President of the United States, this nomination requiring confirmation by the House of Representatives as well as by the Senate, but before she sent the nomination to both houses of the Congress for confirmation, she called Mark. Still heavily despondent over the loss of his wife and children, he had returned to his duties as Governor as some kind of therapy.

"Sally...I appreciate what you're proposing.... The positive side is that I can readily leave this place...this place of such bitter memory...and try to build a new life somewhere else...and actually being in the same city with you...and working directly with you...would be another plus...but there is the negative side.... The time has come to return the federal government to where it was when it was first established by the States.... I feel I can better help to bring that about as a Governor...rather than as the Vice President...."

"Mark...I need you in Washington...and I entirely agree with what you want to do...but there's no reason why you can't do it as Vice President.... Since we are both for it...the effort need not be confrontational between the States and the federal government.... Let's work on it together...," she said with a certain pleading in her voice. "Why not at least come down...and let us talk about it...."

"That's a very fair request...Sally.... Today is Wednesday.... I'll come down in the early afternoon on Friday.... Would that be alright...?"

"That would be fine...Mark...and please plan to spend the weekend.... I just indulged myself...and personally bought a forty-eight-foot day sailer...and I need a crew member...in addition to the usual secret service agents.... The boat is at the Naval Academy...."

"That sounds very nice...," responded Mark, a bit more alive. "I'll look forward to seeing you...."

Being with Sally, even though in a goldfish bowl, did wonders for Mark, and he slowly began to come back to the real world. After three weekends at the White House, interspersed with weekdays in Albany, Mark decided to accept Sally's offer of the vice presidency, not for the vice presidency itself but because it would give him a chance to spend every day, during some time of the day, with her. The Washington press corps were no fools, for they knew that Mark was a White House guest weekend after weekend, and when Sally formally nominated Mark Bernard Rosenblueth to be Vice President of the United States, neither the Members of Congress nor the press corps were at all surprised. Indeed, there was much comment about Sally's and Mark's compatibility, except that if Sally intended to run for election for another term, Mark or she would have to change his or her legal residence, since under the Constitution the Electors of a State could not vote for a President and a Vice President from the same State.

In the Congress, the opponents of the nomination were few in number but they were very vociferous, primarily denouncing the President for nominating a Jew, who would only be a heart-beat away from the presidency itself. And what of these rumors about a likely romantic attachment between the two? One high-level Jew, the Chief Justice, was enough, they insisted. The major newspapers, being directly anti-Israel and indirectly antisemitic, tried to stem the tide of popularity that Mark had achieved, but as much as they did try, they did not succeed, and the nomination was overwhelmingly confirmed by both houses of the Congress. Within a few weeks, Mark moved from the Executive Mansion in Albany to the vice presidential mansion on Observatory Circle. Lieutenant Governor William Stromberg, Mark's old and close friend and political ally, became the next Governor of New York.

TWENTY-TWO

While the new President of the United States was extremely busy getting her official house in order, especially weeding out any person closely connected to James Lancaster, any consideration by the American government to finding and capturing her predecessor had to wait, but even more interested in apprehending James Lancaster, if a greater interest could be found, were the Israelis, who wanted him to answer charges in Israel of attempting to murder several million men, women and children, an attempt that would have succeeded were it not for the valiant effort of their own defense forces.

Only a few days after he became Vice President, Mark recommended to his wife the appointment of his old friend Erich Bauermann, an eminent New York judge and retired army colonel, to become Director of Central Intelligence, and when the nomination was confirmed by the Senate, Bauermann's first task was to trace the circumstances leading to the disappearance not only of James Lancaster but also of Rupert Matthews and Arnold Boswell, the disappearance of all three men obviously one connected disappearance based on information obtained from the White House police and the Ryan deputies.

Born in Germany, Erich had been brought to America by his Jewish parents in 1932 when he was only seven, when they saw the handwriting on the wall heralding the coming to power of the Nazi insanity. Habitually very thorough in his work, he personally interrogated everyone employed by the CIA, in any way employed, to learn everything there was to learn about the many companies formed by the CIA for its various operations. Although the CIA budget was not for public consumption, it was certainly available to the director of the agency, or at least it was supposed to be. Those who appeared to hesitate in answering his questions or producing their records were warned that the only alternative was discharge and prosecution, and finally Erich Bauermann pieced together a skein of organizations and operations under the general umbrella called the Central Intelligence Agency. He was satisfied that on the whole the agency had performed its statutory duties very well, but there were several loose ends, and one of them pointed to a rogue drug operations in Colombia for the private benefit of seven individuals, including Arnold Boswell, Rupert Matthews and James Lancaster, the former president benefiting even when the incumbent president. The remaining four were still high-level officials of the CIA.

Erich reported his findings to Mark in a private meeting at the vice presidential mansion, the meeting private even to the extent of Erich driving his own motor car to Observatory Circle, and during that meeting he suggested the strong likelihood that this particular rogue operation would have its headquarters at a well-guarded place in Colombia.

"I would like to take these four men into secret custody...and have them interrogated using a truth drug.... I am sure that at least one of them knows where that place is...and I would wager that James Lancaster is there...."

"And if he is...how do we get him out...?" Mark asked.

"Mark...we do not get him out.... We inform the Israelis where he is...and let them get him out.... They are much better at that kind of thing...and they want him almost as much as they wanted Eichmann...."

"But they don't have the death penalty...and Lancaster deserves to die...."

"That is true...but they make exceptions for special cases.... They did hang Eichmann...."

"Actually...I do not know whether a charge of first-degree murder against Lancaster would stick in New York.... He could admit to killing Dinah Steinberg...but claim it was an accident during an argument...or at worst for him...unpremeditated murder...murder in the second degree.... But he did abduct Sally and hold her against her will at the White House...a federal facility...and the federal punishment for kidnapping is still death...although he could claim that he did it under some extraordinary powers inherent in the presidency...or whatnot.... I just want to see the man properly tried...convicted...and executed.... I trust the Israeli commandos...but I'm not at all sure I trust the Israeli courts.... We would have to strike a deal with the Israelis that if they do not give him the death penalty they would extradite him to the United States...and we would have to check their laws to make sure they can legally make such a deal...."

"The Israelis would have to be unofficially informed of Lancaster's whereabouts.... There is still much antisemitic feeling in this country...Mark...and those who do not wish us well would greatly exploit our turning him over to the Israelis rather than trying him here...."

"I agree...but I'm sure it can be done without any publicity...although that would rule out any formal prior agreement concerning his extradition...and oral agreements might not be worth anything...." Mark paused. "There might be another problem in trying Lancaster here.... He would be entitled to a jury trial...and could claim that he would not get a fair trial because of all the publicity.... On top of that...it's possible a jury might acquit him...."

"That is true...but there are so many charges against him that I feel the probability of an unreasonable jury in every one of the cases is rather low...."

"Agreed.... Let me talk to the President about all of this...to decide what to do.... I suppose a chance meeting with the Israeli ambassador at a diplomatic White House reception might be a good way to give him the information as to Lancaster's whereabouts...."

"I do not think that anyone else ought to be trusted...Mark...except the three of us...and also Redmond and Wrightson.... They are very fine gentlemen...and I perceive them to be very loyal to the President.... Now...I identified four people at the agency involved in this rogue operation...but there could be more...but on the other hand...I would not like to have the CIA smeared because of a rogue activity.... The agency's work is too important...and by and large it has been doing it all quite well...."

"But the same problem remains.... If we get Lancaster...then our commandos who actually get him would obviously know about it...and it might then be very difficult to justify turning him over to a foreign country...."

Mark met with the President at the White House to report on his meeting with Erich Bauermann.

"He's done a splendid job in a very short time...," Sally exclaimed, "...but I feel this has to be an American affair...or at least a joint American-Israeli operation...."

"I would ordinarily agree with you...Sally.... I can well imagine how the antisemites would shout if they knew we had given Lancaster to the Israelis...but it's well known that they want him even more strongly than we do...if that's possible...and only the three of us know about these two discussions.... It would not be suspect if the Israelis found him...and brought him to justice.... My only concern is that they might not execute him...and that bastard deserves to die...."

"Alright...let us have this understanding with them.... They apprehend him...turn him over to us for trial.... If he doesn't receive the death penalty here...then we turn him over to Israel if they can guarantee a death penalty if convicted...and if not that he be returned to the United States...."

"That sounds about right.... I feel confident they'll buy it...."

"How do we ask them without the entire world knowing about it...?"

"Erich Bauermann wants the four CIA people taken into custody...and interrogated under the influence of a truth drug...but he and I don't know whom to trust for this purpose.... Allen Redmond and John Wrightson have been extremely loyal to you...and both Erich and I feel very positive toward them...but they might balk at this kind of activity...and I would not wish anyone to know about it who doesn't completely agree with it.... But assuming we get the information from the four...you can then hold a diplomatic reception...here at the White House...and I can easily take Samuel Alvarez aside to give him the information in complete privacy.... That part is easy.... The difficult part is the interrogation...." He paused. "You know...Sally...I don't know why that's the difficult part.... Lancaster killed my wife and children...and also put you in considerable personal danger.... I'm ordinarily not a vicious man...but I feel very vicious when I think of him.... I am personally going to do the interrogation...."

"I appreciate how you feel...Mark...and I feel the same way...but before you place them under interrogation...you would have to take them into custody...and who will help you do that...people whom you can trust.... You are the Vice President...and can't be known to have been associated with this kind of extra-legal activity.... This is an extremely delicate situation.... The entire interrogation must be kept confidential...but what about the four men themselves...? Will they not know about it...? And obviously they cannot be trusted...."

"How badly do we want Lancaster...?"

"Very badly.... I would kill him myself if I could...."

"If we want him that badly...then let us inform the Israelis of the identities of our four CIA people...which would cause them to disappear.... Do we want to sacrifice four men to apprehend one...?"

"Well...Mark...under the circumstances...I would say yes.... They're engaged in drug operations...and that carries the death penalty in my book...."

"Then this is how we proceed.... We hold a diplomatic reception...as soon as possible...where I'll privately inform Alvarez whom and what the four are...but that we want the Israelis to turn Lancaster first over to us...we promising to give Lancaster to his country if Lancaster does not get the death penalty here.... I think we have to take our chances of getting Lancaster from them for the first trial...."

Two weeks later, the President of the United States held a reception for the entire Washington diplomatic corps, the formal announcement specifically stating that the reception was in honor of those members of the diplomatic corps who opposed the crimes of her predecessor against humanity. Because those crimes were directed against the Jews, both in America and in Israel, Sally and Mark expected that most of the ambassadors from the hard-line Arab states might not attend, but they forgot that these were diplomats, and diplomats are very much like actors, oftentimes pretending to be what they are not. All the Arab ambassadors did attend, and President Campbell especially singled out the Italian ambassador while Vice President Rosenblueth managed to get the Israeli ambassador in complete privacy for a few minutes without raising any eyebrows. After all, it was one Jew talking to another, probably on some obscure point of Talmudic law.

"I am most grateful to you...Mark...and I know my government will honor my solemn promise to turn that bastard first over to you...but we depend on your promise to turn him over to us if he does not suffer the death penalty in America...."

"Agreed...," as they shook their hands on it.

Several days later, the four CIA officials disappeared, were taken to Israel, there interrogated under the influence of a truth drug to learn where the renegade James Lancaster was hiding in complete luxury. The chief of the Israel secret service reported to the prime minister, and the prime minister decided not to tell his Cabinet of the planned operation to get James Lancaster, the prime minister not trusting his talkative ministers to keep their political mouths shut.

About a week later, the planning to abduct Lancaster was completed, and a rather large team was organized to conduct the operation. All members were then thoroughly briefed.

In the meanwhile, questions were being raised in the American press as to what efforts were being made to find Lancaster and to bring him to justice. Naomi Steinberg was especially concerned, and voiced her concern in a letter to Roger Morrison, who replied in a telephone call that Lancaster had undoubtedly left the country, and that it was up to the federal authorities to find him and bring him back. "I suggest that Joel Seligman might know where he is...," said Roger rather maliciously.

"Joel Seligman was the White House counsel...," Naomi responded a bit testily, "...and defended him as a duty.... I very much doubt he's in any way harboring him...or protecting him.... He did save my life.... And why would a Jew harbor a man who wished all the Jews dead...?"

Israeli agents resident in Colombia confirmed the existence of a large villa on the Pacific coast, the estate complete with its own major airport, and that it had in residence three Americans newly arrived only several weeks before. About a week later, all kinds of European businessmen arrived in Bogota on chartered flights from many different countries for a highly publicized South American meeting of a new multinational corporation, all of them very interested in sightseeing the entire country after their two-day conference. And so the planes that brought them to Bogota were now to be used to ferry them about the country, and only a few days later they all arrived unannounced at that private airport at that private estate. The guards were alerted, and raced to the six Boeing 737s just standing there on the tarmac as close as possible to the residence itself, the pilot of one of them profusely apologizing over his radio for leading the planes into the wrong airport, and asking permission for him to refuel and while doing so to briefly disembark his passengers, to stretch their legs, before the planes took off again. This innocent-sounding request caused the guards to briefly let down their guard, and the passengers took full advantage of the lull by suddenly opening the aircraft doors to kill all of them in sight with silenced handguns. Dressed not in uniforms but in tourist attire, they now raced through the main house, and quickly took into custody six Americans, three of them identified as Lancaster, Boswell and Matthews. Placing all six aboard their aircraft, they took off before the remaining guards could effectively react, and flew northward toward the United States, entering American airspace using a previously filed flight plan, and landed after hours at Dulles International Airport where they were met by Mark Rosenblueth, Elbridge Garry, Erich Bauermann, Allen Redmond and John Wrightson, the five accompanied by a carefully selected force of army rangers. The three were turned over to the five, Mark profusely thanked the leader of the Israeli team, and without any further contact between the Israelis and the Americans, the Israelis took off for the Bahamas, there the European businessmen to refuel and relax for a while before returning to Europe and then back home. The other three Americans were also turned over, but they were flown back to Washington in separate helicopters.

Lancaster protested this treatment, saying it was no way to treat the President. "...and who were those men who kidnapped us...?"

"But you are no longer the President...you miserable bastard...," exclaimed Mark, "...and we have arrest warrants against all three of you...."

"And what have Bosewell and I done...to justify this treatment...?" asked Rupert Matthews.

"I shall very carefully explain it all to both of you when we get you back to Washington...," Erich Bauermann replied.

As soon as they did arrive in the Washington area, all three prisoners were brought before a federal magistrate, a far more reliable magistrate than the one who had issued that arrest warrant for Naomi Steinberg, and they were then taken to the disciplinary barracks at Fort Myers, there to be kept under very heavy guard, each in a separate cell, by the same rangers who were part of the welcoming committee at Dulles. Mark called Roger Morrison in New York that Lancaster was in custody, and to arrange for his extradition from the District of Columbia to New York.

Two days later, James Lancaster was formally returned to the custody of the Senate sergeant-at-arms, but with a rotating force of army rangers always present to ensure that the custody would not again be broken.

The news of the return of the ex-president occupied the electronic and printed press for many days on end as all kinds of telephone calls flowed between New York, Richmond and Washington. The press and many others speculated as to where Lancaster had been and how he was brought back, but no one who actually knew would answer any of the questions being constantly raised, and both he and his two associates were held incommunicado.

The formality of turning Lancaster over to the proper civilian authorities was now under way. He was taken to the office of the President pro tempore of the Senate, there to be officially informed by Senator Abbott of his removal by the Senate. The head of the Capitol Police was waiting, together with several of his officers, to then escort the ex-president to the boundary of the Capitol Grounds, all in a huge cloud of reporters, there at the boundary to turn him over to the Metropolitan Police, all the while a rotating force of army rangers remaining with him. The city police in turn brought him before a judge of the superior court of the District of Columbia to have read to him a formal request of the Governor of New York to extradite James Monroe Lancaster to New York on a charge of first-degree murder. The press cloud grew as it moved along to the courthouse on Judiciary Square, only several blocks from the Capitol, but there was not enough space in the courtroom for the entire cloud.

The judge entered, and took his place on the bench. "Mr Lancaster...we shall hold a hearing in two days...on this New York request...and in the meanwhile I am returning you to the custody of the Army.... I would ordinarily remand you to the custody of your personal lawyer...as soon as we can bring him in...but I am informed that you have already fled the country...while under New York indictment...which is something we do not wish to be repeated...."

Roland Johnson, Esquire, was urgently sent for, and when he arrived in the courtroom, Judge Wrightson, brother of General Wrightson, explained to Mr Johnson what he had told the ex-president.

"I am holding your client in custody...Mr Johnson.... A hearing will be scheduled at ten in the morning...two days hence...and I assume you will be prepared...."

"Both I and my client will be here...Your Honor...."

Roger Morrison came down from New York City to appear in favor of the extradition on behalf of the Governor of New York, and Roland Johnson was of course there to oppose the extradition. The courtroom was filled with reporters, preempting many of the visitors' seats. At the end of the two-hour hearing, Judge Wrightson granted the extradition, and handed the custody of James Lancaster over to William Salinger. The New York City police inspector handcuffed Lancaster to himself, and out went the three accompanied by Lieutenants Thomas Malloy and Juan Ramos to fly from Washington National to LaGuardia in an executive jet.

In Manhattan, Lancaster was held without bail in the Tombs city prison, and Roger finally sat down at his desk with a most audible sigh of relief. "At long last...," he said to Inspector Salinger and Lieutenants Malloy and Ramos, "...we have him where we want him.... I'm going for the death penalty...and hope I can get it.... That man does not deserve to live.... Can you imagine having such evil in the White House...?"

Although the mansion at Observatory Circle on Massachusetts Avenue was the official residence of the Vice President, Mark was staying at the White House as a continuing guest of President Campbell and her two children, both Joshua and Julia home during the summer school recess. They tried to keep out of the way of their mother and the man she was obviously very much interested in, even though she and he could not find any private time to themselves, what with all the secret service agents around.

Joshua Campbell had just finished his freshman year at Princeton where he was a good friend of James Lancaster Jr, and Julia Campbell was also home from school, but from the Sidwell Friends Day School in the Washington area.

As for James Lancaster Jr, the poor young man was still not adjusted to the fact that his father was the rotter he actually was. He refused to accept what had happened, and continued to remain in Princeton rather than go to Richmond to stay with his mother.

With Sally's total support, Mark set about to work with all fifty Governors to forge a return to the nation's fundamental federalism before that federalism had been almost wiped clean by two hundred years of judicial usurpation by the Supreme Court. In this effort, he was indirectly aided by Chief Justice Benjamin who strongly believed in the exercise of judicial restraint, a position he had taken at the Lancaster impeachment trial, and a position he sincerely held.

Mark invited Roger Morrison many times to Washington, whenever Roger could get away over a weekend from his meticulous preparations for the Lancaster trial, and each time that Roger was in Washington, he extended his weekend to spend at least one day with Catherine Custis in Richmond, Catherine continuing to work very hard on her latest novel. Roger had finally adjusted himself to the impossibility of any lasting relationship with Naomi, certainly not of the kind he wanted, and Catherine very gradually took Naomi's place in Roger's interest, in the heart he too often wore on his sleeve for all to see.

After several months, the Lancaster murder trial was scheduled to open in New York City, and that would be the end of Roger's visits to Richmond for quite some time. Roger himself was going to prosecute, and on his last visit to Richmond, both Catherine and Roger realized they would not be seeing each other again for some time, unless a change were made.

"Are you thinking what I'm thinking...Roger...?" Catherine asked as they returned to her home after dinner at the Benjamins.

"I don't know...Catherine...but I'll tell you what's on my mind...and it might be the same...," Roger countered. "I won't be able to see you for some time...and I'll miss you terribly...." He then hesitated, slightly unsure of himself, and then blurted out like a high school boy hopelessly in love, "Catherine...I truly love you...and I want to marry you...not months from now...but by next weekend.... You can write in New York.... That's where many of the writers are anyway...." He paused, now more sure of himself.

Catherine said nothing, but moved so close to him so as to squeeze out the light, and kissed him ever so passionately but gently on his mouth, to which he responded very physically, and so did she. "Of course I'll marry you.... It took you so long to ask...that I almost thought that I would have to ask you...."

They both told Joan while tightly holding each other's hand, and Joan was delighted. "Next weekend...you say.... That's very short notice.... Why don't we have a ceremony only for family and close friends.... Roger...you bring your parents...and invite Mark Rosenblueth...and Mrs Campbell.... And on your behalf...my dear sister...I shall invite Naomi...her mother and grandmother...who have been so kind to me...and of course Mrs Benjamin's brother...Chief Justice Benjamin...and let's also invite Governor Garry...Attorney General Strong...and oh yes...should we invite Joel Seligman...?"

"Why Joel Seligman...?" asked Roger, somewhat

perplexed, "I think he's going to defend Lancaster...and he's a very formidable opponent...."

"He's also a very fine young man...," said Catherine, "...but if you don't want him...it's up to you.... It's your wedding...as well as mine...."

"Of course we'll invite him...," Roger responded exuberantly. "Yes...he is a fine fellow...and it will show that Joel is defending Lancaster only because of his professional integrity as a lawyer...."

"Very good...darling.... I'm very proud of you.... You'll still win...even against Joel Seligman.... I know it...."

Roger postponed his return trip to New York to the following day, and that night, the future bride and groom spent their first night together. Roger had saved all the energy of his lifetime for this one night, and he and Catherine made love over and over and over again all through the night, he especially enjoying her rather plump body as he fully sank into her, but despite very little sleep that night Roger felt very fit in the morning.

As for Joel Seligman, he was his widowed father's only son, and his father was Dr David Seligman, world-renown neurosurgeon practising in New York City. By pure happenstance, Dr Seligman was scheduled to give a series of lectures at the Medical College of Virginia on the Monday and Tuesday following the next weekend, and when Joan called Joel at his apartment in New York to inform him of Catherine's wedding and to invite him on behalf of her sister, Joel readily accepted knowing that this would give him an opportunity to see Naomi Steinberg. After he hung up the phone, he remembered his father telling him about his own planned trip to Richmond, and he then rang his father to suggest they travel together to the capital of Virginia.

Dr Seligman was a very distinguished-looking and quite handsome man of sixty, about five eleven, in excellent physical condition, and a superb neurosurgeon, but any woman who might be seriously interested in him would have to find out for herself the really important things that mattered. He was glad that he and his son, each a very busy man in his own profession, would be traveling together to have that additional time with each other, both on the trip and in Richmond.

Naomi and Joan met the flight from New York at the Richmond airport on Saturday in the late afternoon, and were very surprised to see an older man, who looked much like Joel, coming up the jetway with Joel himself. Joel introduced his father to these two very attractive women, and explained that his father was scheduled to give several lectures at the Medical College of Virginia the following Monday and Tuesday, and had decided to go along with him to keep each other company.

"Oh...then you are the famous neurosurgeon Dr David Seligman...," exclaimed Naomi. "I'm on the staff of the hospital of the Medical College...and when it was proudly announced that the great Dr Seligman was coming down...it never occurred to me...that you might be Joel's father.... How simply marvelous...." But before Naomi could continue, Joan interrupted to invite Dr Seligman to her sister's wedding.

"I'll be delighted to come...Mrs Lancaster...and may I call you Joan...and please call me David.... I'm glad my son was invited and that he suggested I come along...for otherwise I would not have met you...both of you...."

As Joan drove them to her own house, now fully restored to full use, David sitting in the front passenger seat, looking at her at every opportunity when he thought she might not be noticing, but she was noticing and very pleased about it, and both his son and Naomi Steinberg were in the rear seat too busily catching up to pay any attention to anyone in the front. The drive ended too quickly for all of them.

Joan introduced the Seligmans, father and son, to her sister and to Roger, although Joel needed no introduction to Roger. Roger was too happy to have any lingering animosity toward Joel, and actually he had no reason to have any, for Joel was simply a very good lawyer, doing his professional job as best he could. Even the vilest men are entitled to a legal defense, but Roger still did not know whether Joel would be Lancaster's defense counsel in New York.

Roger's parents had arrived with him the evening before, and both they and the two Seligmans were next introduced to each other. Mary Morrison did not know what to make of all this. These people were

Jews, and what was she doing in the same house with the people who had killed her savior? But for the sake of her son, she decided she would put up with this very eminent surgeon and his own outstanding son, for she was certain her savior would forgive her for committing this sin.

Sally and Mark, and Sally's two children, all arrived by helicopter later that day, just in time for dinner at the Benjamin house, with all the wedding guests as dinner guests except Roger's parents, for Mary and George Morrison would not set foot in the home of a Jew. Mark was delighted in Roger's happiness, and Sally was obviously delighted in Mark, and her son and daughter were quite fond of him. He and David Seligman, although meeting for the first time, got along famously, and Sally had to spend much effort warding off Joan's good-natured questions about Sally's own wedding plans. Suspiciously missing from the grand mix were the bride and groom to be, and both Joel and Naomi.

Once completely alone with Naomi, Joel began to unload something that had been on his mind for some time. "Naomi...I've hesitated to say yes to Lancaster's continually urgent request that I defend him...because I didn't know how you would feel about it...and now that I see you once again...and actually for the very first time socially...it's important to me that I know how you feel about it.... If you in any way would hold it against me...I'll not defend him.... I mean it...Naomi...," he said plaintively.

"I understand how you feel...and I must thank you again for saving my life.... James Lancaster is a vile creature...but I know that it's your professional duty to legally defend even the worst people.... No...Joel...I'll not hold it against you.... I hope you'll do your best...but I do hope you'll lose...."

"Roger Morrison has an extremely strong case.... I doubt if any one can win against his evidence...but I'll do my professional best.... If I have some time free...during the trial...on the weekends...may I come down to see you...?"

"I'd be very disappointed if you do not...and if you're too busy to make the trip...and if I can make it instead...I'll go up to New York...," and with that last word they held each other every so lightly and kissed each other's mouth ever so gently.

When Joel recovered, he said, "I think my father will also want to come down.... He's smitten by Joan...."

"And I think she's also very interested in him...as I am in you...."

When Naomi and Joel returned to the others, it was now Joan's and David's turn to be missing, and it appeared that Naomi was quite right.

David and Joel Seligman spent that night, and the following night, as guests of Joan Lancaster. As sorely tempted as both David and Joan actually were to visit with each other, they decided to be patient.

On that same wedding weekend, the President and the Vice President were house guests of the Benjamins, and despite the intrusion of the secret service on the couches downstairs, in the guest rooms and about the grounds, Sally and Mark did manage despite these circumstances to elude them and to make love for the very first time with each other.

"When shall we get married...?" Sally whispered as they moved apart, completely spent.

"I thought you'd never ask...darling.... Shall we make it a double ceremony tomorrow...?"

"No...let's marry in the White House...." She then turned over on her left side, he following on his left side very firmly against her back, and she took his now limp penis gently in her hand and placed him very high between her legs, and very soon after he was no longer limp, and while they were lying as they were, she guided him into her, and they slowly enjoyed being together for quite some time. After coming once again and at the same time they both fell blissfully asleep.

TWENTY-THREE

The following day, a Sunday, Roger and Catherine formally became man and wife in the home of Catherine's sister Joan, the civil ceremony performed by Chief Judge Seth Coleman of the Virginia Supreme Court, an old friend of Chief Justice Benjamin who was also present. Catherine and Roger deliberately wanted a civil ceremony because at least half of the guests were Jewish, and they did not want the part about the Holy Trinity thrown in their faces, but Roger's parents were very disappointed in not having a real wedding ceremony for their son, and Mary Morrison felt compelled to tell him so as soon as she could after the ceremony. Even the presence of the President and Vice President and Chief Justice of the United States was not enough to make the mother and father of the groom delighted in their own son's wedding.

Catherine and Roger joined their guests in a catered dinner in the same large house, George Morrison insisting on saying grace in the name of the Holy Trinity, and as the hour drew close to midnight, off they went on their honeymoon, no one even knowing where they planned to spend their first night, perhaps in the Commonwealth Park Hotel?

The next morning, Joan insisted on driving her house guest Dr David Seligman to his first lecture at the Medical College of Virginia, and decided to sit through it all even though she knew she would not understand a word, and for some reason she felt extremely proud when he received a prolonged standing ovation in the lecture theatre. Naomi was there of course, but Joel had to return to New York to prepare preliminary motions for the Lancaster defense. He had begun to miss Naomi even before he left her.

Before he had left New York for Richmond, David Seligman canceled all his appointments in New York for that week, and had intended to take a brief holiday, perhaps on the Outer Banks of North Carolina, before returning to a rather rigorous schedule the following week. Instead, he now wanted to spend all his time with Joan, and fortunately for him, she was of the same feeling. By the end of the week, David proposed in a very old-fashioned manner, and Joan in a very old-fashioned way accepted, the wedding not to take place of course until Joan received her final divorce decree from the Virginia courts.

"I'm not going to be very happy down here...with you in New York..." she said. "I intend to apply for an appointment at Columbia or New York University...

and put my children in the Riverdale School...or some other good school...and never let you be alone...or me be alone...."

"That's a marvelous idea...darling.... My apartment is in the west Eighties.... It's very large...with large rooms and high ceilings...one of those old but very well kept buildings.... It's a co-op with four bedrooms...and four baths...certainly large enough to hold all of us...with your three children at home.... When do we tell them...?"

"Let me break the news after you leave on Sunday...and I'll be up the following week after I pack myself...and them.... I'm sure they'll be very proud of you...as I am...and love you...as I do...."

"And as I love you...darling Joan.... What marvelous good fortune we met...."

Earlier the same week, Sally and Mark had to return to Washington, and on their flight back they were trying to figure out every possible way they could elude the secret service agents in the White House unless he occupied a bedroom in her private apartment, but that would not be seemly, certainly not in the White House. So they decided that they would visit the Benjamins as often as they could, and make love there, at least until they married.

"I have a better idea...," said the President to the Vice President, speaking in a low voice as though they were earnestly discussing affairs of state. "Let's get married...soon.... Why put it off...?"

"No good reason that I can think of...," responded the Vice President to the President. "How about a month from now...? That should give us enough time to make it a proper state occasion...as I'm afraid it will have to be...."

"Can't think of a better time...Mr Vice President...."

"Nor I...Madame President...."

The formal announcement of President Campbell's forthcoming marriage to Vice President Rosenblueth made waves throughout the world. Would the ceremony be Christian for the bride, or Jewish for the groom, or a hybrid for both of them, or could it be, no it could not be, that either of them would convert to the other's religion? What if the President converted to Judaism? A Jew in the Oval Office. Unthinkable! There was enough food for the gossips of the world, and certainly of the United States, to last for some time.

The announcement was made by Sally on a Sunday, at a specially called news conference, when her children were at home, with her children at her side, and Mark standing next to Joshua. After some unusually polite questions about certain trivialities, the senior member of the White House press corps rendered the traditional "Thank you...Madame President...."

Very soon afterward, together with their mother and their stepfather-to-be, both Joshua and Julia essentially asked the same question about religion. "I think you both ought to be of the same religion...," said Joshua very maturely.

"...and I agree...," added Julia, sounding very

grown-up. "And if you decide...Mom...to become Jewish...then we shall too.... The whole family should be the same...."

"That's a very sensible attitude...Joshua...Julia.... I'm very proud of you...but it might be that your new Dad might want to convert to Christianity...."

"Oh...if I were he...I wouldn't...," responded Joshua very quickly. "I can imagine how difficult it would be for Dad to stomach the usual antisemitism...as a new Christian...but for a Christian to become a Jew...that would mean just going back to his religious roots.... Don't you think so...?"

"What I think...is that you are both the most sensible and lovable children in the world.... That's what I think...." And with that, Sally hugged each of her children, as Mark approvingly looked on. "Then it's settled.... All three of us will convert to Judaism...and we'll have a Jewish wedding ceremony in the White House.... And if some people don't like it...they will not have to vote for me in the next election.... How does that sound...?"

"Go to it...Mom...."

Mark was seated on a couch next to Sally while Joshua and Julia sat in upholstered chairs facing them. Mark took Sally's hand and held it, not to let it go, and then leaned over to kiss her as their two children applauded rather loudly.

Mark was a member of the leading reform congregation in the District of Columbia, the Washington Hebrew Congregation on Massachusetts Avenue at Macomb Street. He made an appointment to privately see the senior rabbi in his vice presidential mansion, and after the usual preliminaries, Mark told a startled Rabbi Jacob Aaronson that the president and her too children wanted to convert to Judaism, and to do it within the following month.

"As you know...Mark...we have regular classes to prepare people for conversion...but obviously we cannot use them to prepare the President...and her children.... Oh my...this will certainly cause quite a stir.... I shall personally meet with them...at the White House...with my wife...over the next two weeks...and I think that would be sufficient.... The conversion ceremony would then take place at the temple...unless the President prefers a private ceremony...at my home or in the White House.... Are you sure the President really wants to do this...?"

"Absolutely...rabbi...and she and her children are doing it for their own sakes...not for mine...."

Mark reported back to Sally, and Rabbi and Mrs Aaronson visited the White House for about an hour a day over the next two weeks, which Sally managed to fit into her busy schedule. Her children, still home for the summer recess, spent most of the next two weeks with the rabbi and his wife and their own two children, Paul, 18, and Deborah, 16. On the third weekend, on a Sunday afternoon, in a private ceremony in the White House and in the presence of their families and close friends from Washington, Richmond and New York, Sally and her two children were converted to Judaism, and plans for Joshua to go through a bar mitzvah ceremony would come later. The leading clergymen of the Protestant churches in Washington, and the Catholic Archbishop of Washington, were there as special guests of Rabbi Aaronson.

The following weekend, in a public ceremony at the White House, in the presence of governors and senators and representatives and diplomats and many others, and especially in the presence of families and friends, Sally and Mark became man and wife in a reform Jewish wedding ceremony performed by Rabbi Aaronson. Joshua was best man for Mark, Julia was maid of honor for her mother, and Sally was "given away" by Chief Justice Benjamin. The ceremony, but not the festivities afterwards, was broadcast on all the major networks.

After the dinner and dancing and other festivities, Sally and Mark left on a brief week-long honeymoon, but where do a President and Vice President take a honeymoon knowing that the President must always be available to the Secret Service in case of a national emergency? The summer recess now over, Joshua returned for the week to Princeton, and Julia spent that week at school but at home after school with Rabbi and Mrs Aaronson, she greatly admiring a very good-looking and athletic Paul Aaronson, remaining with them until her parents returned the following weekend.

Joan and her three younger children were now living in New York City in Dr David Seligman's apartment, the children enrolled in the Riverdale School along the Hudson in the western part of The Bronx. Joan negotiated with Columbia's Teachers College for a professorship beginning the following fall, an appointment as a full professor with immediate tenure. The tenure was not that important to her except as an indication of the high professional regard in which she was held. Everyone was very busy during the day, but the nights were more and more delightful as both David and Joan shed many chronological years together.

Joan did her best to expedite the awarding of her divorce decree, and she actually managed to get it just before she discovered that she was one-month pregnant. She and David were married the following weekend by the senior rabbi of Temple Emanuel, David's reform congregation, in a private ceremony in the Seligman apartment attended only by family and very close friends, including the President and Vice President, but with the notable absence of Joan's oldest child James Jr. Joel was his father's best man, Abigail her mother's maid of honor, and Joan was "given away" by Kenneth Strong. Entrance to the apartment building was tightly controlled by the Secret Service, and the other occupants bitterly complained, ostensibly because of the access controls but actually because they were not invited.

It was now Joan's and David's turn to go on a honeymoon, and off they went to parts unknown for two weeks while her three younger children stayed with their new brother Joel Seligman in his apartment. But before the Seligmans left on their honeymoon, Joan and Sally confided to each other that each of them was pregnant.

TWENTY-FOUR

The trial of James Monroe Lancaster for the murder of Dinah Miriam Steinberg opened ten days after the senior Seligmans returned from their honeymoon and Joan's three younger children returned to their parents' apartment, the children reluctant to leave all the fun of staying with Joel. Joel needed that ten days for final preparation, and he fully understood why Naomi planned never to appear in the courtroom, even to see him in action. She had no testimony to give in this murder trial, and the emotional strain of having to again see the man who had murdered her sister was too much. Most of the evidence against the defendant was documentary, and very solid, and the witnesses were the police officers involved and Justice Berger. As for Catherine, radiant and obviously very happy, and not being otherwise emotionally involved, she lived in the courtroom to see Roger at his best, and she later planned to write a book about the trial.

Like Naomi, Joan never stepped foot in the courtroom, to avoid having to see the murderer she was once married to, and like Naomi she had no testimony to give in New York County, but her eldest son James Jr did come up from Princeton whenever he could, to sit in the visitors' gallery as though some magnet were pulling him to the place of judgment of his father. He sat in the back of the large courtroom, and never made his presence known to either his father or to this new step-brother of his who was defending his father and whom he had never met.

The selection of a jury proved to be extremely difficult. Who was not aware of the great drama that had taken place in the nation's capital when the defendant in this murder trial was the subject of an impeachment trial on the same issue? And who had never read or heard about the disappearance of the defendant, and his re-appearance? Those potential jurors who claimed they knew nothing about what had happened in Washington could not likely be people with much intelligence, and a murder trial required jurors with a reasonable degree of intelligence.

Judge Charles Abrams, a veteran of twenty-three years as a judge of the New York County Court, was presiding, and he took it upon himself to dismiss many in the jury pool who had formed an opinion or who seemed incapable of making a sensible decision as to guilt or innocence. After five days of voire dire, Judge Abrams called both Roger and Joel to his chambers after recessing the court for the weekend.

"Well...gentlemen...," said the judge, "...what are we going to do...? This man has been indicted...and must go to trial...but so far I see no potential juror qualified to render judgment.... I shall certainly not dismiss because of this difficulty.... Any ideas...?"

"I suggest you draw twelve jurors at random from the jury pool...," suggested Roger Morrison, the prosecutor, "...and empanel them.... As simple as that.... Otherwise we'll get nowhere.... What do you think...Joel...?" And this was the first time that Roger was emotionally able to easily call Joel by his first name.

"I think it's a very good idea...and I agree we would otherwise get nowhere...."

"I'll go along with that...," said the judge, "...if you...Joel...formally stipulate that the selection of the jury in this way...without the use of any challenges...either peremptory or for cause...would not be the basis for an appeal...."

"I think that's fair...Your Honor...and I'll so stipulate in open court...but only after I've had an opportunity to speak to my client.... I'll be seeing him over the weekend in the Tombs...."

"Fine...," responded Judge Abrams, "...and if it's agreed by Monday morning...then I'll personally select the names of the jurors from a goldfish bowl...."

A panel of twelve jurors was empaneled on Monday morning, chosen at random from the jury pool. Of the dozen, seven were white, four black, and one Hispanic. Five were professionals and had college degrees. Another four had low-paying service jobs, and the remainder were on welfare. Seven were men, and five were women. Three were Catholic, two Jewish, one Muslim, and six Protestant.

After a lunch recess, Roger presented his opening argument right after the court reconvened at two o'clock.

"Your Honor...ladies and gentlemen of the jury...the People of the State of New York will prove...beyond a reasonable doubt...that the defendant James Monroe Lancaster...did commit the premeditated murder by strangulation of Dinah Miriam Steinberg.... The evidence presented by the People will be primarily documentary...supported by the testimony of several witnesses for the People who will testify as to the authenticity of the documents.... The People will ask for the death penalty...," that last remark causing quite a stir in the courtroom.

Joel realized that James Lancaster had indeed strangled Dinah Steinberg, and that the evidence against him, as brought out in the impeachment trial, was conclusive. With this in mind, Joel made the opening statement for the defense.

"Your Honor...ladies and gentlemen of the jury.... The impeachment trial of the defendant in Washington was a political trial...without the usual safeguards ordinarily accorded to a defendant because the only possible punishment would be removal from office.... Please do not assume therefore...that my client has been proven guilty beyond a reasonable doubt...by the Senate in Washington.... That was not the constitutional standard before the Senate...and in actuality...the Senate could remove any President...by a two-thirds vote...upon impeachment by the House of Representatives...without any evidence at all...." Joel paused, and watched for any live faces among the jurors, and did detect a few, to which he would deliver his arguments in the course of the trial. Joel resumed.

"My client did kill Dinah Steinberg...but the killing was not first-degree murder...and that is why we have pleaded not guilty to that charge in the indictment...a charge that the defendant did kill Dinah Steinberg with premeditation...." The courtroom burst into a crescendo of noise, and the judge had to bang his gavel down on his desk many times before order was restored. Joel continued, "James Monroe Lancaster...at that time a United States Senator from Virginia...loved Dinah Miriam Steinberg...and he thought she loved him.... It is true that he was married and had four children...but he is not on trial here for being unfaithful to his wife.... He is on trial for his life...and you...ladies and gentlemen of the jury...must not let any of his personal behavior becloud the main issue...and the main issue is whether the defendant killed Dinah Steinberg with premeditation...or whether he killed her in an uncontrollable last-minute rage...or perhaps in self-defense...or perhaps accidentally.... No one now alive was in that room...in the victim's apartment...at the time of the tragedy...no one except the defendant...and he will take the witness stand for the defense...when it is our turn...to show that...on the issue of the indictment...the defendant is not guilty...." The courtroom was once more in an uproar, and it took quite some time to bring it to order.

"I shall clear the courtroom if there is another outburst...and as for the members of the press...you are not to leave this courtroom except when this court recesses.... Mr Seligman...do you have any further remarks to make at this time...?"

"No...Your Honor...."

"Then this court stands recessed until tomorrow morning at ten...and I would like to see both counsel for the People and for the defense in my chambers...."

"What are you trying to do...Joel...?"

"The People can't prove that Dinah Steinberg did not have a gun.... The defense can claim that she was threatening to kill him...that he lunged forward to knock the gun from her hand...or that in an unpremeditated rage he tried to kill her...and without realizing it...he actually did.... That's what my client will testify to...and I don't think that even Roger...as good a prosecutor as he is...will be able to shake that story...."

Roger sputtered, "But we found no gun in the apartment...."

"And we'll argue that there was a gun...with Dinah Steinberg's fingerprints on it...but that it was suppressed...because Roger very quickly became obsessed with Dinah's sister Naomi...and was most anxious to get her killer on the maximum penalty...."

Before a very angry Roger could respond, Judge Abrams asked, "Then what are you getting at...Joel...?"

"I don't want to besmirch the memory of Dinah

Steinberg...but I will if it means saving my client's life.... It's his life that's at stake...and I would be less than a competent lawyer if I didn't try to save it...."

"Alright...Mr Seligman...what do you propose...?" asked Roger, finally recovering from the verbal onslaught against his case.

"I propose that my client plead guilty to a charge of second-degree murder...and that will save his life...."

"But what of Dinah Steinberg...?" asked Roger.

"There's nothing we can do to bring her back.... As you know...Roger...Naomi and I are in love with each other...yet she perfectly understands that as a lawyer I have to do what I can.... If saving Lancaster's life means my losing her...I'll still have to try to save his life.... You do realize that my injecting this important doubt...which reflects on the integrity of your case...could be enough to result in a verdict of not guilty on the present charge.... If I were you...Roger...I would accept my offer.... And please also realize that Lancaster is a lawyer...and is quite aware of his defensive position...."

Roger thought and thought for what seemed like a long time, but actually for only a few minutes, and finally said, "Yes...you're right...Joel.... You're a good lawyer...and with the highest integrity as a lawyer...and I hope I don't have to come up against you again.... Yes...Your Honor...the People will ask you to consent to the defendant pleading guilty to the charge of second-degree murder...."

"I shall consent...but you realize...Joel...that I can still sentence the defendant to life in prison without possibility of parole...."

"I realize that...and so does the defendant...but it would at least save his life...even though it would mean spending the remainder of that life beyond bars.... And I also realize that both Albany County...and Henrico County...and the District of Columbia...can all levy charges against him...but I very much doubt that any conviction on likely charges in those jurisdictions would result in the death penalty...even if he were found guilty of conspiracy and incitement in the death of Mary Rosenblueth.... So if that would be your sentence...Your Honor...that ends the prosecutorial phase of the criminal justice system...as far as former President Lancaster is concerned...."

"I don't agree with that conclusion...Joel...," said Judge Abrams. "In my professional opinion...Lancaster committed a crime against humanity for ordering that massive attack against Israel...and I would not be too surprised if the Israelis ask for his extradition...."

"But they have no death penalty...," said Roger.

"They had one for Adolf Eichmann...," Joel commented, "...and might reinstate the penalty for Lancaster.... A most interesting point...Your Honor...."

"I'd even convert to Judaism...," exclaimed Roger, "...if it meant getting another crack at that horrible man...."

A few minutes after ten o'clock on the following Monday morning, a stunned courtroom heard James Monroe Lancaster plead guilty to second-degree murder in the death of Dinah Miriam Steinberg, and then heard Judge Abrams sentence James Monroe Lancaster to life in prison without any chance of parole. All hell then broke loose as the reporters tried to beat each other out of the courtroom to report their stories.

Lancaster was handcuffed and led away without any sign of any kind between him and Joel, and Joel preferred it that way. He had saved the man's life, and that was enough. He now had to face Naomi, her family, Joan, and Mark for what he had done, for despite Naomi's prior assurances, he knew her reaction would be very negative.

After James Lancaster Sr was handcuffed and taken out of the courtroom to spend the remainder of his life behind bars, and before Joel himself left the courtroom, James Lancaster Jr came over to him, said "Thank you...," and then quickly left the courtroom before Joel could recognize him.

As soon as Joel got back to his apartment, he called Naomi in Richmond, at her hospital, and while he waited for her to respond to the paging for her, he began to break out in a cold sweat. Was it all worth it if he were to lose her? Naomi answered the page, and was informed that there was a long-distance call for her, which she then took in her office. She was very cold as Joel explained to her what happened.

"I heard it over the TV even before you called.... I thought Roger was going for the death penalty.... Why is that miserable creature going to live for the remainder of his life...while my sister lies buried in the ground.... How could you allow something like this to happen...?"

"Naomi...please.... There was reasonable doubt in this case as to whether the murder was premeditated...and any good defense lawyer would have seen it.... If Lancaster had not been able to plead guilty to a lesser charge...there was a likelihood that he might have been found not guilty of first-degree murder because of that doubt...."

"Oh...why do you lawyers always play such games...? He killed my sister...and he should die for it.... A life for a life...." She began to cry.

"Naomi...please...," he pleaded again. "I wasn't willing to take any chance that Lancaster might have been found not guilty...and there was a chance...even though a small one.... The prosecution didn't have a completely air-tight case for first-degree murder...and Roger Morrison...realizing it...agreed to this deal.... It was the best that I could do...for you...."

"Alright Joel...can you come down to Richmond tomorrow...and explain that to my mother and grandmother...? And when you return back north...explain it to Mark...and then to Joan.... I'm sure that the only way for a reasonable doubt to have been raised...was for you to raise it.... Why did you have to raise it...? That's what I would like to know...."

"I think that Mark and Joan will understand...and I hope your family will...and I especially hope you will.... Yes...I'll arrive tomorrow afternoon.... Can you meet me at the airport...?"

"No...I can't.... I expect to have a very busy day.... Just go straight to the hospital...and then we can go to my house together.... I don't think you ought to arrive there without me...."

"Is it that bad...?"

"Yes...it is.... My mother is furious...and you had

better explain it all...very very carefully...and if you can't...please don't come down...ever...." She hung up.

Joel then called Mark at the White House, and Mark was considerably more understanding.

"Yes...I was always a bit concerned by that loophole in a case for first-degree murder.... I spoke to Roger about it even before we identified the fingerprints...but he put it aside...hoping that no one would raise the question.... He insisted there was no misconduct in suppressing evidence...and I told him that I wasn't implying that he would do such a thing...but that it could be...could be...could be that one of the police officers did it.... I agree that it's enough of a reasonable doubt against a first-degree case...and if you did not raise it...some other good lawyer as Lancaster's defense counsel would have.... I don't know how good a lawyer Lancaster himself actually was...but even he could have seen it.... I feel you really did the best thing...under the circumstances.... As for Mary and the children...it would be very difficult to prove conspiracy and incitement by Lancaster.... I know Henry II took responsibility for the death of Thomas a Becket...but under our law he did not have to...and of course being the King his confession did not mean a thing except some religious penance.... The actual killers in Albany...including Jefferson Smith and Roy Carpenter...will be tried for felony murder...and undoubtedly convicted...but that will not bring Mary and the children back...." He paused for a while. "When shall Sally and I be able to see you again...?"

"I'm going down to Richmond to try to patch things up with Naomi...and her family.... Her attitude when I talked to her...just before I called you...was that I had gotten Lancaster off...."

"Let me call her.... I'll explain the situation to her...before you arrive...and that should make it easier for you...."

"I'd greatly appreciate it...Mark...and may I see you and Sally on the way back to New York...?"

"Just let us know when...and we'll look forward to it.... Try to bring Naomi with you...say for the Sabbath meal next Friday.... Sally and the children really enjoy the ceremony...and they would all love to see you...."

His stepmother Joan was also understanding when Joel then called her, and she also promised to call Naomi that evening to try to place the entire situation in its proper prospective. With two wonderful people like Mark Rosenblueth and Joan Seligman on his side, Joel felt he could not possibly lose. But he was still very apprehensive that even their explanations to Naomi and her family might not adequately placate her. He must have some back-up position, but he did not know what position that ought to be.

TWENTY-FIVE

There was only one mid-day nonstop flight from New York to Richmond, and Joel Seligman was on it the next day, a Tuesday, but holding his breath all the way. He had spent a sleepless night despite the support he received from Mark and Joan, and he did not particularly look forward to what could possibly happen when he saw Naomi.

The flight landed on schedule, and as Joel quickly walked up the jetway to the terminal building, there was Naomi waiting for him, and when she saw him she smiled and ran toward him. Their kiss and embrace was about the most it could be in a public place.

"I thought you were ready to shoot me...and I willingly came to be slaughtered...."

"Darling...Mark called...and then Joan called...and even Roger called...all to say that your conduct in the whole matter was exemplary...and all that sort of thing.... I'm sorry I was such a bitch.... Please forgive me...."

"With all my heart...," he responded as they walked past departure gate after departure gate until they reached the main ticket lounge. "Mark asked us both to go up Friday to join Sally and him for the Sabbath at the White House.... Let's get our tickets now...."

"Yes...Sally talked to me when Mark called...and she very much wants us to come...and of all things...she said she wants us to come as man and wife...."

"Well...she is the President of the United States...and when the President says come as man and wife...that means we shall have to come as man and wife.... What do you think...Dr Steinberg...?"

"Oh...I entirely agree...and I never thought I would receive a proposal of marriage in an airport...."

"As good a place as any...."

And then regardless of the passersby, they kissed most intimately.

"Let's get the tickets...and then pick up my car...and go home...and tell my mother and grandmother...."

"And how do they feel toward me...?"

"Well...Joan spoke to them at great length...and if you have to ask them formally for my hand in marriage...I'm sure they will consent...."

Mrs Steinberg and Mrs Benjamin did heartily approve, but they pointed out that they could not possibly arrange a proper wedding for Naomi before the Friday deadline.

"Well...then Joel and I shall to go up not as man and wife...and then we'll come right back down again...and arrange for our wedding day...."

Naomi and Joel were house guests of the Rosenblueths the following weekend, but occupying separate bedrooms as a punishment for disobeying a direct order of the President, all in good humor. Sally and Mark were delighted by their wedding plans and promised to come to Richmond in the absence of a national emergency.

That evening, Sally did indeed look so womanly as she placed a white lace shawl over her head, lighted the Sabbath candles, and intoned the brief Sabbath prayer. It was especially at that time that she was the woman of the house, not the President of the United States.

After dinner, Mark took Joel aside for a private talk. "I'm going to form a working relationship with all the Governors...to develop plans...and the means for implementing those plans...to return the United States to the original concept of a Union of States.... Will you become my close associate in this very important cause...?" Before Joel could even answer, Mark continued with a smile, "You must admit...Joel...that you're a brilliant lawyer...and I feel you're a very fine person to the bargain...unless I'm completely wrong on both counts.... I want you to work with me to bring this all about...."

For one of the very few times of his life, Joel was at a loss for words, but finally said, "Mark...I would be glad to...and I greatly appreciate those very kind words...."

"They're well deserved.... Now let me tell you how I propose to go about doing all of this.... First of all...you'll have to move to Washington...and give up your private practice...at least temporarily.... Sally intends to formally meet with the Governors to propose the establishment of a Council of Governors as a formal organization with the Vice President as chairman...but only as presiding officer...not as the boss...and you'll be the executive director to actually run things...." While Joel continued to be at a loss for words, Mark continued on. "The President will formally propose to the Congress that it enact legislation to set up this council...and she will also ask the Governors to obtain the authorization of their legislatures to also set up this council.... The council will not come into existence unless the Congress and every State agree to it.... Senators and members of the House have become very responsive to their States...more so that in the past...and the States are more than interested.... So...how does that strike you...?"

"Right between the eyes...Mark.... An excellent approach...and I'll be more than proud to play my part.... I'll of course have to get Naomi's approval...but I see no reason why she can't obtain a good position somewhere in the Washington metropolitan area...."

Naomi did most heartily approve, but plans for her wedding were more urgent, the ceremony being scheduled three weeks from that weekend. Formal invitations went out to all their families and close friends, including Roger and Catherine, and they also included Rabbi and Mrs Aaronson to give Sally's daughter Julia another opportunity to be with their son Paul.

In the meanwhile, Joel and Naomi found a fine townhouse in Olde Town Alexandria, the old colonial section of Alexandria, an independent city in northern Virginia, and furnished it with many antiques from her home in Richmond, supplemented by the purchase of new furniture.

Sally and Mark and their two children, both Joshua and Julia now formally adopted by Mark, the First Family arrived at Richard Henry Lee Drive the day before the wedding, and were all guests of Mrs Steinberg and Mrs Benjamin while all the other members of the family and close friends stayed at Joan Seligman's Richmond house, still retained and maintained by the senior Seligmans.

Rabbi Jacob de Cordoba, a longtime friend of the Steinberg and Benjamin family, and senior rabbi of the oldest Sephardic synagogue in Virginia, the synagogue where Judah Benjamin had worshipped more than a century before, Rabbi de Cordoba conducted the old orthodox Sephardic wedding ceremony, in classical Hebrew, old Spanish and modern English. And during the many hours after Joel crushed the drinking glass under his foot, a good time was had by all, especially by Julia and Paul and by Joan's children and Sally's children, all finding one another. But James Jr was not among them.

Naomi and Joel re-surfaced again in the Washington area two weeks later, and moved into their new Alexandria house. But before Joel got down to work, and before Naomi took over her new duties as assistant medical director of a small new hospital in Alexandria, they went to New York to see the senior Seligmans and to Richmond to see Naomi's mother and grandmother. Joan looked more radiant as she grew much larger, and Dr Seligman was as proud as a peacock and making sure that his wife had the best medical care available.

Joan privately asked Joel after dinner whether David could adopt her minor children in New York without James Lancaster's consent. John Lancaster, the younger son and now legally an adult wanted to be adopted, and could be without anyone's consent other than his own, but James Jr obviously would not want to be, for he never saw his mother since the Senate trial of his father. The question only pertained to Abigail and Gabrielle, who very much wanted to become Seligmans. Joan did not hint about any plans for conversion, for herself and her daughters, and Joel did not feel it proper to ask. Mark Rosenblueth, within weeks of his marriage to Sally, had adopted both Joshua and Julia, and all of the First Family were officially Rosenblueths, but Joel did not have a ready answer to Joan's question, and said he would research the matter very soon, and let her know.

Some weeks later, and within only several days of each other, Sally gave birth to a daughter, named Frances Miriam after her mother and Mark's mother, and Joan to a son named Aaron Robert after his paternal and maternal grandfathers. Both mothers and both fathers were doing very well, and the infants exceptionally well.

For all intents and purposes, Mark was acting president during the several weeks before and after his daughter's birth, but no one in Washington seemed to make an issue of it, for everyone knew the nation was in his very capable hands, even those not liking the Rosenblueths conceding that point.

In New York, Joan's happiness was tempered by her eldest child's constant refusal to see her, and when Joan phoned him to tell him that he now had a new brother, his reaction was rather nasty.

"All of this would not have happened to my father...if you had been a proper wife to him.... Do you know where I go on weekends and during my school breaks...? I go up to Sing Sing...to visit my father everyday.... He's still my father...not that Jew you married.... How could you do such a thing...?"

That was quite a verbal blow, and almost as effective as a physical one. Joan fell ill, and it was all that her physicians could do to prevent her from becoming worse. It took many weeks of loving care by her husband, her son John and her two daughters to pull her back, and when she finally did get back, she realized that for the sake of her family she would have to completely forget her eldest child as she had completely forgotten his father.

Naomi and Joel returned to Washington, and took up their separate daytime activities, she at the hospital in Alexandria and he in the Executive Office Building. It did not take many more months before Naomi told Joel that she was going to have a baby, and Joel responded in the usual old-fashioned way. That same evening, they received a call from his father that Joan and Abigail had been physically threatened when her eldest son visited the apartment while Dr Seligman was at Mount Sinai Hospital, and that she had another relapse.

"Where is he now....?"

"Back at Princeton...I believe...."

"I think that perhaps we ought to call Roger Morrison in on this one.... I know how busy he is...but he might still find some time to do something about this young monster.... If he can be put away for a time...that will give me some breathing space...to figure out a permanent solution.... Naomi is expecting...and I don't want to involve her at this time...but on the other hand...we can't neglect Joan.... I'll talk to Roger...." He paused. "No...on the other hand...I will not talk to him.... There's really very little the law can do about a so-called family situation of this kind...and I would rather not expand the circle beyond the two of us...."

The following Friday evening, James Jr drove up to Ossining, New York to visit his father over the weekend at Sing Sing State Penitentiary. James Sr, especially more haggard this time than on his son's usual visits, was glad to see him, but the first thing he asked, as he always asked, was "When are you going to get even for me...for what she did to me...and for marrying that damn Jew.... Imagine her letting that dirty Jew go inside her.... It's disgusting...."

"I'll take care of it as soon as I can.... I promise...Dad.... I have to see her when she's home alone...without the others...."

"Alright...but the sooner the better.... You're my only reason for surviving in this awful place..."

James Jr visited his father as much as he could over that weekend, and early Monday morning drove down to New York City, into Manhattan, and stopped on the street around the corner from the Seligman apartment house. His brother John and his two sisters were away at school, and James Jr had checked to make sure that Dr Seligman was at his office. He then called his mother at the apartment, hanging up as soon as she answered. She was apparently home alone.

He skillfully got passed the security guards, and took the stairs rather than the elevator to the eleventh floor. Standing in front of her apartment door, he rang the doorbell and then jumped out of the way. Joan absent-mindedly unlocked the door when she saw no one in the peephole, to look outside into the hall, and that was enough for her son to force his way into the apartment.

"What are you doing here...?" she asked indignantly. "I thought I told you I never wanted to see you again...after the way you treated me last time.... What do you want...?"

"I'll tell you what I want.... I want what my father wants...and I'll show you what my father wants...."

"I'll call the police if you don't leave...," she cried,

rushing toward the telephone. Her son grabbed her with one hand before she could reach it, and put his other hand over her mouth to prevent a scream. Holding her this way, he dragged Joan to her bedroom, and threw her down on the bed with himself falling down directly on top of her.

"I'm going to release my hand over your mouth...and if you scream...I'm going to kill you.... So help I will.... You stopped being my mother after what you did to my father.... Will you keep quiet...?"

Joan nodded that she would, and James Jr released his hand.

"Now you will remain very quiet while I take off all your clothes...."

"My clothes...? Why my clothes...? What are you going to do...?"

"I'm going to show you once again what a real man is like...not that Jew you married.... Just pretend it's your real husband...rotting away in some filthy hole...who's inside you...," and he ripped her clothes off and then his own.

Joan started to scream, but back went his hand onto her face.

"I told you I'd kill you if you screamed...and I mean it.... I really mean it...."

As though he personally could not wait any longer, he quickly tore the rest of her clothes off while Joan lay quivering and terrified on her back, her body now stark naked on the bed just below his own naked body as he now stood on hands and knees above her ready to pounce, his body very stiff and erect, and when she crossed her legs to try to protect herself, he grabbed her neck and threatened to kill her if she did not quickly raise her knees and spread them apart. Even more terrified, Joan did just that, and he plunged himself, without further warning, sharply into his mother's body.

Joan screamed in great pain, and while he was inside her and with his full weight on top of her, with nothing between them, he increased the grip around her neck with both hands and began to strangle her.

"I told you not to scream...," as he moved very rapidly up and down inside her, all the while increasing the pressure of his hands around her neck, and it was only the sudden release of an early orgasm that caused him to also release her neck before his hands killed her. He rolled over on his back alongside his mother, fully spent, and Joan immediately got out of bed and ran to a drawer in David's dresser, there to retrieve a 38-calibre pistol. She aimed it at him with one hand, and began to use the telephone next to her bed with the other.

He reacted by moving quickly over the bed toward her, but Joan threatened to use the gun if he came any closer. He did come closer, and she fired, not once but many times until the gun clip was empty. James Jr lay dead on the bed in his own pool of blood.

Joan ran into the nursery to make sure that her baby was alright, and indeed he was. He had slept through his mother's ordeal, for which Joan was most grateful. What if he had cried, causing the deranged James Jr to strangle him?

Joan immediately called David at his office, and was told by an officious secretary that the doctor was busy.

"You tell him that his wife is on the phone and that it's an emergency...," she said hysterically. A few seconds later, Dr Seligman was on the phone.

"David...you must come home right now...right now...right now...."

"Darling...what is it...? I have a serious problem with a patient...."

"Well...your wife has a far more serious problem than your patient has.... I'll expect you in a few minutes...," and she hung up.

She then called her sister, who was in the Morrison apartment diligently working on her latest novel.

"Catherine...it's Joan.... I must see you and Roger...right away.... It's an emergency...damn it.... Yes...both of you...right now...," she screamed.

Joan did nothing and touched nothing as she waited, standing and still completely naked, for her husband and sister, and her sister's husband, to arrive. David came within five minutes, almost running all the way, and was aghast when he saw what he saw.

"Joan...darling...what happened...?"

"He raped me...and then tried to kill me.... My own son raped me...and tried to kill me.... I killed him to defend myself...with your gun.... No...don't touch me and don't touch him.... Leave everything until Catherine and Roger get here...," and they came about ten minutes later. After they all saw the bruises on her body and on her neck, she put a robe on.

Joan related every second of what had happened from the time her son first rang the doorbell, leaving no gory detail out.

"Joan...I don't want to seem callous...," said Roger, "...but I'm going to have to have you examined very carefully... including the bruises around your neck...and see if we can get his fingerprints off your neck.... We'll also have to extract some of his seminal fluid from your body...and compare it with what is left in him...and also to find indications of forced entry...."

Catherine began to protest. "Don't you see what happened here...? Why does my sister have to go through all of that...? Hasn't she gone through enough...?"

David answered before Roger could. "Roger is doing all this to protect Joan...in case someone begins to accuse him of bias in favor of his own sister-in-law...."

"I understand...Roger...," said Joan. "What do we do now...?"

"I'll try my best to keep this quiet...and I think I can.... We'll need photographs...and examinations by authorized people...and I'll choose only those whom I can trust not to babble to the press...." Roger then called Inspector Salinger, and told him to come over right away, "...and bring Malloy and Ramos...and a body bag...with you...and also a good camera.... And also bring Dr Jensen...the medical examiner...yes...the medical examiner himself...not an assistant...."

The three detectives arrived before Dr Jensen did, and after being quickly briefed, began to go about their business. They photographed everything in the apartment, but waited for Dr Jensen to photograph Joan's body in some privacy, to extract some seminal fluid from her body, and to give her a pelvic examination.

In that, Dr Seligman did what he could to assist, as his assistance was requested, all the while doing his best to comfort his wife.

The naked body of James Monroe Lancaster Jr was removed in a body bag after being thoroughly photographed and medically examined, and Joan, now a bit more composed, gave a formal statement to Inspector Salinger.

David took his brother-in-law aside. "Her son was seeing his father at almost every opportunity...and this is not the first time he threatened her.... It's obvious his father put him up to this.... Is there anything that can be done against that monster in Sing Sing...?"

"I don't know...David...but let me think about it.... You realize of course that it might not have happened...if I had gotten the death penalty against him...," obviously blaming Joel, "...but I'll see what can be done...for Catherine's sake...."

David then called Joel and asked him and Naomi to come up from Washington as soon as possible, relating without details the tragedy that had just occurred. David did not mean James Jr's death but the rape he committed against his own mother.

His sisters arrived home after their brother's body was taken away and all the outsiders had left. They realized that something was very wrong when they saw their mother's face, but their Aunt Catherine took them aside to tell them without details what had happened. The two girls ran to their mother and began to cry, and it was their mother, who would always be their mother, who comforted them.

In Washington, Naomi and Joel dropped what they were doing, and took the Metroliner to New York to avoid driving most of the way after dark. When they arrived at the Seligman apartment, they found Joan and David, the children, and also Catherine, Roger previously having to leave with the police to make sure everything was kept quiet.

And over the next several weeks and with considerable skill, and without breaking any laws, Roger managed to keep the press out of this affair, and despite his busy schedule he turned his attention to James Sr. As for Joel, he blamed himself, and silently vowed that James Lancaster would not be allowed to live.

TWENTY-SIX

Sally sent her proposal to Congress to form the Council of Governors, and at the same time Mark presented the proposal to all fifty Governors assembled at the vice presidential mansion. The residence for the time being not needed for its primary purpose, it was now the headquarters for the proposed Council of Governors.

During the next few months, Joel plunged heavily into his job as executive director of the council. Congress enacted the authorization and also an appropriation for the participation of the federal government, and each state legislature also enacted its own legislation authorizing membership of its Governor in the council and appropriating funds for that purpose. Thus fifty-one legislative bodies were in complete agreement on the need for a fundamental change in the federal structure of the nation back to where it began, as a federation of sovereign States.

Naomi worked at the hospital until about her seventh month, and then took a long leave of absence to end well after the baby was born, but the more she thought of it, the more she did not want to go back to work on a regular schedule, and she certainly did not have to do so for the money. Both families genetically contributing to the life-in-being were wealthy, but she did want to do something meaningful in her profession even though part-time. Through her father-in-law's considerable influence in the medical profession, and also because of her own outstanding qualifications, she obtained an appointment as a clinical associate professor of medicine at the George Washington University School of Medicine, which would take only a few hours of her time each day, and then on a very flexible schedule. She though of what Joan had done to devote her primary time to her children as they were growing up and that Joan had given only secondary time to her profession.

Naomi resigned from the hospital in April, her baby was due in June, and her appointment at the medical school would begin in September. She would even be able to take her child to her university office while there, and arrange for one of the female graduate students on campus to play baby-sitter.

Almost to the day, Naomi gave birth to a healthy boy, named Jeremiah after her father and Samuel after one of Joel's great-grandfathers. Congratulations poured in, and in groups of varying size those of the family and friends in Washington and in New York and Richmond went to Alexandria to visit. Mrs Benjamin, now a great-grandmother was a bit too sickly to travel, and so little Jeremiah went to visit her when he could arrange for his parents to drive him down to Richmond.

Sally and Mark visited the junior Seligmans when Jeremiah was all of seven days old, and Julia came with her parents to play with the baby. Joshua Rosenblueth was in New York City, in a summer session at New York University, and only incidentally because Abigail Lancaster, now Abigail Seligman, just happened to be in the same city.

At the first opportunity at the mansion on Observatory Circle, Mark again took Joel privately aside, but this time not to discuss federalism but to say that his daughter Julia was pregnant, and that Paul Aronson was the father.

"When Sally and I questioned her about it...she said that Paul and she loved each other...and they wanted to be married...."

"Then why not let them get married...and live in the White House while they both finish their education.... From what I can tell...although I have not had much contact with him...Paul Aronson seems to be a very fine young man.... He was certainly well-mannered when I met him...."

"Yes...Sally and I both think very highly of him...but don't you think they're too young...?"

"Not if they're mature enough to truly love each other.... It appears that Julia is...and what is your assessment of Paul.... I'm sure you know him better than I do...."

"I would say that he's also rather settled and mature.... He received a strict upbringing from his parents...and he's not frivolous...."

"Well...with fully supportive parents...both emotionally and financially...let them marry and obtain their sexual fulfillment through married love rather than carnal appetite.... The ancient Jews always knew what they were doing...and everything they did was right...and that included having their children marry at thirteen...at puberty...just when the sexual urge very strongly begins...."

"You're right...Joel.... I'm glad I talked to you.... When we get back home...Sally and I will talk about it...and then we'll talk to the Aronsons...."

"Just a matter of curiosity...what does Paul plan to be...? What will he study...?"

"He wants to be a doctor.... Well...I think we can always use another doctor in the family...if he's a good one...but with Paul's outstanding academic record so far...I think he'll make a very good one...and I'm sure David will also see to it...."

Sally and Mark talked to Rabbi and Mrs Aronson during a private dinner at the White House. At first, the rabbi almost exploded, that his son had done such a thing, but Mark immediately suggested that the two get married if they truly loved each other.

"Julia is ready to enter college.... She plans to go to

George Washington...and as I understand it...Paul is entering his senior year...and will then enter medical school.... Let him finish at George Washington and continue on in their medical school.... We would enjoy their living with us while they both finish their education and finally get settled...."

Sally interrupted to say with a smile, "...and I'm sure they'll find two sets of very devoted grandparents to do some baby-sitting for them...and I would admonish both of them to avoid another pregnancy until their education is completed...."

Ruth Aronson at first did not know what to say, but she finally found her tongue. "Oh...Mrs Rosenblueth...you and your husband are such fine people.... I'm so glad that Paul found Julia...and it's not because this is the White House...and all that sort of thing...but really nice families are so few and far between...and I am...," and then she broke down and began to cry. Sally got up and walked over to her and put her arm around her daughter's future mother-in-law to comfort her.

Paul and Julia were overjoyed, and both pledged to avoid another pregnancy until they finished all their studies. They were married in a private ceremony in the White House by Rabbi Aronson with Joshua as best man for Paul, and Sally as matron of honor for her daughter, with only family and close friends present, and as most of their close friends were becoming united to themselves and to the families by marriage, they all began to coalesce into one family, in New York, Washington and Richmond.

The young bride and groom went on a two-week honeymoon, using part of a generous wedding gift from the senior Seligman, and escorted by very understanding secret service agents, and both returned walking on the same cloud to take up residence in the White House. They enrolled in George Washington for the Fall semester, at the same time that Naomi would begin on the medical faculty, and now Paul would also have the company of at least one secret service agent to and from his classes.

Joshua Rosenblueth remained with his parents for a few days before going back to New York with the senior Seligmans and their children, including little Aaron and especially Abigail. Two weeks later, when Joshua returned to Washington to visit his parents, it was at a family dinner at the White House, with the senior Seligmans and Abigail also present, that Joshua announced to two not-too-surprised sets of parents that both he and Abigail loved each other and also wanted to be married. The family precedent having been set, all that remained for the parents to do was to make sure that their two children were emotionally ready, and indeed they were. So, not long after one family wedding in the White House, there was to be another family wedding, but this time in New York City at the home of the bride's parents, which was to remain their home until they too completed all their studies.

It was not until Joan Seligman became the mother of the bride that she finally and fully came out of her long emotional turmoil, but not quite fully, for the lingering memory of the evil man she first married and of the son she first bore continued to remain with her, but it did recede far into the background. David, having tried all this time since the tragedy to rescue his wife from psychological oblivion, was so delighted with her spontaneous recovery that he strongly suggested they go on a very extended honeymoon right then and there, putting all other things aside. She placed her arms around him, and they kissed with such loving tenderness that both were now ready to make another baby. And while they were away, John Lancaster, now John Seligman, and his sister Gabrielle lived with the junior Seligmans in Alexandria, John also attending George Washington University and his sister going to the neighborhood public school in Alexandria. As for very little Aaron Seligman, Joel's half-brother, he shared the same room with his very young nephew Jeremiah Seligman, Joel's son. Naomi and Gabrielle provided both of them with all the loving care the two little ones could hope for from two loving women, for Gabrielle was growing up faster than her family realized. And John Seligman, while living with his step-brother Joel, renewed an acquaintanceship with Deborah Aronson at a dinner at the White House, they beginning to date with ever-increasing frequency.

After the press had its fill reporting the unheralded wedding of the President's daughter, and about a month later the wedding of the President's son, things began to settle down more or less back to normal, and back went Joel to his duties and responsibilities in the mansion on Observatory Circle, his duties for the new

Council of Governors.

The first recommendation of the council was for Congress to restrict the appellate jurisdiction of the Supreme Court, which under the federal constitution Congress had the power to do, so that the court could no longer hear appeals from the State supreme courts. It took considerable pressure by the Council of Governors to get Congress to act, but act Congress eventually did, and President Rosenblueth quickly signed the bill into law.

Once the victory was won in that congressional battle, it was somewhat easier to get the Congress to further amend the Judiciary Act of 1789 so that no federal court could order the transfer of a case from a State court, and no federal court could act on any matter adjudicated by the State courts nor could any federal court declare any action by a State to be unconstitutional under the federal constitution. It was for the State's own courts to make any such determination.

The third recommendation was the most difficult to implement, but the threat by the Council of Governors that it would ask the States to convene a constitutional convention to achieve the same goal if the Congress refused to constrain itself, the third recommendation was that the Congress be permitted to appropriate funds, that it be permitted to spend, only in those areas of power specially delegated to it by the States in the federal constitution. Along with many other things, this eliminated federal interference in the educational systems of the States, and left it up to the legislature of each State to decide what policies ought to be adopted and implemented.

These measures greatly shifted the balance of power in the nation from the federal government in Washington to the fifty state governments in their fifty state capitals, and the importance of the state legislators and officials greatly increased.

With these initial reforms accomplished, Mark and Joel turned their attention to other matters in the campaign to restore the States to their rightful sphere of sovereignty.

Even though Sally's term had about two more years to go, Mark began to think of her re-election and the strong likelihood that he would be her running mate. There was of course the very practical political question of their religion, but there was also a constitutional question, for according to the Twelfth Amendment, the presidential Electors chosen by the State of New York would not be able to vote for him as Vice President if they were to vote for Sally as President, and of course their vote for Sally would be far more important than any vote for him. In a close election, this might mean that Sally would hopefully become President but the vice presidential candidate of the other major party could become the Vice President, which might cause all kinds of problems in Sally's next administration.

There were two ways to avoid this. One would be for Sally and Mark to establish legal residence in separate States, but this would require a legal separation, and that was something neither Sally nor Mark would even think of doing. Their marriage was far more important to them than any public office, no matter how high. The other solution would require a constitutional amendment to eliminate this restriction on the presidential Electors. So this second route was the one that Joel took when he began to lay the groundwork for new amendments to the federal constitution. Should he go solely through the States, or should he try to have the Congress initiate the amendments? And he had no more than twenty-four months to get this particular one through, but if the Council of Governors were to very strongly support the measure, it would very likely sail through in less than half the time.

There was actually a third alternative, not requiring a constitutional amendment nor a legal separation, and that would be for Sally and Mark to establish their legal residence in a State having only three electoral votes, and hope that the election would not be so close that the loss by Mark of three electoral votes would cost him the election as Vice President.

/

WENTY-SEVEN

Despite all the efforts to further delay the trial of Jefferson Smith and Roy Carpenter, and of the three hundred and sixteen of their accomplices, all three hundred and eighteen for the felony murder of Mary Rosenblueth and her children, the trial was finally scheduled to begin in the county court of Albany County.

The long delay was caused by the refusal of the electronic press to turn over the extensive video camera footage they had taken of the accused during their march to the governor's Executive Mansion and during the relatively brief period the crime was actually committed. The District Attorney of Albany County insisted that the footage was important prosecution evidence, but the press refused to provide the tapes. Totally annoyed, the Albany DA asked the county grand jury for an indictment against the chief executive officer of each television network on the charge of obstruction of justice. But the networks had their corporate offices in New York City, specifically in Manhattan, and the head of each network simply refused to appear in Albany to answer the indictment. District Attorney Max Armstrong of Albany County then obtained a fugitive warrant against each corporate officer named in the indictment, a warrant that Roger Morrison was more than happy to execute. The fugitives were simultaneously arrested by Inspector Salinger, and by Lieutenants Thomas Malloy and Juan Ramos, and at that point they agreed to give up the tapes, but Max Armstrong did not have the indictments quashed. He would attend to them later at his leisure.

During all of this, the networks had their lawyers appeal the actions taken against them, but the New York courts at every level held that the administration of justice was relatively more important than the freedom of the press organizations to do whatever they pleased, and the courts could not see any legitimate issue involving freedom of the press in all of this. So, with the tapes now in the possession of the district attorney, the murder trial was placed on the court docket to begin in about three weeks.

"I am going to ask Max Armstrong to let me prosecute that human filth...," Sally said one morning to Mark at breakfast, "I knew Mary.... She was an outstanding woman...and your children...Mark...every time I think of them...I shudder.... I want to do it...." But when she saw how badly her words were affecting

Mark, she said, "I'm sorry...Mark.... I should not have said what I said...about Mary...and your children.... It just brings back a very painful memory...."

"It's alright...Sally.... I appreciate how you feel...but you can't do it.... You're the President.... To avoid violating New York law...you would have to be paid by Albany County to do this.... In order to be paid...you would have to take leave without pay from the presidency...which is literally impossible.... It can't be done...assuming Max even agrees...unless you resign as President...and that would be absolutely absurd.... And all of this also applies to me.... Don't you think how much I would want either you or myself...or both...to prosecute.... Max is a good prosecutor...but with all due modesty...you and I are much better.... I'm sorry...darling.... I wish it could be done by either or both of us...but it can't...."

"You realize what might happen.... Max is good...but I don't think good enough against a really outstanding defense lawyer...and I suspect that Jefferson Smith has enough backing in this country to raise a great deal of money for a very good one.... There's even a Jefferson Smith Defense Fund...which advertises on TV.... I've asked the FCC to look into the obviously antisemitic overtones of their fund-raising ads.... TV and radio stations are not supposed to accept that kind of ad...." She paused. "I don't want them acquitted.... I want Smith...and the actual murderer...to receive the death penalty...."

"I want exactly what you want...darling.... Now let me see... who would be a proper match for the best legal minds in the country...? Roger is very good but I don't think that Max as a county DA would bow out to let another county DA do it for him.... We need a really brilliant lawyer...even without prosecuting experience...but with enough experience in the criminal law...and we have one right in the family.... Joel...!"

"Of course...but what of his present work...? Can he be spared...? You would have a much better feel about that then I...."

"Yes...I think so.... We've already gotten the major measures through Congress...and the proposal by the Council of Governors for a constitutional convention is slowly wending its way through the state legislatures.... I think he can be spared for about six months...and it certainly won't take that long to try the vermin in Albany...and then Max could handle any appeals...."

"Well...let's ask him...and if he says yes...then we'll ask Max.... If Max agrees...then all he has to do is appoint Joel an assistant DA while Joel is on leave without pay from his present position.... It could work...and I would have full confidence in Joel getting convictions...at least of Smith and that Roy Carpenter...."

Joel was in full agreement, feeling that this would help make up for the horrible crime against his stepmother, a crime he still felt he somehow contributed to. The next step was for Mark, alone, to go up to Albany to see his old friend Max Armstrong. This did not appear to the press to be too unusual, merely the former Governor of New York visiting his former capital city to see his former Lieutenant Governor.

"It's great to see you again...Mark...," Max welcomed Mark into his office. "To what do I owe this pleasure...? And how is that wonderful wife of yours...? She's turned out to be one of our best Presidents...."

"Thanks for those nice words about Sally...with which I wholeheartedly agree.... Max...we've known each other for a long time...so I'm not going to play diplomat with you.... I'm sure you realize how anxious I am that Jefferson Smith and Roy Carpenter go to the death house...."

"No more anxious than I am...Mark.... What disgusting people...and we'll get prison terms for all the remaining 316...now that we finally got the tapes...thanks in no small measure to Roger Morrison...."

"Max...you're a good prosecutor...one of the best...but you're going to be up against some very expensive and very good legal talent.... I understand that the Jefferson Smith Defense Fund has already raised several million dollars.... Even Rainey...the former secretary of the interior...contributed a large sum...right after he resigned from the Cabinet.... He would not continue to serve under a Jew...is what he actually wrote in his letter of resignation.... Can you imagine putting something like that in writing.... It's frightening...."

"And you want me to get some very good talent too...?"

"Look...Max...even the best of us can use help.... It's no reflection on your ability...but if I myself were in your position...I would do exactly what I'm suggesting you do...."

"You know...Mark...you're entirely right.... I've thought about it a great deal...and the last thing I would ever want to experience in my life is the acquittal of those two...and the others...or a reversal of a conviction on appeal.... Of course I can use some outstanding talent.... Any recommendations...?"

"Yes...Joel Seligman...."

"Of course.... He's the fellow who beat Roger in the Lancaster murder trial.... But wasn't he Lancaster's lawyer in the Senate impeachment trial...? He's very good...but is he available...? I though he's working for you in Washington...and I must say that so far I welcome the changes you are both helping to bring about...."

"Yes...he is available...and most anxious to take a long leave of absence and become your assistant district attorney for this case...."

"Great...! He has the job...but how do you know he would take this case...?"

"I asked him before I came here...."

The two friends laughed.

When Joel told Naomi that he had agreed to take on the job of prosecuting Smith and Carpenter, Naomi's only reaction was, "I wonder if I can take a leave of absence from GW...and go with you.... Jere and I would not be in the way.... I would otherwise miss you too much...."

"Darling...try to arrange it...and if Max Armstrong agrees that I be the prosecutor...we'll rent a large apartment in Albany...."

"Nonsense...," said Governor William Stromberg of New York when he learned from Max Armstrong that Joel and his family were coming to Albany, "...they are going to stay right here...in the Executive Mansion.... And if Sally and Mark Rosenblueth want to visit...before...during...or after the trial...this is also where they shall stay...." So that is where the junior Seligmans did stay after Naomi insisted on a leave from George Washington and got it after direct intervention by the university president.

Joel brought in Robert Ginsburg and a younger lawyer Jonah Montague as his associates, Robert the former U S Attorney for the District of Columbia and assistant district attorney of New York County, and Jonah, 28, an outstanding graduate of the Columbia University Law School and working for Robert in the New York law firm of Ginsburg & Redding, both taking leaves of absence from the firm, and they along with Joel were appointed assistant district attorneys of Albany County. Robert, now divorced, and Jonah, never married, found a large furnished apartment to share, Robert still disappointed that he did not prosecute the Lancaster murder case as Roger had promised when Robert had moved from Washington to New York.

The trial began two weeks later in a blaze of press coverage rivaling the Lancaster trial in New York, actually breaking a record for any trial in the State outside of New York City, and the coverage was to continue with that intensity throughout the entire proceeding.

Sally and Mark were entirely right about the legal talent that Smith and Carpenter were able to get. It was rumored that their defense fund had reached almost fifty million dollars, and both Sally and Mark, and many others, wondered whether these dollars came from just a few wealthy antisemites or from a very large number of much less wealthy antisemites. While neither situation was welcome, the second was more ominous than the first.

Jackson George was chief defense counsel. A graduate of Harvard Law School, he had immediately made a brilliant career of successfully defending the prodigal sons and daughters of wealthy families, the sons and daughters accused of serious crimes, crimes they felt they could always get away with if they had a good lawyer, and each one of them certainly had the proverbial good lawyer.

"The only thing I can say...," said Joel to Max in a meeting with Robert and Jonah in Max's office, "...is that we are going to have a challenge...but we'll win...so help me God...we shall win...."

"I have complete faith in all three of you...," said Max, "...and if anyone can do it...you can.... Please remember that I...and my entire office...will be available to you.... This is the most important case in the history of this county...."

The trial began the following morning. Max Armstrong, Joel Seligman, Robert Ginsburg and Jonah

Montague appeared for the People, and Jackson George and five other lawyers appeared for the defense. There being only places for three lawyers and the two primary defendants at the defense table, the other three lawyers took their places in the front row of the visitors section just behind the defense table. Smith and Carpenter were to be tried first, and then the remaining three hundred and sixteen, and Smith and Carpenter were presenting a joint defense using the same defense team. To the charge of first degree murder had been added the charge of making an insurrection against the State of New York.

Jackson George was about fifty years old, not a tall man, about five feet nine, and he had a certain air of false geniality about him that deceived most prosecution witnesses before he trapped them and twisted their statements.

As preparation for the trial, the prosecution team had obtained and read the transcripts of the last ten cases that Jackson George had tried. As in any war, it is important to know all about the adversary, not personally, but how he performed on the battlefield.

The presiding judge was Chief Judge Frederick Manning of the Albany County Court, a judge of eleven years with a reputation of cracking down on lawyers, on either side, who tried to perform any tricks, and the chief judge had assigned this case to himself because of its national importance.

TWENTY-EIGHT

On the very first day, even before jury selection began, Max Armstrong introduced Joel, Robert and Jonah to Judge Manning, and stated that Joel would be the chief prosecutor representing the People, pointing out that all three were members of the New York Bar. Max remained in the courtroom for the remainder of the day as Joel took over. Then John Lindsey, one of the six lawyers for the defense and the only one a member of the New York Bar, introduced Jackson George and his four colleagues, announcing that Mr George would be chief defense counsel.

The same initial problem arose in this trial that had arisen in the Lancaster trial, but this time Joel was on the other side. How does the court find a jury of twelve impartial persons, each with a reasonable level of intelligence but without having formed an opinion in the case? Changing the location of the trial to another county in the State would not solve that problem, for the entire country was well aware of what happened. The electronic press had seen to that as a form of entertainment.

Jackson George was not at all cooperative, and insisted on exercising his challenges for cause, hoping to sabotage the trial right from the very beginning. At first, Judge Manning permitted him to do this, but after a reasonable number the judge allowed him no more. George took exception, but the judge knew that a conviction would not be reversed in New York State on the ground that the judge did not allow challenges for cause beyond some reasonable limit. Exasperated, the judge called both Joel Seligman and Jackson George into his chambers, and told them he was going to select the jurors purely at random, by using a goldfish bowl right in the courtroom, much as in the Lancaster case.

A jury was selected that very afternoon containing a mix of men and women of different religions, races and education levels. Joel and his two associates were not particularly happy with the jury, for it seemed to contain a few rather uneducated people, and they were concerned about the possibility of a "hung jury," or even worse the possibility of an acquittal regardless of the evidence for the People. But Jackson George was even less happy, for he felt that the best he could get was a "hung jury." The jury were to be locked up in one of the better in-town hotels, and were to remain incarcerated and guarded in that way for the duration of the trial when not in the courtroom, for Judge Manning did not want this case tried in the press.

"Mr Seligman...are you ready for your opening statement...?" asked Judge Manning.

"Yes...Your Honor.... Ladies and gentlemen of the jury...the People will show by conclusive evidence...beyond a reasonable doubt...that Jefferson Smith and Roy Carpenter committed the premeditated murder of Mary Rosenblueth...of her two children...Saul and Miriam Rosenblueth...and of Martin Angleton and Sidney Lansing...as the result of the deliberate shooting down of the helicopter in which Mrs Rosenblueth and her two children were passengers....and Mr Angleton and Mr Lansing were the pilots.... The two defendants were part of an uncontrollable mob of 318 people marching on the governor's Executive Mansion in Albany to deliberately murder Mark Rosenblueth...then the Governor of this State.... Governor Rosenblueth insisted that his family leave the Executive Mansion for safety...but that he as Governor would remain.... When the helicopter took off...one of the defendants...Roy Carpenter...acting under the order of the other defendant...Jefferson Smith...deliberately fired a missile...using a hand-held launcher...that struck the helicopter...thus causing it to crash.... All of these facts...ladies and gentlemen of the jury...we will show by conclusive evidence.... The People will ask for the death penalty for this heinous...unconscionable crime.... Thank you...Your Honor...."

"Mr George...."

"Your Honor...ladies and gentlemen of the jury.... We will not dispute the evidence...showing that the defendant...Roy Carpenter...fired the weapon that destroyed the helicopter...and we will not dispute the fact that Jefferson Smith ordered that the weapon be fired...but we have pleaded not guilty to the charge of first-degree murder and insurrection because whatever the defendants did they were justified in doing.... Opposing Mark Rosenblueth...and even killing him to oppose him...was justified...and the killing that arose from the behavior of the defendants was therefore justified.... Showing justification will be the essence of the case for the defense...."

Justified! Joel thought, in what possible manner could the murder of a woman and her two children be justified?

The case-in-chief for the prosecution went rather slowly, as Joel, and oftentimes Robert or Jonah in his stead, presented the evidence. Robert Ginsburg presented the video tapes of the electronic press, tapes that not only showed the motions and faces of the defendants but also clearly had recorded their voices. In the witness chair to buttress the visual evidence were the reporters and cameramen who had taken the motion pictures and who had been witnesses to the entire continuing scene.

"Then why did you not do something about it...if you felt that the defendants were about to commit a crime...?" asked Jackson George in the cross-examination of one of the reporters, trying to show that even the reporters did not feel that an unjustified action was about to be committed and then actually committed, but he did not get the answer he expected.

"We don't interfere in anything we're reporting.... Our purpose is to report it...not play any role in what we have been sent by our news organization to report...."

In the re-direct examination of this particular witness, Jonah asked whether he and his colleagues would actually refrain from preventing a murder even if they were in a position to prevent it, and the answer was that they would refrain from preventing the crime. Are these people from another planet? again thought Joel.

Jackson George did his best to try to damage the credibility of the witnesses and of the tapes, as any good defense lawyer would, in order to instill in the jury's collective mind some substantial feeling of a reasonable doubt. But re-direct examination by Joel or Robert or Jonah skillfully put that reasonable doubt aside.

The prosecution's case went on for many days, and at the end of the last day, the judge heard the usual motion that the case be dismissed because of the prosecution's failure to make a case, a motion Judge Manning denied. Judge Manning then recessed the trial until ten o'clock the following morning, at which time the defense would present its case-in-chief subject to the cross-examination of defense witnesses by the prosecution.

At about a quarter past ten the following morning, Judge Manning announced the beginning of the presentation for the defense. "You may call your first witness...Mr George...."

"We do not intend to call witnesses...Your Honor...and our sole piece of evidence will be the very copy of the Bible that your bailiff has been using in this trial to swear in the witnesses for the prosecution...." A loud noise rumbled through the courtroom, and Joel instinctively now realized how Jackson George intended to justify the killing of Mary Rosenblueth and her two children, and how he intended to justify the motivating desire to kill Mark Rosenblueth. Judge Manning, a look of some perplexity on his face, banged his gavel down many times to reduce the noise to a bare, unheard whisper. "May I use that copy of the Bible...Your Honor...?"

Still somewhat perplexed, Judge Manning ordered the bailiff to give the copy to him. It was a copy of the Jewish Holy Scriptures, renamed by Christians the Old Testament when plagiarized, and of the Christian New Testament, both bound together to make up the Christian Bible, and this particular Christian Bible in English was a copy of the King James Version first published in the year 1611.

Joel stood up, and asked, "Your Honor...if Mr George intends to use the King James Version of the Christian Bible...may we have a brief recess to obtain our own copy...if the court does not have an additional copy for me...another for Mr Ginsburg...and another for Mr Montague...."

"I am sure that the court clerk can provide you with other copies...within a few minutes.... Mrs Appley...would you be so kind as to obtain several other copies.... We will recess for fifteen minutes...."

Alone in a conference room assigned to them for the trial, Joel met with Robert and Jonah.

"I think his strategy is obvious...," said Jonah. "Whether you know it or not...Joel...my family are English Jews...descended from one of the branches of the Montague family...and I can smell the beginning of a very antisemitic activity...of a kind used on some occasions in the distant past in England...."

"I agree...," responded Robert, "...and I wager he'll use the passages in the Gospels that damns all Jews...for eternity...because of the Roman execution of the rabbi...Jesus of Nazareth...."

"Yes...," said Joel, "...I realized that...as soon as he asked for the Christian Bible.... We can't permit him to use such a defense.... He would be using the courtroom as a forum for the worst antisemitic filth imaginable.... Those passages are among the foundations of two thousand years of hell on earth for the Jews.... Now...the question is...how do we stop it...? Jackson George is really a snake...defending two snakes...and no better than they are...to use the Christian Gospels to justify the murder of a Jewish woman and her Jewish children...in an attempt to kill a Jew...Mark Rosenblueth...trying to destroy a good Christian...James Lancaster...."

"I think we need a session with Judge Manning in his chambers...," suggested Jonah. "He's been very fair...and he might be able to make such writings inadmissible...on the grounds that it involves Christian teachings...and I don't mean the Jewish teachings in Christianity...but the anti-Jewish teachings in

Christianity...in the enforcement of the laws of a secular State...."

"Very good...," exclaimed Joel, "...but it's imperative that we completely keep this away from the jury.... Jackson George has thrown a bundle of dynamite into the courtroom...and we must defuse it before it goes off.... Now for tactics.... I feel we ought to go back into the courtroom...and immediately ask for a another recess for George and me to meet with Judge Manning in his chambers.... I can always use as a reason...if I need one...in requesting the meeting...that the defense appears to be a most unusual one...and that therefore the prosecution is entitled to have some advanced understanding of the general nature of the case for the defense...in order to be able to prepare rebuttals...."

"I think that should work...," Robert commented. "I can't think of a better approach.... Can you...Jonah...?"

"No...I cannot.... It's very good...."

"OK...," Joel said, "let's get back into the courtroom...and do our best...."

"Your Honor...may we approach the bench...?"

Judge Manning beckoned both Jackson George and Joel Seligman to come up to his raised desk. "What do you have in mind...Mr Seligman...."

"This defense strategy is most unusual.... I feel that Mr George and I ought to meet with you in chambers for a short while to ascertain its basic nature.... It is only fair that the People have some general idea of the defense's case in order to be able to prepare suitable rebuttal.... The defense has caught us completely by surprise...and just as the People are not supposed to catch the defense by surprise...a reciprocal responsibility falls on the defense...."

"What do you think....Mr George...?"

"I have no objection to such a meeting...and I suspect that Mr Seligman's motivation for the meeting is other than strictly honorable...."

"That kind of talk will not be permitted in my courtroom...Mr George...even outside the hearing of the jury.... Please return to your chairs...gentlemen...."

Judge Manning called a recess for one hour, and asked both Joel Seligman and Jackson George to meet with him in his chambers.

"Alright...Mr Seligman...what is it...?"

"Mr George is an excellent lawyer...but so am I.... I would wager any amount that Mr George intends to introduce those passages in the Gospels of the New Testament...those passages that damns the Jews for eternity...just because someone wrote...several centuries after the event...that the Jews shall always be held responsible for the death of Jesus...a rabbi from Nazareth.... If I were Mr George...and completely oblivious of the consequences...that's what I would do to try to justify the killing of Jews...but do the passages justify the killing of two Christians...the pilot and co-pilot of that helicopter...?"

"But they were helping the Jews to escape the wrath of God...!" exclaimed Jackson George most vehemently, "...and they too deserved to die...."

Judge Manning was appalled by this verbal outbreak,

and needed a moment or two to compose himself. "Mr George...I have seen all kinds of evil presented in my courtroom...but never before by a member of the bar.... I shall not permit you to enter the Bible in evidence...unless you also intend to enter the Ten Commandments...from the Old Testament...and especially the Commandment Thou shalt not kill...!"

"Then...Your Honor...we have no case.... You have destroyed the case for the defense...and I shall not permit you to do this...."

"Mr George...it is obvious that what you want to do is to use my courtroom as a pulpit to preach antisemitism...as my Sunday school teachers preached antisemitism...to incite another American Kristallnacht.... I am sorry...Mr George...but I will not have it.... If you have no further defense...then I shall expect both you and Mr Seligman to present your closing arguments to the jury...."

"Judge Manning...you are a Christian...and I am a Christian...and the defendants are Christians...and these three prosecutors are Jews...at least two of them are...and you as a Christian will permit these Jews to crucify two Christians...."

"Mr George...I have really had enough from you.... Now you and Mr Seligman will both go back into the courtroom...and present your summations...for otherwise I shall hold you in contempt of court...and I am warning you...Mr George...that if you insinuate this defense in your summation...in any way...I shall hold you in criminal contempt of court...and will then sentence you to the maximum prison term allowed by the laws of this State.... Your summation will deal with the flaws...as you see them...in the prosecution's case.... Nothing more...! Do you understand me...Mr George...?"

"Yes...I do...but if the defendants are convicted because of your refusal to permit me to present our defense...as I see it ought to be presented...then we shall of course appeal...."

"You are entitled to an appeal...Mr George...but you will find the appellate courts of this State equally inhospitable to your efforts to use the law courts to preach antisemitism...."

Jackson George followed the strictures of the judge in his summation, feeling that all he had to do was to transfer his efforts to the appeal courts. He and his associates, and their clients, were not going to miss any opportunity to use the institutions of a free society to spread whatever filth they wanted to spread.

Judge Manning issued his instructions to the jury, and it took them only three hours and forty-five minutes to return a verdict of guilty. Following the required pre-sentencing investigation and report, Judge Manning awarded to both Jefferson Smith and Roy Carpenter the punishment of death!

TWENTY-NINE

Although Judge Manning could keep rabid antisemitism out of his courtroom, he could not prevent Jackson George from announcing to a large number of reporters, right on the steps of the courthouse, why he lost the case. Antisemitism, in its most virulent form, was once again now out in the open, but at least it had not been permitted in America to legally justify homicide, not yet.

Joel and Naomi prepared to leave Albany with thanks to Governor and Mrs Stromberg for their hospitality, and before they actually did, Joel together with Robert Ginsburg and Jonah Montague had a farewell meeting with Max Armstrong. Max remarked how flabbergasted he was by the defense antics in the trial, but in his own thoughts, he was glad that Joel was the prosecutor, rather than he, because it was possible, just possible, that Max might not have caught the significance of the request to enter the Bible as a defense exhibit, might not have caught it early enough to prevent it from happening.

Since Robert and Jonah were returning to their homes in New York City, and the junior Seligmans wanted to see the senior Seligmans before they moved on to Washington, all of them traveled together in a rented luxury sedan with Jonah doing most of the driving, with Robert in the front passenger seat occasionally relieving him, and with Joel very comfortable with Naomi and Jeremiah in the back seat. After a few days in New York the junior Seligmans planned to return to the Washington area, and the first thing on Joel's agenda there would be a meeting with the Rosenblueths.

When Jonah reached the Seligman apartment house after the long drive from Albany down the New York Thruway, Joel suggested that both he and Robert come up to his parents' apartment to meet them, and to have some refreshment. The result of their acceptance was an invitation to dinner from Joan Seligman, very gladly accepted, and it was at that dinner that a pubescent Gabrielle met Jonah Montague. Joan quickly sensed her daughter's interest, and also the glimmer of a reciprocal interest by this Mr Montague in a very attractive and bright and rather mature young lady. Could anything meaningful come out of a romance between an older man of twenty-eight and a very young lady of thirteen going on fourteen?

After Robert and Jonah left quite late that evening, and the junior Seligmans left the next day, Joan decided to have a little talk with her younger daughter.

"I know what you are going to say...Mom...but didn't Julia Rosenblueth marry at seventeen...and Abigail at...."

"I get your point...Gaby...but just take it easy.... I know how difficult it is for anyone going through your years.... As Joel once pointed out...that's one of the reasons for the marriage at puberty among the ancient Israelites...and why the Rosenblueths agreed to Julia marrying young.... Just take it easy.... Let's see how this young man feels.... Let's see what he's really like.... Let's see what his family background is.... Joel mentioned that he comes from an old family of English Jews.... In other words...darling...be patient...."

"Of course I'll be patient.... I'm still a child...yet I am a woman...but can you sort of invite Jonah to dinner sometimes...together with Robert Ginsburg for the time being...you know...just to give me and Jonah a chance to see each other again.... He seems like such a nice man...."

Joan smiled. "Yes...he does...and I think you are a very fine young lady...and yes...we shall certainly invite him from time to time...but as one woman to another...let's not make it too obvious...."

Although he had kept Sally and Mark continually informed by phone from Albany of developments in the trial, this first dinner meeting with them at the White House now gave Joel the opportunity to fully discuss the bombshell that Jackson George had thrown into the trial, and its aftermath.

"Sally and I felt that something like that would happen...but I'm surprised he alternatively did not use... as a mitigating excuse...the exhortion by James Lancaster to violence against the Jews...although as a lawyer he fully knew that would probably get him nowhere...."

"Well...my dear sirs...," said President Rosenblueth, "...the time has come for this President to undo the harm done by her predecessor.... I intend to go on the major networks...and speak to the nation on this evil...and specifically against Jackson George and his kind.... Yes...I know that I'm not supposed to interfere in a continuing criminal case...and the case in continuing because of the appeal...but this is really not an ordinary criminal case.... It is something else...and I shall interfere in it regardless of what you want to call it...."

"I completely agree with you...Sally...," said Naomi. "This is a threat...not only to the American Jews...all six million of us...but also a threat to our free American society.... The two murderers in Albany were apparently sacrificed...by a group of American neo-Nazis...to publicize their horrible propaganda...and Sally must use her full prestige as the President to scotch the snake.... If any form of official sanction is given to a doctrine that justifies the killing of Jews...just because they are Jews...then who are next...the Catholics...?"

"Yes...," said Sally, "...there's still a great deal of anti-Catholic sentiment in the United States...certainly not as strong as the anti-Jewish...but strong enough to be a potential problem....."

"Well...," said Mark, "...I'm not at all sure I agree with either of you...." And that statement seemed to cause a verbal bombshell, right in that private dining room.

Joel, deep in thought, said nothing, but Sally immediately asked, "For God's sake...Mark...why not...?"

"Let me start from the beginning.... The agony of the Jews goes back to ancient times...well before the life of Jesus.... The Jews lived as a small nation surrounded by the pagan world...and that world included the Greek and the Roman...both pagan civilizations revered throughout subsequent Western civilization.... The Jews were hated even then because they would not in any way tolerate homosexuality...infanticide...the glorification of prostitution.... As a matter of fact...among the more cultured Greeks and Romans...sexual intercourse with one's wife was only for the purpose of begetting legitimate children.... Sexual intercourse with prostitutes...euphemistically called courtesans...and homosexual intercourse...were considered to be on a much higher civilized plane.... As a matter of fact...homosexual carnality was called Greek love...and infanticide...well...that was but one step away from human sacrifice.... The ancient Jews would not accept any of this...not a bit...and for this they were called stiff-necked.... And the reason they would not accept Christian theology when it came along...espoused by a Hellenized Jew...was because it was pagan.... After all...if they wouldn't accept Roman paganism...why should they accept this Greek version...?" Mark paused, and Sally and Naomi, and Joel too, waited patiently for him to continue.

"And for their refusal to accept a pagan theology...the Jews were...for two thousand years...reviled by the Christians.... The Gospels of the New Testament are as antisemitic a literary collection as you would find anywhere...and when the two primary Christians festivals...of Easter and Christmas...are celebrated...even today...the antisemitic story of how Jesus came to be executed is celebrated each time...twice a year...and once weekly on Sunday...as they have been for two thousand years...as a verbal assault on the Jews.... Historically...these two pagan festivals were the occasion for massive physical violence against the Jews throughout all of Christendom.... Christendom has become a bit more civilized...and does not permit outright pogroms...but the behavior of the Jefferson Smiths and the Roy Carpenters is actually sanctioned by Christian history.... Martin Luther was a rabid antisemite...and so was William Blake...one of the leading English poets...and so was William Shakespeare...even at a time when there were no Jews in England.... The Vatican...and only very recently...has tried to mitigate the antisemitism of the Gospels...but not one word of the New Testament has been changed...and people can now read...and be lectured to as if they were idiots unable to understand what they are reading...and we still have the Gospels presented at every opportunity as though they represented the highest level of God's achievement...where in actuality they could not have possibly been inspired by God...."

"Then what can be done...?" asked Naomi.

"The problem is actually more complicated...," responded Mark, seemingly avoiding her question. "We now live in an age of almost complete moral breakdown.... I use the word moral strictly in the Jewish sense.... We see the dawning of an age of homosexuality...of infanticide...euphemistically renamed abortion...of glorified prostitution.... Judaism now faces...not only the inexorable continuation of the embedded hatred of the Christian Gospels...but also the hatred of our modern-day pagans who exult in homosexuality... infanticide...glorified prostitution.... It's a battle that Judaism cannot hope to win...against a combination of theologically devout Christians...Christians who have forgotten...or even ever knew...that their morality is actually Jewish...and outright pagans...who hate the stiff-necked Jews just as the ancient pagans hated the ancient stiff-necked Jews.... Sally...you can go on the air and urge everyone to be tolerant...but man is not built that way.... The ancient Jews tried to maintain their morality in the isolation of their small kingdoms...but they were powerless against the pagans...the Assyrians...and the Romans.... Today...Israel reborn...in some tenuous way a restoration of the ancient state...tries to survive in a sea of mankind totally hostile to it...and the Jews of the Diaspora still try to lie low...not to make waves...as they try to survive as Jews in a non-Jewish world...." Mark suddenly stopped.

"Then you say we can do nothing...," Sally said, "...but something has to be done...."

"No...I agree that something ought to be done...but

I doubt whether any good will come of it.... Lancaster...when he was an embattled President...officially opened the floodgates of antisemitism...resulting in Mary's death...and in the death of my children...and it was only the innate decency of a trial judge in Albany County that did not permit antisemitism to flourish in his courtroom.... But there are many other trial judges in this country...and by the laws of probability...I'm sure we can find at least one who will not prevent his courtroom from being used as a forum for antisemitism.... Jackson George and his crowd will find that judge...and they will kill a Jew in that county just because he is a Jew...and then the press will have its usual gala field day covering the trial.... Yes...Sally...go on the air...and try to stem the tide.... What I have been saying is that I very much doubt it will be very effective...but I do agree that for you to do nothing might be even worse.... Right now...I just don't know...."

"I can't help but agree with Mark...," added Joel, "There have been times...rather recently...since the Albany trial...when I felt that the murder of Naomi's sister might have been the ultimate antisemitic act...." He paused. "...and then there's the question of the next election.... Both of you are very vulnerable to an antisemitic attack...and I'm sure it will arise.... There has been...almost from the time you became President...Sally... much spoken and written about those Jews in the White House.... Are you aware of the basic antisemitic attitude of Roger Morrison's parents...clearly shown in Richmond when Roger married Catherine...? It's true they are ordinary people...but the country is filled with ordinary people...and being extraordinary does not make a person not antisemitic.... I'm not saying that you should not run for re-election...but we should be prepared for this kind of attack...."

"I never doubted it...Joel...and I fully realized what I was doing when I converted to Judaism...but the Jews...when they could stand up...never backed away from a fight...and we should not back away now.... As a matter of fact...while you were both in Albany...Mark and I met with quite a few delegations of leaders of American Jewish organizations...who asked us not to run in the next election...that we would simply make it difficult for the American Jews...to which Mark very forcefully replied...," she smiled a very loving smile at her husband, "...in his inimitable fashion...that the only road for the American Jews to take is to hold their heads high and do what they think it right...or else to transfer both their persons and wealth to the State of Israel...to face a different kind of fight for Jewish survival...that any attempt to temporize would only whet the appetites of their enemies that much further.... You should have heard him...," said his wife, most proudly.

It was at this point in time that the chief of the secret service White House detail broke into the privacy of the President's private dining room to say that a very large ugly mob was marching down Sixteenth Street on its way to the White House, led by Jackson George, and shouting Death to the Jews. "The Metropolitan Police can't stop it.... They can only slow it down...and it's growing very rapidly...."

THIRTY

Sally immediately picked up the telephone to call Allen Redmond and General Wrightson, and instructed them to bring in every military unit from Maryland and Virginia at once, to stop and contain the mob, to arrest its leaders.

"There might be bloodshed...Madame President...," said the Secretary of Defense, "but I realize it can't be avoided...."

"What do we do...to eventually stop this sort of thing...?" rhetorically asked the chairman of the Joint Chiefs.

The military responded promptly to the orders of its leaders, for it appeared that the virus had not spread too strongly, not yet, through the armed forces. Both Allen Redmond and John Wrightson stood squarely behind the President, both of them well respected by the armed forces, a respect they continued to earn.

The mob ran at the first sign of heavily armed troops before them and helicopter gunships above them and Maryland state militia units behind them. Jackson George and the other leaders were arrested and held without bond for trial, and Sally commented to Mark in the privacy of their breakfast room the next morning, "Here we go again.... When does it all stop...?"

Joseph Langdon, the U S Attorney for the District of Columbia, was a holdover from the brief Lancaster administration because Attorney General Raymond Singleterry felt at the time that there was no need to replace him. But now there was a need, not only to replace him but also to replace Raymond Singleterry, for in the first few days after the arrest of Jackson George, Langdon and Singleterry did absolutely nothing. Both of them were invited to resign, which they did. Raymond Singleterry was immediately replaced by Thomas O'Leary, in private practice in New York City, formerly Sally's chief deputy attorney general in New York State, before then the Judge Advocate General of the Army, and originally a New York University law graduate. And at O'Leary's recommendation, Langdon was replaced with Robert Ginsburg, the former U S Attorney for the nation's capital, all the while the Washington Chronicle bitterly criticizing President Rosenblueth, a habit as deeply embedded as a narcotics addiction. The Senate confirmed the O'Leary and Ginsburg nominations the following day.

Robert moved back to Washington from New York,

but Jonah was reluctant to join him, having found Gabrielle Seligman more interesting the more time he spent in her company. But after a few days of hesitation, he did decide to join Robert, and Gabrielle immediately implored her parents to let her live with her step-brother Joel in Alexandria, a prospect that Naomi quickly endorsed having decided to join in this conspiracy.

As for Thomas O'Leary, widower, grandfather, former collegiate football star, and successful New York lawyer, he overnight became one of the stars of the Washington social scene, but first to the urgent business at hand.

The very day after their joint arrival in Washington, Thomas and Robert went to the District of Columbia jail to interview Jackson George, trying if they could to offer the prisoner his life in return for information on the true ring-leaders behind these insurrectionary movements, the people who were providing the money and the direction.

"You realize you face the death penalty...for felony murder...," warned the Attorney General. "Several innocent people were killed by your mob...in the course of your insurrection.... Now...if you want to save your life...you had better give us some information.... Now...where does the money come from...?"

"Much of it actually comes from abroad...," said Mr George to the not-too-surprised Messrs O'Leary and Ginsburg.

"Do you know where...?"

"Not really...but I would guess most of it comes

from the Middle East...."

"Who gives you the money...?"

"John Rainey...and he practically commutes between Houston and the Middle East...."

"Do you have other names...?"

"Yes.... Alpherson Zegretta...of Phoenix.... Barbara Smythe...of New York.... And Abdullah Aboudi...of Houston.... They are the people with whom I have met...to plan strategy...."

At Attorney General O'Leary's direction, the U S Attorney for the District of Columbia immediately obtained federal warrants for the arrest of the three named by Jackson George, and the warrants were efficiently enforced by the local FBI offices in those three cities. Those arrested were brought before federal magistrates in those federal judicial districts, all held without bond, then transported by the special planes of the U S Marshals Service to Washington, and committed to the District of Columbia jail. Robert very carefully arranged for none of the three and none of the leaders of the Washington mob to be part of the jail's general population, but to instead keep them all isolated from each other and from the other inmates.

This time at the new Attorney General's request, Joel again took a leave of absence from his position with the Council of Governors, was temporarily designated the President's special legal counsel, not to be a prosecutor but to be an investigator, to try to ferret out the other conspirators who were nourishing the latent antisemitism in the United States, to find out who had conspired against the lives of the then Governor of New York and now against the President and Vice President of the United States, solely because of their Jewish faith.

The secret service guard around Sally and the other members of her family was doubled, one was set up for Chief Justice Benjamin, and now their children were further restrained in what they could do, but it was all for their safety. The guard around the White House grounds was quadrupled, and the usual tours of the White House were suspended.

Joel began to investigate some of Lancaster's old associates, the ones who had been close to him during his entire political career, and who were his primary fund raisers. Joel did not feel that Lancaster had suddenly become antisemitic just because he was under such heavy pressure from Mark Rosenblueth, but that Lancaster himself was planning sooner or later while President to make an overt government move against the American Jews, that it was only the issue of the murder of Naomi's sister that had re-directed his major plan.

And then there were several Arab diplomats with whom James Lancaster had been very friendly when a Senator and continued to be when he became President. What role, if any, did they play? Even if they were as guilty as hell, the Attorney General could not have them arrested because of diplomatic immunity, but they could be declared undesirable by President Rosenblueth and forced to leave the country. In any case, the heads of many Arab diplomatic missions in the United States had found it very difficult to deal with a woman President, especially with a Jewish woman President, and American diplomatic relations with those Arab nations had quickly become very formal.

While Thomas O'Leary was back in his office in the Department of Justice Building, planning a concerted nationwide legal offensive against the conspiracy, in cooperation with the attorney general of each of the States, a plan to be presented to President Rosenblueth for her approval and to the Council of Governors through Mark Rosenblueth for their approval, Robert and Joel interviewed each of the three persons recently arrested and now languishing in the District of Columbia jail. Their very expensive lawyers were still unable to get them out on bail, and jail was not the kind of experience each once particularly liked. They were more used to their country clubs, the traditional breeding places for the more sophisticated American antisemites. Robert and Joel felt that the most vulnerable of the three was Barbara Smythe, and they were right.

Mrs Smythe, a very wealthy widow in her sixties, ordinarily well-groomed and now unable to understand why she was being charged with conspiracy, the chairwoman of many New York City campaigns to raise funds for the arts, a significant contributor in her own name, Barbara Smythe simply hated the Jews. Was there a crime in that? she asked. No, said Joel, if that was as far as it went, but that hatred became a crime when the hater caused someone harm because of it. When Joel asked her why she hated the Jews, she could not at first answer, even though she would have answered if she had the answer, and when the answer finally did come it sounded right out of the Nun's Tale, from Chaucer's Canterbury Tales, a bitter reminder of the blood libel levied against the Jews since the twelfth century, the libel embedded in the literature of the English-speaking world.

With an offer of considerable leniency before her, Mrs Smythe literally became a fountainhead of information, and began to implicate so many prominent people, in politics, in business, in the universities, in the press, in the entertainment world, even in the churches, that Joel felt that this information had to be independently verified. It was as though a particular stone had been overturned leaving a large multitude of crawling creatures now in full view.

And even if Joel were able to corroborate this information and then prove in a courtroom that these "sustaining patrons of the arts," these "pillars of the community," were actually part of a massive conspiracy to make Amerika Judenrein, and as part of that conspiracy to kill the three most important public figures in the United States, three because Chief Justice Samuel Benjamin would have to be included, then what? Might it not all be turned around by their very able defense counsel, and publicized by the press, that this was not a trial of Christian conspirators against the American Jews but that instead the entire criminal justice proceeding against the conspirators was in itself a Jewish conspiracy again them as stalwart American Christians.

Once Joel and Robert left the District of Columbia jail, they immediately went to the Attorney General's office to meet with Thomas O'Leary, to discuss the astounding information they had just gotten from Barbara Smythe.

"This list reads like a social who's who...," commented the federal attorney general, "...and as we all realize...that is going to make this an extremely difficult case.... We're up against a profound dysfunction in our society...and I'm aware of where it came from...a dysfunction now manifested by very serious criminal behavior...and from time to time will again break out in the form of criminal behavior.... We can try to punish everyone involved in this current outbreak of the disease...but how do we cure the disease itself....? I've known Sally and Mark too long...and respect them too highly...to feel that they...or anyone else...should be sacrificed to the misguided...who demand their heads in the name of a fellow Jew...."

Jackson George and henchmen pleaded guilty to felony murder and to the making of an insurrection, and were sentenced to spend the remainder of their lives in a maximum-security federal prison without possibility of parole.

To the astonishment of those listed in the social register, Mrs Barbara Smythe pleaded guilty, although to a much lesser felony charge, and was sentenced to the time she had already spent in prison, to be followed by ten years of probation.

The other two named by Jackson George once again pleaded not guilty to the charges of conspiring to murder the President and Vice President and to make an insurrection, and their trials were placed on the docket of the U S District Court for the District of Columbia.

As though to give thanks for the very swift collapse of the Washington insurrection, Sally and Mark hosted a dinner at the White House for all of their family and close friends. Jonah Montague escorted Gabrielle Seligman. Allen Redmond came with Mrs Alberta Redmond, John Wrightson with Mrs Martha Wrightson, Robert Ginsburg with his new fiancee Hannah Weissmann. And the entire family came from New York, Richmond and the Washington area. Thomas O'Leary escorted his stunning New York law partner Sian McAlester, she in Washington from New York just for this dinner. Also attending were Samuel Alvarez and the ambassadors of Italy, Spain, Denmark and the Netherlands, together their wives, the ambassadors who had strongly supported Israel in the midst of Lancaster's attempt to destroy the Jewish state and continue the Nazi holocaust.

As to the basic question Thomas O'Leary had restated in that meeting in his office with Joel and Robert, and which inexorably now came up in the course of conversation after dinner, neither he nor any of the family nor any of their close friends could come up that evening with an answer, but in a moment alone with Mark Rosenblueth, Umberto Rossi asked for a private meeting the following day with Mark and his wife.

THIRTY-ONE

"Sally...," said Mark the following morning at breakfast, "...after dinner last night...during our milling about among our guests...Umberto Rossi briefly took me aside to ask for a private meeting with both of us...to include Samuel Alvarez...Niels Bohr...Pieter van der Vere...Count Nordlinger...and the new Spanish ambassador...Jose Martinez.... Undoubtedly about Lancaster...."

"I would assume so.... He'd ordinarily go through the Secretary of State to ask for a meeting.... It's been some months since Lancaster went to prison in New York.... Whatever happened to all the other criminal charges against him...in Virginia...and here in the District...and the federal charges...?"

"They were all eventually dropped because none of them would result in the death penalty.... None of them would be any more punitive than in New York...."

"We did promise Alvarez we'd extradite Lancaster to Israel if he were not executed in the United States...and Samuel's been very patient...but off-hand I don't know how to make good on that promise without stirring up the antisemites...."

"Neither do I...but we must make good in some respect on the promise.... Shall I arrange the meeting...?"

"Yes...and please make it as soon as possible...say early next week...which ought to be enough time to give that brilliant mind of yours a chance to work out a solution to the dilemma...."

Mark returned the smile with a kiss over the table. "But not before the genius of Mrs Rosenblueth comes up with an answer...," which now prompted another kiss, but this time from the President to the Vice President. "Shall I talk to Joel about it...?"

"Yes...I think that would be a good idea...," said Sally. "We need all the legal brilliance we can get for this one...." She paused. "Now would be a good time to inform Tom O'Leary of the situation...and to bring him in on the meeting...."

"Of course.... I'll talk to him...although he's been very heavily occupied...personally...with his law partner...while she's been in Washington.... Interestingly...she's Jewish...not Catholic...."

"Very interesting indeed.... One doesn't ordinarily think of an Irishman...or Irishwoman...being Jewish...."

"Well...there are at least four synagogues in Dublin...."

"She impressed me as being very bright...as well as extremely attractive...," commented Sally. "Perhaps she might also attend the meeting.... I think she can be trusted...but perhaps you might further look into it before you actually invite her...."

Mark went to Observatory Circle that afternoon, after completing some urgent work in the White House, to talk to Joel, and there related how Lancaster was found and brought back to the United States.

"And I suppose the Israelis and their European friends want him put on trial for crimes against humanity...."

"Absolutely correct.... We have a request from Umberto Rossi for a meeting of the ambassadors with Sally and me at the White House...and we want you and Tom O'Leary to attend.... I still have to brief Tom as I just briefed you...."

"I think you should also invite Sian McAlester.... She's a brilliant lawyer...and has already had several cases involving international law.... Her father was one of our prosecutors at Nuremburg...."

"Do you think she can be trusted to keep this all confident until we work out a practical way to turn Lancaster over to the Israelis for trial...?"

"I think so...and incidentally...she and Tom plan to get married...."

"Well...good for Tom...and for her...."

"As we speak...Mark...I'm trying to formulate in my mind the legal arguments on both sides of an Israeli request for extradition.... I'm sure you and Sally will have your heads full trying to work out the political aspects.... American antisemites...and we know there are quite a few...and many of them in high places...will have a field day emphasizing...over and over again...how un-American it would be to turn a former President over to the Jews to persecute him...just as they persecuted Jesus...although they didn't persecute Jesus...but the truth usually does not count for much in these situations...."

"Sally and I are both entirely aware of the problems...both legal and political.... It might set a dangerous precedent to subject a President to this potential jeopardy.... It might inhibit him in his conduct of foreign affairs...."

"Oh...I think a very clear distinction can be made for what Lancaster did against Israel.... The alleged nuclear blackmail of the Israelis could have been very quickly proved by displaying the nuclear bombs...but even then...those bombs could have been planted by Lancaster's orders.... And if it were argued that Lancaster had no congressional sanction...either by an authorizing resolution...like the Gulf of Tonkin resolution which was the legal hook for Kennedy bringing America into the Vietnam morass...or by a declaration of war...or by a congressional appropriation of funds for the military operation...then Lancaster could argue that he had no time to get the sanction...but on the other hand this was not a situation where a decision had to be made with a time limit...although Lancaster could argue that if he did not act quickly...those nuclear bombs could have been set off.... And then one asks what bombs...? which takes us through the whole vicious cycle once again...."

"No question...no question at all about that circular argument.... As for the political situation...I'm sure you can imagine how it would appear for an American government to turn a former President over to any foreign country for trial...for something he did as President...even though what he did was criminal...."

"Well...Mark...something has to be done to demonstrate that a President can't use...with impunity...the awesome military power of the United States to just go ahead and destroy another country...making this decision himself.... You asked me to help bring this country back to the federation of States that this nation was intended to be...and that Constitution...that compact the States entered into...that compact requires that war-making be sanctioned by Congress through a declaration of war.... The President is authorized by the Constitution to act on his own only in the case of invasion or domestic insurrection...but not to wage aggressive war against another country without congressional approval...."

"I entirely agree...Joel...but what is the mechanism...? The Israelis have a case...and the only reason they still exist is because of their own military fortitude...."

"You know...Mark...after Joan was raped by her own son...obviously goaded into it by his father...I felt that I would arrange some way to have Lancaster killed in prison.... He truly does not deserve to live...and I'm sorry I was instrumental in saving his life.... Having him killed can still be arranged...which would make this Israeli request moot...but as I think more about it...I feel that an example has to be made...not of Lancaster personally...but of any President who engages is the monstrous abuse of power that Lancaster did.... If there were only grounds for trying him for crimes against humanity in an American court...."

"And have him acquitted by a sympathetic jury...? Or have a jury deadlock...? That's too risky...."

"What about an international tribunal...set up by the countries that have diplomatically supported Israel...? Then the Jewish factor does not so forcefully enter...."

"That is a possibility...but none of the countries has a death penalty...and the judges chosen by them might follow the policy of their countries...." He paused. "Let's start all over again on this.... It seems to me that Israel would formally request extradition through diplomatic channels... but that the request would then be transmitted to the Governor of New York since Lancaster is in the custody of New York.... The decision would have to be made by the State of New York...as to whether the State wishes to turn him over for trial to another jurisdiction...and we can consider that the State of Israel...although a foreign country...is but another jurisdiction.... As a matter of fact...if Bill Stromberg decides not to give him up...then I feel there's nothing that can further be done...."

"Let's take a step back for a minute...Mark...and look at the forest instead of the trees.... What if Lancaster's crime against Israel were his only high crime...not one additional to the murder he committed...would we extradite him...?"

"I doubt it.... We cannot extradite ex-Presidents to every country that feels it has a grievance against him...or her...no matter how justified it might be appear to some.... Which of course means that we would be acting against Lancaster only because he is already incarcerated...not because the extradition has sufficient merit of its own...."

"Exactly...which means we must have a mechanism for trying him...in America...for his crime against Israel.... We cannot have an ex-President answer to a foreign country...no matter how worthy that country might be...."

"You're entirely right...Joel...but what is that mechanism...? It cannot be ex poste facto...which would be unfair to anyone accused...."

"Well...America and its allies in the Second World War established the crime...the crime against humanity...fully legalized in America by congressional sanction.... It was not limited in its definition to apply only to the leaders of those countries vanquished in battle...although that might have been what the definers had in mind...and from a strictly legal point of view it would not pass constitutional muster because it's too vague...but it's all we have.... I think there would be sufficient justification for establishing an ad hoc court...under a special Act of Congress...to try Lancaster on the charge.... Congress has the constitutional power to establish courts...whether standing or ad hoc...and the only rule would be that the crime exist at the time it was committed...."

"A brilliant idea...Joel.... If Congress will act...then that solves all the political as well as legal problems...and I do agree it might be the only way.... And so as not to violate the restoration of federalism that you and I have been working so hard to achieve...I feel the federal government ought to formally ask the State of New York for extradition rather than assert some federal superiority over New York...."

"Absolutely...and it would emphasize how our system of federalism ought to work.... One sovereignty...the federal...requesting extradition from another sovereignty...but only because the State has custody of the person.... If Lancaster were not incarcerated by New York...then extradition would not be required...for then the federal sovereignty would have direct jurisdiction over the person...."

"That is so...."

"Well...then the next step is for Sally to send a message to the Congress asking for the establishment of special court to try Lancaster for crimes against humanity...."

"Just to make sure...Mark...I would suggest you first talk to William Stromberg in Albany.... For some strange reason...he might not extradite...."

"Yes...of course.... Actually...it would be the courteous thing to do anyway...."

That evening at dinner, Sally conditionally agreed with the approach proposed by Joel Seligman, saying, "...but only if each house of Congress acts with a two-thirds majority.... We are establishing a potentially dangerous precedent...Mark...and I feel that it ought to require an extraordinary majority in each house.... Otherwise...any party returning to power could use this very heavy mechanism against the newly former President...for strictly partisan purposes...and I'm sure they would always be able to conjure up some country willing to assert that it was unduly threatened with annihilation during the previous administration...whether or not that assertion had any foundation in fact.... As for Bill Stromberg...I doubt he would refuse.... He's been our good and loyal friend for many years...and I don't think he would have any political fallout since this would be an American trial of an ex-President...."

"Actually...the more I keep thinking of this entire problem...the more difficult it appears to obtain a proper trade-off between punishing an ex-President for crimes against humanity committed while in office...that on the one hand...and protecting a ex-President...which you will be one day...against partisan abuse of such a precedent.... At least in the event of a President committing a crime...we have the mechanism of impeachment and Senate trial for removal.... Even if you ask Congress to act with a two-thirds majority...your successor could act against you asking for a simple majority vote.... This is going to require more thought...to protect you against a vindictive successor...."

"When you were Governor of New York...Mark...the legislature was the first in the country making the commission of crimes against humanity a statutory crime under state law...."

"Now that you mention it...I remember it clearly...and it was very specific.... The statute made it a crime punishable by death for a President to wage an undeclared war without any sanction by the Congress...such as supporting appropriations of money...and if any citizen of New York was killed as a result of such a war...all of it very specific to make it constitutional under the New York Constitution....

There has been no case that would give the federal supreme court the opportunity to declare it repugnant to the federal constitution...and now that the court can no longer invalidate State laws...the New York statute is still intact...but the statute does allow the trial court the discretion to alternatively sentence a convicted defendant to life imprisonment without parole.... We have to hope that Lancaster would receive the death penalty...."

"Then let New York prosecute Lancaster.... They have him in custody...."

"But the crime was committed when Lancaster was in the District of Columbia...not in New York.... New York might have jurisdiction over the criminal...but it doesn't over the crime...."

"Maybe it does...and it would if Lancaster carried out some part of his aggression against Israel while physically in New York...."

"Well...Lancaster did announce the naval expedition against Israel when he was visiting the Brooklyn Navy Yard...but I think Bill Stromberg would have to obtain the unanimous support of the Governors before bringing Lancaster to trial in New York...just as I did on the charge of murder.... Now that we have a formal Council of Governors...we have a proper mechanism for this...and requiring unanimity would prevent abuse...."

"You needed unanimous support...Mark...because Lancaster was the incumbent President...but an ex-President is a private citizen...and I see no way that any Governor would need any support at all to bring an ex-President to trial on a charge of committing a crime under state law even though not a common-law crime...especially if that law reflects a compelling State interest in protecting the lives of its citizens...."

"True...and I have to always remember that I must look at Lancaster in this situation as an ex-President...and not as a convicted murderer...to avoid setting any kind of precedent that might boomerang against you...which is the very last think I would wish to happen.... We might wish to act honorably in this matter...but that would not require any successor of yours to act honorably...."

"I completely agree...." She paused. "We keep going around in circles...Mark.... Consider a President who has the support of fifty-one senators and two hundred and sixteen representatives to simply go out and destroy another country using America's military might...with no objectively good reason.... It requires only a simple majority and a presidential signature for a constitutional declaration of war.... Such an aggression could never be considered a crime against humanity under American law...yet from a very objective point it might be.... The only possible hook on which we can hang Lancaster is that he acted without a declaration of war.... Even Hitler followed all the appropriate German procedures...in effect at that time...when he declared war on Poland...and after Pearl Harbor on the United States.... I think we have to act against Lancaster legally...not morally.... There's too much immorality in this world...for us to act morally in our affairs with other nations.... And in no way would I wish the United Nations to be involved in any of this.... All that you and I...and our families...can be personally thankful for...in the case of the Jewish state or of any other worthy country...is that it was able to defend itself.... So...let any State of our Union of States try Lancaster...any State that has had a law defining it to be a crime for a President to conduct an aggressive war without a constitutional declaration of war.... And if Lancaster has mitigating circumstances that he can argue...then that's what trials are for...."

"That should be the only meaningful definition of a crime against humanity by an American State...or by the federal government...as applied to the President.... It would apply to Lancaster...but not to you...and it would deter any future President from waging an undeclared war.... It would also prevent any future President from using the United Nations organization as an excuse to wage an undeclared war.... Let me check the New York statute...and statutes of the other States.... Sally...you've come up with the answer to this riddle...."

"I hope so...."

"I know so.... After I check the law...and if New York's statute is properly drawn...then I'm going up to Albany to talk to Bill about this matter...."

THIRTY-TWO

A quick visit to the law library of the Library of Congress confirmed that sixteen States had laws defining a crime against humanity but that only three of them defined the crime specifically in terms of an American President waging war without a congressional declaration of war, a declaration required by the federal constitution, the three States being California, Illinois and New York, all three using almost identical language and all three apparently enacting their laws in reaction to the Korean and Vietnam "wars." The other thirteen States defined the crime only as against the leaders of a foreign state making war against the United States. Every State law provided for the death penalty if any citizen of that State was killed as the result of the military action, and it was in that way that each State made a crime against humanity a matter of compelling interest to the State.

When he returned to the White House, Mark called Allen Redmond at the Pentagon to get a list of all officers and enlisted men killed as a result of the naval battle in the Mediterranean, and of those killed in the American invasion of Canada, the list to include the State of official residence of the person who died.

"Allen...can you have a copy of that list sent to me before six this afternoon...?"

"Yes...of course...Mark.... Shall we fax it...?"

"No...use a trusted messenger...and have it sealed...."

The list arrived at five o'clock, and included nine officers and men from New York killed in the naval action, but more than two hundred killed in the invasion of Canada.

The Vice President reported to the President at dinner, saying, "I'll call Bill Stromberg this evening to ask him to meet me tomorrow...just where he is.... I'll fly up in the morning...and should be back by the end of the day...."

"I'm gratified that New York and the other two States drafted their language to make their definition of the crime one of appropriate interest to the State...."

"So am I...." Mark smiled. "And who was Attorney General of New York when the wording was first drafted...?"

"I stand properly accused...," Sally verbally returned the smile. "But you realize that a person could be extradited for this particular crime only between New York...Illinois... California.... If Lancaster were anywhere else...we might not be able to touch him...even though extradition among the States is required by their federal constitution.... Even our federal statutes do not define the crime in the same manner...and we obviously can't change them to cover a prior act.... It's fortunate Lancaster is already in the custody of New York...."

"And it's also fortunate that we have reverted to our original federalism...to where the federal Supreme Court may no longer review the judgments of the highest court of each State...."

Mark left the next morning on a fast White House helicopter escorted by four army helicopter gunships, arriving in about two hours on the lawn of the Executive Mansion in Albany, Bill Stromberg and his wife waiting for him to join them for lunch. After lunch, Amy Stromberg excused herself, and Mark presented the whole story to his old friend.

"I was actually thinking in the same direction...Mark...but felt there was no urgency.... But from what you just related to me...there is an urgency.... Do you want me in Washington to attend that meeting...?"

"Yes I do...Bill.... It would give everyone direct assurance that New York will proceed.... And it seems to me that if the accused were not in New York...that New York would simply proceed in the usual way to have him extradited...."

"Correct...but obviously unnecessary in this case.... We already have that rat where we want him...but you must realize...Mark...that the statute requires that the Attorney General of New York prosecute in such a case...and that the trial be before the New York Court of Appeals...one of the very few situations in which the court has original jurisdiction...."

"Yes...of course...I remember that the Attorney General is automatically the prosecutor...which is going to present a problem...."

"It certainly is.... Richard Cunningham was a close friend of Lancaster's...just as Askins was...and he might deliberately lose the case.... I don't know what we can do to prevent that.... Lancaster does have a defense.... He can assert that he invaded Canada under his constitutional duty to repel an invasion from Canada...that the American Jews were in a state of insurrection...and that Lancaster had the constitutional duty to suppress insurrections.... You and I know these assertions are all hogwash...but it could introduce enough doubt...even before a court trying him without a jury...to have him acquitted...unless the prosecution very strongly demolishes the defense...and I doubt Cunningham would do that.... Actually...I feel he's more politician than lawyer...and may not have a sufficiently good grasp of the constitutional implications in the case...and Dick is not know for his willingness to take advice.... I ought to know...."

"That's a great problem.... It would be very desirable for Lancaster to be tried in New York because its statute is very specific.... I don't recall reading any passage in the law that would allow by-passing the Attorney General...."

"I don't remember off-hand...but as you well know Richard Cunningham was independently elected with you and me on our party ticket...and it would be very difficult to by-pass an elected official...."

"Well...we'll have to talk to him...and see whether we can persuade him to stand aside in favor of a prosecutor you would designate...."

"Not very likely.... This would be a very high profile case...and good for Cunningham's political career if he wins...which would mean he might challenge me for the governorship in the next primary election...."

"What happens if he stands aside...or resigns his office...?"

"Then I designate the prosecutor...."

"There's a vacancy in the Northern District of New York.... Do you think he would be suitable...and do you feel he would accept...?"

"I feel he'd make a very good judge...and I base that assumption on his prior experience on the state bench.... It's only his long previous connection to Lancaster that bothers me.... As to whether he'll accept...I feel he might.... I'm sure his wife would appreciate having her husband in a prestigious job...without having to campaign every few years.... You'll have to ask him...."

"I will...after I talk to Sally.... We need the best prosecutor there is...."

"As for the defense...there is some basis for one in this case...and I have no doubt that some high-priced lawyers will come out of the woodwork just as they did to defend those people who killed Mary.... Oh...I'm terribly sorry...Mark.... I didn't mean to open old wounds...."

"Not to worry...Bill.... Mary and our children are still very dear in my memory...and Sally knows that...but I've been much more fortunate than most men in having been married to two of the finest women ever created.... A few men are fortunate in having one...."

"Which is my category...Mark...and I hope I go before Amy does.... Back to the prosecutor...if I'm able to name him.... Shall it be Joel Seligman...?"

"Yes...and it would give him a chance to expiate the sin he wrongly feels he committed by saving Lancaster's life in the murder trial...."

"If Joel had not seen the loophole in the prosecution's case...I'm sure Lancaster would have.... But he did exceptionally well in the Jefferson Smith case...managing to instantly understand the defense strategy.... Then it's Joel if he agrees to it...and both Amy and I would look forward to having him and his family staying with us again during this trial in Albany...."

"I know he'll agree to it.... I plan to schedule that meeting with the ambassadors on Monday...and it's now Wednesday.... Can you and Amy come down by Friday afternoon...in time for our Sabbath dinner...and then spend the weekend with us...? It's been too long a time since we've had some social time together...and your coming down will also give you and Amy a chance to renew your acquaintanceship with Joel and Naomi Seligman...."

"Oh yes...the most beautiful woman in Washington...so they say...."

"I would agree.... Then shall Sally and I expect both of you Friday afternoon...?"

"Without question.... We'll look forward to it....

Amy's younger brother Ernest Cartright was recentl widowed by an automobile accident...and is stayin with us...but I don't think he'd mind being left alon until next week.... He's an orthopaedic surgeon o leave from his hospital in Rochester.... No chil dren...."

"Bring him with you.... I'm sure he'll enjoy weekend at the White House.... Oh...and one mor thing...Bill.... I'd suggest you place Lancaster in isol tion...to make sure nothing happens to him before t trial...."

Mark returned to Washington by six that afternoo and reported directly to Sally after she was finish with the meeting she was in.

"Well...Mark...that seems to take care of it...a very nicely too...if we can replace Cunningham wi Joel.... I'll have the FBI run a standard backgrou check on him...very quickly...and talk to Joe Bent and Martin Siegel as to whether there would be trouble confirming him in the Senate.... I do reme ber his judicial career before he ran on your ticket replace me...and it was rather good...." She paus "We have to realize there's still the possibility...eve Lancaster is convicted...that he'll not receive the de penalty...but this upcoming trial would give us at l a second chance against that murderer.... I'm g Amy and Bill are coming down tomorrow...."

"They're bringing Amy's brother with them...at invitation.... He's staying with them after his wi recent death...."

"Fine.... Tom casually mentioned to me before

meeting actually began...the one I just got out of...that Sian McAlester also has her younger sibling...her sister Clara McAlester...with her...in from California.... She's a history professor at the Claremont Colleges...and perhaps might be able to provide Dr Cartright with some needed female company...."

That same early evening, Mark called the ambassadors, beginning with Samuel Alvarez, to invite them all to a meeting at the White House for the following Monday at two in the afternoon, and the next day he had a meeting with Joel, again at Observatory Circle, to relate his visit in Albany. And in the meanwhile, Sally was very busy touching base with the two Senators from New York, and afterwards calling Richard Cunningham to offer him an appointment as a federal district court judge, an offer he most readily accepted without any hesitation. She doubted the FBI would come up with any information that would rule him out.

"Mark...," said Joel, "...that completely takes care of every single aspect of the problem.... We would be able to rightfully go after Lancaster...yet will not set a precedent that might ever involve Sally.... A truly outstanding arrangement...."

"The New York statute requires the designation by the Governor of an ad hoc prosecutor if the Attorney General of New York stands aside...or is not available for other reasons...and Sally is offering Richard Cunningham a federal district court judgeship...not as a quid pro quo to stand aside...but to achieve the same

result by appointing a man with very good judicial qualifications.... Now...if he does accept...both Bill and I want you to prosecute...." Joel's face brightened.

"I'll nail the bastard...and atone for my sin...all at the same time.... You know...it's a good thing Naomi and I kept that co-op apartment of mine in Manhattan.... I think that would be the best place in New York State to prosecute...or does the statute require a specific location...?"

"Yes...it does.... The trial will be without jury before the New York Court of Appeals as part of their original jurisdiction...which means of course that it will be held in Albany.... Bill Stromberg has already invited you and Naomi...through me...to live at the Executive Mansion when you're again in Albany...assuming that Cunningham accepts Sally's offer.... She said she'd call him today...but I won't know the result until I return to the White House.... I'll let you know this evening...."

"I still have to check with Naomi.... It would mean another move...but I feel she'll approve.... I'll let you know tomorrow...."

"Bill and Amy Stromberg will be down early Friday...together with her recently widowed brother...and Sally is also inviting Tom and Sian...and Sian's sister visiting from California.... And of course the Aaronsons will be with us.... So...if you and Naomi have anything really personal to discuss with Sally or me...let's get together just before dinner...or after dinner.... Do you think Jonah Montague...your assistant executive director...can take care of the Council of Governors...or do we need someone else during your absence...?"

"No...Jonah will be an excellent replacement...and he'll always have you if he really needs help...which I doubt will be too often...."

"One last point.... Although the New York law provides for the death penalty...it is not mandatory.... The court could sentence him to life in prison without parole...but it gives us a second chance against him...and we are depending on you...Joel...to get the death penalty...."

"I'll get it...!"

Despite their membership in a reform congregation, Sally and Mark had decided to adopt the more traditional custom of celebrating the opening of the Sabbath at home, and so the following Friday at sundown, with all their dinner guests present, the woman of the house placed her white lace shawl over her head, lighted the Sabbath candles, and intoned the Sabbath prayer in Hebrew and English. The dinner conversation was lively, and Ernest Cartright, seated next to Clara McAlester, the younger image of her sister, Dr Cartright appeared to have left his melancholy elsewhere.

"Sian and I plan to marry in two weeks...," Tom O'Leary announced. "Just a private ceremony by Rabbi Aaronson in our house in Georgetown...and everyone here is of course invited...."

"Your townhouse is too small...," proclaimed the President. "You'll be married here in the White House...and we shall do our best to keep the press from spoiling the occasion...."

"Thank you...Sally...," said Sian. "Tom and I would very much appreciate it...but did not wish to impose...."

"You mentioned Rabbi Aaronson...Tom.... Does that signify anything...?" Mark asked with a broad smile.

"Well...yes.... As you know...Sian is one of those rare creatures...not only one of the most delightful women alive...but also a Jewish Irishwoman.... I'm only a nominal Catholic...and a candidate for conversion...but that can wait until after we are married...when I shall become another of those rare creatures...a Jewish Irishman...."

"...and one of the most delightful men alive...," added Sian to the smiles of everyone.

The next day, in the morning, the Rosenblueths and their house guests attended the regular Saturday services at the Washington Hebrew Congregation, the weekly presence of the First Family always a press event, and in the afternoon, everyone at that dinner the night before, everyone except Naomi Seligman, Amy Stromberg, Clara McAlester and Ernest Cartright, they all met in one of the White House sitting rooms to discuss any lingering problem relating to the upcoming Lancaster trial, and any anticipated difficulty with the ambassadors the following Monday. The meeting did not last very long, for no one could see any problem or difficulty, not even Tom O'Leary and Sian McAlester, especially now that Joel would be the prosecutor replacing Richard Cunningham, but Bill Stromberg and

Joel Seligman, together with their wives, took the opportunity after the meeting broke up to renew their acquaintanceship since the Smith-Carpenter trial.

"I'm very grateful to you...Bill...for giving me this opportunity to hang James Lancaster...."

"As you know...death is the penalty if he's convicted...but it's not mandatory...and you do realize that the defense can argue that what Lancaster did was part of his effort to repel an invasion...and to suppress an insurrection...."

"Yes...I realize that...but I feel confident we can overcome that defense...although I do admit it won't be easy.... I assume I can choose my assistant prosecutors...."

"Yes...of course...any reasonable number.... I'll have to formally appoint them after you choose them.... I'll formally appoint you the special prosecutor...but not before it's necessary...and only after Cunningham is confirmed by the Senate.... He doesn't know of this upcoming trial...and I don't feel we're doing anything untoward by not informing him of our plans.... Once I formally designate you...that will begin the heavy press coverage.... I've already had Lancaster placed in isolation...and well guarded...to make sure nothing happens to him in prison.... We all fully appreciate the significance of this trial...and we don't want to lose the defendant to some other prisoner's illicit knife.... Do you have your chief assistant in mind...?"

"Yes...Sian McAlester...if she'll take the assignment.... She's an exceptionally good trial lawyer...with much criminal law experience in New York...and some cases involving international law.... She and Tom are getting married...as you know.... Well...we shall see...."

"Her sister has already proved an effective tonic for Amy's brother...."

The six ambassadors arrived on Monday at two in the afternoon at the White House, the reporters at the gate immediately noting the diplomatic tags of the cars and the flags of the six countries. They had previously recorded the arrival of the Attorney General and his fiancee, of Joel Seligman, and of Robert Underwood, the Secretary of State. William and Amy Stromberg were still house guests of the Rosenblueths.

The President opened the meeting in one of the sitting rooms of the White House, first introducing everyone present to each other.

"We greatly appreciate this opportunity to meet with you...Madame President...," Umberto Rossi then said as he opened the meeting on behalf of the ambassadors.

"It Is always our pleasure to meet with the staunch friends of our country...," said the President. "We have given the subject of this meeting much thought...and every American present is familiar with the situation.... We are as anxious as all of you to ensure that James Lancaster receives the punishment he truly deserves for his attempt...for personal reasons...to use the armed forces of the United States to destroy two friendly nations.... But you must appreciate that we cannot simply hand a former President over to a foreign state for trial for something he did as President...no matter how criminal that act might have been.... Just consider the implications of such a move.... Fortunately...however...we do have a solution to the problem...an excellent solution.... The State of New York has a criminal statute...enacted before Lancaster began to make war against Canada and Israel...defining a crime against humanity in terms of the compelling interest of the sovereign State of New York.... Governor Stromberg intends to prosecute James Lancaster under that statute...the law carrying the death penalty...which partially explains why Governor Stromberg is with us.... I shall ask Governor Stromberg to explain the statute to you...."

"Thank you...Madame President.... Gentlemen...the New York statute provides that the crime is committed by a President if he engages in warfare against a foreign country without a declaration of war by our Congress...which is required for legal warfare under our federal constitution...and if as the result of that illicit warfare...any citizen of the State of New York is killed...meaning any officer or enlisted person holding his official domicile in the State of New York...making him a citizen of New York.... About a dozen New York citizens were killed in that naval engagement in the Mediterranean...and more than two hundred in the invasion of Canada.... Once I...as Governor...take the necessary first steps...the machinery under New York law will begin to move...." There was a considerable pause.

"Madame President...," exclaimed Samuel Alvarez,

"...that is a most excellent solution to the problem...and we all understand why you cannot extradite an ex-President to another country.... I doubt any of us would do that ourselves.... I know I shall be present in New York...to attend as many of the sessions of the trial as I can...to witness history being made at this unprecedented trial.... May I congratulate you...Governor Stromberg...for New York being so enlightened...."

"And I wish to add my congratulations...Governor Stromberg...," added Umberto Rossi. "Will the trial be held in Manhattan...?"

"No...in Albany.... Under our law...it will be a trial...without jury...before our highest court...the New York Court of Appeals...but you do realize...gentlemen... that all the procedural law of the State of New York will be in effect...including indictment by grand jury...and we ask everyone present in this room to keep all of this confidential until I formally make the appropriate announcements in Albany...."

"We would expect no less...and do no less...," exclaimed Count Nordlinger of Sweden.

"I must remind you all...," said Governor Stromberg, "...that although the New York law provides for the death penalty...it is not mandatory.... The court may...in its discretion...award the punishment of life imprisonment without parole.... We shall all hope that the court does not apply that alternative...and shall do our best...not only to obtain a conviction...but also to get the death penalty...."

THIRTY-THREE

The trial opened several months later in Albany, in the courtroom of the New York Court of Appeals, Chief Judge Collingwood presiding, Joel Seligman and Sian McAlester O'Leary leading the prosecution, and a battery of very expensive lawyers, led by Belford Smythe, son of Barbara Smythe, appearing for the defense, Mr Smythe and his associates sitting at the defense table with the defendant James Lancaster, the defendant dressed in a dark business suit, but his face hardly recognizable ever since the death of his elder son. The preliminary defense motions were all denied, including the one to have the criminal statute declared unconstitutional because it did not provide for trial by jury. The presiding judge read the indictment by a special Albany County grand jury, the indictment charging James Monroe Lancaster, when President of the United States, with making undeclared war against Canada and against the State of Israel, both unlawful wars resulting in the deaths of two hundred and sixteen citizens of New York, nine in the war against the State of Israel, and the remainder in the war against Canada, to which indictment the defendant had pleaded not guilty the previous week.

After Judge Collingwood then carefully explained the criminal statute under which James Lancaster was being tried for his life, Joel Seligman opened the case for the prosecution. Vice President Mark Rosenblueth, Governor William Stromberg, Attorney General Thomas O'Leary, District Attorney Roger Morrison, and a large number of ambassadors in addition the original six were present that opening day despite the inconvenience of the location, and so were Barbara Smythe and her friends for the defendant, all the while that Joan Seligman was holding a graduate seminar in Manhattan at Teachers College on the education of gifted handicapped children, and Naomi Seligman was spending her few hours a day treating patients in one of the Albany hospitals.

"Conviction will require the unanimous vote of all the members of this court...," emphasized the Chief Judge, "...from which there can be no appeal...and for which the maximum sentence is death..... As in all trials in the State of New York...the prosecution will have the burden of proving the guilt of the defendant beyond a reasonable doubt.... And I need not remind counsel...for the People...and for the defense...that there is no jury.... This court is the trier of the facts as well as of the law...and there will be no need to use theatrics of any kind...which might ordinarily impress a jury...."

Joel explained in his opening statement that the prosecution would prove beyond a reasonable doubt the three points required under the statute, that Congress had not declared war against Canada or against the State of Israel, that the land invasion of Canada and the massive naval offensive against the State of Israel were indeed ordered by James Monroe Lancaster, at the time the President of the United States, and thirdly that two hundred and seven citizens of New York were killed in the land battles and nine citizens of New York were killed in that naval action.

"We are also aware as to what the defense will contend...that the defendant acted within his constitutional power to repel invasions and suppress insurrections without the consent of the Congress...but we shall show that there was no invasion and no insurrection...."

To prove the first point, Joel presented certified copies of the journals of both houses of Congress to show no record of a declaration of war enacted by the Congress, nor any action taken to support the two wars undertaken by the President. He buttressed this documentary evidence by presenting the testimony of the Secretary of the Senate and of the Clerk of the House, each of them unequivocally stating that according to his records no such legislative actions were taken during the time that the defendant was President.

In his cross-examination of Timothy Sutton, the Secretary of the Senate, Mr Smythe asked whether the Senate had taken any action to prevent the hostilities against Canada and the State of Israel.

"No...the Senate did not...but...," and before Mr Sutton could complete his answer, Mr Smythe interrupted him to say, "Then the failure of the Congress to act would be a constructive declaration of war...."

Joel jumped to his feet, and loudly voiced his objection.

"That is the most preposterous legal principle ever conceived by the mind of man.... To assert...as defense counsel is asserting...that the failure of Congress to prevent the President from waging an undeclared war is a constructive declaration of war...is a gross absurdity...and the absurdity in this particular case is further compounded by the fact that the defendant was foisting a virtual dictatorship on Washington...using his private army division at Fort McNair...arresting many Senators and members of the House of Representatives.... Under those conditions...how could Congress take any action...even if wanted to...? ...although its failure to take action could not possibly be construed to be a declaration of war...under any set of circumstances..."

"My assertion of a constructive declaration of war is held by many legal scholars...Your Honor...," countered chief defense counsel.

"The People's objection is sustained...," exclaimed Chief Judge Collingwood as the presiding judge. "Mr Smythe...I know of no reputable legal scholar who has argued such a notion...and certainly no court that has ruled in favor of your assertion.... You are of course free to present expert witnesses...but this court will not permit any witnesses except reputable ones...."

Then Sian O'Leary presented the testimony of the editors-in-chief of the major Washington newspapers, and of the chiefs of the Washington bureaus of the major news services, that they published no news of any declaration of war, or of any action to sanction the war, which they certainly would have had there been such momentous action taken by Congress. The defense declined to cross-examine.

Joel then presented the testimony of George Marbury, chief of the Washington bureau of the Dallas Morning Post, that he and other reporters, both of his paper and of several others, had been taken on a thorough and unencumbered tour of the Israeli Embassy, and that they found no evidence of a bomb.

"Might not the bomb have been hidden...?" asked Belford Smythe in cross-examination.

"Mr Alvarez...the ambassador...gave us free rein of the entire building...even their secure areas...and authorized us to bring in technical experts and workmen of our own choice to monitor the building and to break away any suspected hiding place that might have been mortared up.... We spent more than twenty-four continuous hours...using a very large number of personnel in rotating shifts...and could not find anything...."

Sian O'Leary then presented Admiral Joseph Meridan, now retired, but at the time the commander-in-chief of the Mediterranean Fleet, who testified as to the orders he received directly from then President Lancaster.

"I protested the order...realizing that it was motivated by a President both very antisemitic...and wishing...." The defense interrupt to object to the witness characterizing the defendant as "antisemitic," asserting that such a characterization was for the judges to make.

"Your Honors...," said Mrs O'Leary in response to the objection, "...it is relevant that the witness give his own impression at the time...as an indication of his state of mind when he received such a fateful order from the President of the United States...."

"Objection is overruled...," intoned Judge Collingwood. "You may answer the question...Admiral Meridan...."

"As I said...I realized he was antisemitic...and that he wished to divert the attention of the world away from the criminal charges by New York against him for murder...."

"Then why did you obey such an order...realizing that it was not lawful...realizing that you could very likely also be held accountable for what might then happen were you to carry it out...?"

"We in the armed forces are conditioned over our entire careers to obey the orders of a superior...and the President is the commander-in-chief.... In retrospect...I should have disobeyed it.... Under the circumstances...I should not have carried it out...but my conditioning caused me to carry it out...."

"I have no further questions of Admiral Meridan...Your Honor...," said Sian O'Leary, rather sweetly.

"Do you have questions to ask the witness...Mr Smythe...?"

"Yes...Your Honor.... Admiral Meridan...did you know there was no American declaration of war against the State of Israel...?"

"Yes...I did...."

"But you still carried out the order...."

"As I said before...I realized it was unlawful for that reason...and I already explained why I carried it out...."

"Then you...in your own way...aided the President.... Have you been given immunity for your testimony here...?"

"I have been advised by my own lawyer that I am not subject to this New York criminal law...that only a President is...and there was therefore no immunity to be given.... I was not subpoenaed to give this evidence.... I wanted to give it.... I did a terrible thing...by obeying the order of an evil man...(defense counsel tried to stop him, but he continued)...and the only way I can right this wrong is to present the facts...as I know them...at this trial...." The courtroom was in an uproar, which was dissipated under the repeated banging of the gavel.

"I have no further questions of this witness...," said Mr Smythe.

"It's a bit late...," announced Judge Collingwood. "We shall recess until three o'clock this afternoon...."

Joel and Sian joined Mark, Tom, Bill and Roger to have lunch in a special dining room in the federal courthouse nearby, where the four spectators were congratulating the two prosecutors for their presentations so far.

"It's obvious that the defense will not contradict the facts...," said Joel, "...but will instead insist that the military actions were in effect a suppression of an insurrection by American Jews and the repulsion of an invasion from Canada.... It's going to be difficult to prove what is not...and I'm not at all sure the burden ought not to be on the defense...but we are prepared...and will assume the burden...and I feel will prevail...."

At three o'clock, Sian presented the testimony of General John Robertson, the former Chief of Staff of the Army, now retired, that he was ordered by the defendant to quickly plan and implement the invasion of Canada.

"Did the defendant give a reason...that the United States were being invaded by the Canadians...?"

"No.... He told me very directly that we were invading Canada to punish the Canadians for providing refuge to the many American Jews fleeing for safety there...."

"Did you have any information...General Robertson...of any prior incursion by the Canadian armed forces onto American soil...or of any hostile act taken by Canada...that could be reasonably interpreted to be an invasion of the United States by Canada...?"

"None whatever...."

"No more questions...at this time...."

"Do you wish to cross-examine...Mr Smythe...?"

"Yes...Your Honor.... General Robertson...how would you know there were no hostile acts being imminently contemplated by the Canadians against this country...which President Lancaster wished to thwart by a pre-emptive attack...."

"Mr Smythe...the Secretary of the Army was in Ottawa meeting with the Canadian Minister of Defense.... During the course of his visit...he was taken on a thorough tour of all Canadian planning facilities at the ministry...and if there were any plans they would have been apparent to a practiced eye...."

"But Secretary Cedrics was a civilian...."

"He was when Secretary...but he was a retired army three-star general...who had resigned his commission to become Secretary...as General Eisenhower had done to become President.... General Cedrics was a very experienced military officer...and when he returned to Washington...he sent me a thorough memorandum of his visit to Ottawa...which would have related anything indicating preparations to invade the United States...but it does not.... I have given the original copy of that memorandum to Mr Seligman...."

"And General Cedrics...why is he not here to present his own memorandum as evidence...?"

"Because he was killed in a car accident in Washington...several months ago.... I also have the original of a very long report he had prepared relating to our unprovoked invasion of Canada...."

"I will ask you the same question that I had asked Admiral Meridan.... If you felt that the order to repel the invasion was illegal...why did you execute it...?"

"I did not execute it.... I refused to execute it...and was arrested by the so-called President's Division...and held to be tried by court martial.... Major General Luke Martins...the head of that private army division of Lancaster's...he executed it...after he was promoted to lieutenant general as a reward to carrying out an illegal order...."

Realizing that his cross-examination was eliciting no evidence favorable to the defendant, but instead further evidence very damaging to the defendant, Belford Smythe suddenly said, "No further questions...."

Sian O'Leary then handed the original copies of the memorandum and report to the presiding judge to be entered as written evidence along with the oral evidence just presented by General Robertson, and despite the fact that she was dressed in a simple business suit, she could not disguise her considerable beauty, which was not lost on the all-male court.

"May it please the court...," said Joel Seligman, "...we now intend to prove the absence of an insurrection...which is not an easy thing to do...for it will appear to replicate the kind of testimony much more suitable for a war crimes trial at Nuremberg...although this crime for which defendant is being tried is characterized in the statute itself as a crime against humanity...."

"Your Honors...I object to Mr Seligman's characterization of this trial as a war crimes trial.... Mr Lancaster is a patriotic Christian...trying to defend this country against the evil influence of the Jews...."

"Mr Smythe...," Judge Collingwood exclaimed. "I

personally object very strongly to the disgusting remark you just made.... You may defend...when it is your turn...on the basis that the defendant did what he did to suppress an insurrection...and/or to repel an invasion...but you will avoid any defamatory statements in doing so...or in cross-examining prosecution witnesses.... You are not here to sway a jury according to its religious biases...but to defend your client accused of a capital crime.... If you do not adhere to these guidelines...we shall hold you in criminal contempt.... You are not making it easier for yourself by engaging in that kind of speech...and if you persist...we shall consider that you are not competently serving your client...and will remove you...which as you know a trial court has the authority to do...."

Saying nothing, Belford Smythe sat down as a loud murmur swept the courtroom, and several reporters stood up indicating their intention to leave the courtroom to file their stories.

"Representatives of the press will be permitted to leave the courtroom only during a recess...," announced the Chief Judge to prevent an incipient disruption as more reporters stood up to leave. "Mr Seligman...do you have another witness...?"

"Yes...Your Honor...the People call Samuel Mendelssohn...."

"Mr Mendelssohn...please state your full name...and your occupation...."

"Samuel Aaron Mendelssohn...physician and surgeon...practicing in Boston...."

"Please tell us what happened to you the day following Lancaster's address to the nation that nuclear bombs were in the Embassy of Israel in Washington...and at Israeli consulates throughout the United States...."

"A squad of armed marines from the Boston Navy Yard came to my office to arrest me on a charge of insurrection...the sergeant in charge making it very clear that the accusation was made solely because I am a Jew.... When I protested...I was conveyed...very roughly...to my home...forced to leave several patients behind in my office in need of urgency medical care...where a search was conducted without a warrant...the search uncovering two Hi-Standard target pistols...and two single-shot rifles...both very accurate rifles...also used in sports shooting.... They were not used for hunting because our religion forbids us to kill animals except for food or in self-defense...but they were quite capable of being used in the same manner that the colonists used their weapons.... I belong to a prominent shooting club...with members of every religious persuasion...but only the Jewish members were arrested...and for some reason...I was released...."

"Was there any plan in the Boston area for American Jews to rise in rebellion against either the government of the Commonwealth of Massachusetts or the federal government...?"

"None whatever.... We were of course ready to defend ourselves against attack...from anyone...but it would have been foolhardy for us to otherwise use our weapons.... What we were planning to do...right after that Hitlerian speech by the defendant...was to move our families as soon as we could to Canada...for safety.... And to do that we had the voluntary assistance of many of our non-Jewish friends...."

"Were you ever attacked...?"

"Yes...by armed uniformed men claiming to act for their new savior.... They looked and behaved like Nazi brownshirts...."

"And what was your reaction...?"

"Since they were not our regular Boston police...we used our weapons to defend ourselves...something they did not expect...and the bullies ran...."

"And then what happened...?"

"They returned with a marine colonel from the Navy Yard...to arrest us...and the colonel charged us all with insurrection.... We refused arrest...which prompted the next Hitlerian speech by Lancaster...."

"Were the Boston police involved...?"

"Yes...to help us protect ourselves against the bullies...and actually to try to arrest them...but we had opposition from marine personnel at the Navy Yard.... It was a basic conflict between the Massachusetts authorities...and Lancaster's henchmen...and whatever of the armed forces he could muster to support him.... If there was any insurrection...Mr Seligman...the entire country seemed to be in insurrection against that monster in the White House...."

"Thank you...Dr Mendelssohn.... No more questions...Your Honor...."

"Do you have any questions...Mr Smythe...?"

"None that I would ask of a Jew...?" responded Belford Smythe with considerable disdain.

"I warned you...Mr Smythe...about your manner

and language.... The laws of slander do not apply to the courtroom...but contempt of court does.... Just a friendly reminder...Mr Smythe.... Mr Seligman...do you have more witnesses...?"

"No...Your Honor...the prosecution rests...."

"It is rather late.... The defense will begin its case tomorrow morning at ten.... Court is in recess until then...."

THIRTY-FOUR

"The defense calls President Lancaster...," proudly announced Belford Smythe the following morning to open the defense.

A grim-looking man stood up, slowly looked around the courtroom with some considerable disdain, and then walked over to the witness chair to take the oath to tell the truth, the whole truth and nothing but the truth. But the oath made no mention of opinions or attitudes.

"Mr President...," said Belford Smythe, "...please tell the court what prompted you to order an attack against Israel and against Canada...even though there were no declarations of war by Congress...."

"I had to act without Congress because most of the members were part of the conspiracy to sell this Christian nation down the river...to the Jews.... The Senators...the Congressmen...none of them could be trusted...and I had the constitutional duty to protect and preserve the Constitution of this Christian land against all enemies...foreign and domestic...the solemn oath I took as President of the United States of America.... And our enemies were the nefarious Jews...all led by Mark Rosenblueth.... There was an armed Jewish uprising threatening to kill every Christian clergyman in the land...and Canada was aiding that uprising.... As for that human cesspool called Israel...it was an abomination in the sight of God...and I was determined to obliterate it...at the same time that I would destroy the Jewish enemy from within...to finish the divinely inspired task...left incomplete by that great man...Adolf Hitler...the task to rid the entire world of the Jews...especially to rid this Christian land of the Jews.... Just as Hitler sought power primarily to eradicate the Jewish menace...so did I...and I would have been successful had it not been for that murder charge falsely brought against me...all of it orchestrated by the Jewish conspiracy...."

A beaming Belford Smythe said, "No more questions...." But questions had already formed on the face of almost everyone in that courtroom, questions generated by the vile statements of the witness.

Lancaster began to leave the witness chair, his movement prompting Judge Collingwood to tell him to remain where he was, and then asking, "Mr Seligman...do you wish to cross-examine the witness...?"

Before Joel could reply, Lancaster shouted, "I will not be questioned by a filthy Jew.... I refuse to be questioned by that Judas...."

"You knew you were subject to cross-examination...Mr Lancaster...," exclaimed the Chief Judge. "If you do not make yourself available...then all your testimony on direct examination will be stricken...."

Lancaster moved slowly back into his chair as Joel stood a considerable distance from him, the witness staring at his former defense counsel with such hate that it made Sian rather uncomfortable.

"Mr Lancaster...," the cross-examination began, "...if you hated the Jews so much...why did you have anything to do with Dinah Steinberg...a Jewish woman...?"

"Your Honor...," shouted Belford Smythe, "...I object to that question.... It is not relevant to the direct examination...."

"But it is relevant...," insisted Joel Seligman. "Direct examination revealed the defendant's attitude toward Jews...."

"Objection is overruled.... You may continue...Mr Seligman...."

"All Jewish women are sluts...whores...," exclaimed James Lancaster, "...but they always rejected me.... I killed that woman because she also rejected me.... She wouldn't even go out with me.... A Jewish slut has no right to reject a fine upright Christian gentleman...."

"How did you get into her apartment...?"

"Your Honor...," Belford Smythe again objected. "I really do not see the pertinence of this question.... It is as though the prosecution is re-living my client's previous trial...."

"I shall allow the question...."

"I waited for her in the hall...around a corner...and when she appeared at her door to unlock it...I seized her...and forced my way into the apartment...to quickly rid the world of that Jew.... It was the beginning of my campaign to make this great nation free of the corruption of the Jews...," the witness said very proudly. The courtroom gasped at the defendant's confession of first-degree murder.

"No more questions...Your Honor...," said Joel Seligman.

The stillness was almost unbearable until Judge Collingwood asked, "Do you have another witness...Mr Smythe...."

"No...Your Honor...the defense rests...."

"Do you plan to present expert witnesses for that concept you previously asserted...of a constructive declaration of war...?"

"No...Your Honor.... I doubt we can present witnesses who would be acceptable to the court.... But even more importantly...we have presented the President as a witness in his own behalf...and I am sure that he has convinced this honorable court of the justification for the actions that he took.... He is a patriotic man who has tried to serve his country to the best of his great ability despite the efforts of the Jews to thwart him.... Everyone knows that the world is under a massive Jewish conspiracy to control everything...to make everything impossible that is Christian...noble...and pure...."

"Then deliberately killing a Jewish woman would fit

in with your client's vision of his manifest destiny...."

"Yes...it would...Your Honor...."

"You do realize...Mr Smythe...that your client confessed in open court to the first-degree murder of Dinah Seligman...."

"It does not matter...since he pleaded guilty to second-degree murder in that case...."

"We shall see whether or not it matters...," responded the Chief Judge, rather testily. "We recess until tomorrow...when we shall hear the summation for the People...and for the defense...on the issues of this trial...."

In his summation the following morning, Belford Smythe presented an emotional picture of a harried President, attacked by domestic enemies on all sides, doing his best to honor the oath he had taken as President of the United States of America to preserve and protect and defend the Constitution, cutting corners of necessity to defend this beloved land of his.

Joel then made the summation for the People of the State of New York, very carefully and clearly pointing out the facts, facts unable to be disputed by the defense because they were not disputable, all the facts in support of the requirements of the criminal statute. He then very slowly refuted the position of the defense, by saying that no man was above the law, that the road to dictatorship was paved with the cutting of corners, by a leader doing things beyond the law to achieve what he alone felt ought to be achieved. "This is a democracy...where the people rule...where the people rule through their elected representatives.... This is not a dictatorship...where one man can decide all things...where he can use the awesome military power of our country for his own personal purposes.... The founding fathers gave the power to declare war to the Congress...not to the President.... They had just achieved their independence from a country where war was declared by the King...not by the people's representatives...."

Joel Seligman completed his summation by thoroughly demolishing the defense contention that the citizen opposition in Boston was an insurrection, and that Canada had invaded New York, demolishing the attempt by the defense to make Lancaster's actions fall within the constitutional responsibilities of the President.

But above all, it was the confession of the defendant that he had deliberately murdered Dinah Steinberg, a confession that he had committed a murder in the first degree, a confession that continued to ring through the minds of everyone in that courtroom, especially through the mind of Roger Morrison, a confession skillfully elicited by Joel Seligman to expiate his sin, that confession was the best summation for the prosecution.

Two days later, a verdict of guilty was announced by Chief Judge Collingwood to a standing James Lancaster and Belford Smythe, no emotion appearing on the face of the defendant as he heard the verdict as though he fully expected it and perhaps even welcomed it for the martyrdom it might bring. Once the noise of the spectators disappeared, and the courtroom was quiet again, Judge Collingwood pronounced the sentence of death, still no emotion on the face of James Lancaster, the pronouncement of the sentence marking the end of the trial. James Monroe Lancaster, at one time President of the United States, and guilty of the premeditated murder of Dinah Steinberg, James Monroe Lancaster was taken back to Sing Sing State Penitentiary, but this time to death row, to await execution for her death and also for the wrongful death of two hundred and sixteen citizens of the sovereign State of New York, one of the United States of America.